MORTICE IN AMERICA
MORE JUSTICE – MORT STYLE!

Mortice in America: More Justice – Mort Style! © 2024 A J Wilton

All Rights Reserved. No part of this book may be reproduced in any form or by any electronic or mechanical means including information storage and retrieval syst ems, without permission in writing from the author. The only exception is by a reviewer, who may quote short excerpts in a review.

This book is a work of fiction. Names, characters, places, and incidents either are products of the author's imagination or are used fictitiously. Any resemblance to actual persons, living or dead, events, or locales is entirely coincidental.

Printed in Australia

Cover and internal design by Shawline Publishing Group Pty Ltd

First printing: June 2024

Shawline Publishing Group Pty Ltd

www.shawlinepublishing.com.au

Paperback ISBN 978-1-9231-0189-0

eBook ISBN 978-1-9231-7103-9

Hardback ISBN 978-1-9231-7115-2

Distributed by Shawline Distribution and Lightning Source Global

Shawline Publishing Group acknowledges the traditional owners of the land and pays respects to Elders, past, present and future.

A catalogue record for this work is available from the National Library of Australia

MORTICE IN AMERICA
MORE JUSTICE – MORT STYLE!

BOOK THREE

A J WILTON

ALSO BY A J WILTON

You Killed My Wife
Mortice: Justice Mort Style!

DEDICATIONS

I used to work with a bloke named Mort.

A Vietnam vet, he was a hardworking, no-nonsense bloke. Sadly, even with a loving and supportive family, Mort struggled with day-to-day life after his years serving his country.

This story is dedicated to him and all who have served their countries. Thank you.

This is an act of fiction, so please forgive me if my imagination doesn't fit with reality. My aim is to entertain not write history!

All characters and events are figments of my imagination.

ACKNOWLEDGMENTS

My thanks to the following for their guidance and support:
- My two daughters Shannon and Courtney for their proofing, help and guidance.
- Friends Milz and Roger for more proofing!
- My wife for her patience!

1

Pig, Suzie and I are walking back toward 'Entertainment Central', the hub of the Invictus Games in Victoria BC from the small boat harbour.

We had been out whale watching, following a pod of orcas, which had been awesome, watching these ruthless killers gliding along. Apparently in sleep mode where they simply cruise. Fascinating to watch.

The trouble is, it was a bitterly cold and breezy day and we were in an open zodiac boat, so no protection from the elements. Even though the tour had provided us with dry suits – both rather tight on Pig and my large bodies! We were all freezing. Suzie's teeth had been chattering, she was so cold. Her fingers had gone blue and the tour guide suggested her toes most probably were too. (Helpful!)

Being Queenslanders with our tropical warm climate, we simply don't have the right cold weather gear (or thick blood!) for these bitter temperatures. Besides, it is meant to be summer!

We were walking as quickly as possible, all with our own plans on how best to warm up quickly. Long hot shower or bath, with maybe a shot of hot Irish whisky. An Irishman, a member of the elite British SAS squadron, had told me once on a long bleak and bitterly cold Afghan night he was dreaming of just that!

Suddenly, Pig says, 'Hunter, three o'clock.' I don't look. If Pig says Hunter is at three o'clock, then Hunter is at three o'clock.

Instead, I reply, 'I thought I saw him on Thursday, but only fleetingly.'

Pig replies, 'Interesting, I also thought I saw him at the track just before my ten-thousand-metre race as well.'

Suzie has been looking from me to Pig and back again and to her credit, has not tried to look to the three o'clock position. But she does ask, 'Who is Hunter?'

I reply, 'He was a lieutenant in the US Marines. We worked with him a few times in Afghanistan. A good guy. Was then anyway.'

I continue, 'Okay, let's find out what he's up to and why he hasn't come out and said hi. You two keep heading into the crowd. I'll go around and find out what's going on.'

Suzie looks at me and says, 'Don't take too long or you will have to de-ice me.'

I smile and say, 'A nice long hot kiss will do that pretty quickly, but not out here in the crowd. They might get jealous!' I give her a reassuring squeeze on her arm and deviate away from them. At the same time, I take the newly bought Seattle Sea Hawks beanie, common headwear around here, and pull it down on my head and droop my shoulders, thus changing my body profile. I've learnt to do this and had to do it a few times in the past.

I'm a big unit after all, so a little difficult to not stand out in a crowd.

Hunter, who I can now see still standing at the top of a small rise overlooking the crowded harbour area, doesn't appear to have noticed my peeling away.

I move slowly through the crowd off to his left until I'm out of his sight.

Then I move quickly through the thinner crowds here in the background, approaching him from directly behind.

I slow my pace as I get closer, keeping an eye out for any obvious partner working with him. Whilst Pig and I worked with Hunter and his Marines unit a few times in Afghanistan and certainly shared many a beer with them in the mess, we had not stayed in touch with him. So have no idea who or what he is doing now. Certainly not why he would be spying on us. Or are we simply being paranoid?

It would be unusual to have only one person running a reconnaissance mission. Then again, I have no idea who or what he does these days.

Time to find out.

I wait until a group of three move further away from Hunter and slip up behind him. My right hand tightens around his neck and my left plucks his earpiece and throat mic off him.

I say, 'Not a sound and don't move.'

He deflates, saying, 'Shit. Where did you come from?'

I don't loosen my grip, as yet I don't know if he is friend or foe.

I say, 'You have three seconds to tell me why I don't crush your larynx and you collapse.'

'F…K. It's okay. I had a bet with Campbell you wouldn't see me for three days. Now I have to shout him a fancy dinner.'

'Why are you spying on us? You friend of foe?'

He jerks a little as if startled by my question. 'Shit, man, friend. I work with Campbell in the FBI. We were going to show our hand tomorrow but wanted to see how good your skills still were.' A pause then he says, 'Man, I could never be foe. You're good people.'

'Our skills are better than yours obviously. This is the third time we have seen you,' I reply.

'Shit,' is his response before continuing, 'Campbell is in the office over there.' He points with a nod of his head to an office building on the other side of the square. 'Let's go and see him.'

'First things first. Which pocket is your FBI badge in?'

'Inside coat pocket, left-hand side.'

He pulls the zip of his puffer jacket down to give me easier access. I'm still holding him around the neck, so he knows one wrong move and he will go down. I use my left hand to slip inside his jacket and before retrieving his badge, I feel around for any holster but don't feel one. I grab his badge wallet, pull it out and flick it open.

It's a real FBI badge or a bloody good imitation. It shows Hunter Buchanan with an FBI ID number.

'Okay, let's go and have a chat with "Sunshine", shall we?'

'Sure, but don't call him that for all our sakes. Please. Where's Pig and Suzie?'

'So you know Suzie's name. What's going on?'

I am on edge again. I don't like that they have not only been watching us for three days but have dug up enough to know Suzie's name.

'Let's go see Campbell. He will lay it all out for you.'

I reply, 'Let's go. I will be one pace behind you. Any false move, you know what I will do from there. Pig will find us.'

As always in these situations, Pig's and my phone act as two-way radios. They might look like Apple iPhones – but they aren't!

Pig and, I suspect, Suzie will have heard the conversation and will follow, at a distance, to act as back up and certainly monitor to see if Hunter in fact does have back up as well.

Hunter leads me around the outskirts of the 'Entertainment Central', the centrepiece of the Invictus Games with temporary bars, clubs, a stage and seating for five thousand, all built over the inner harbour, right in the heart of town.

It's an awesome location and it has been buzzing 24/7 through the entire Games.

We head off around the edge of the gathering crowd, all getting ready for the night's festivities, this being the second to last night of these Invictus Games.

As we reach the far side of the crowd and head into Humboldt Street, Hunter slows outside the imposing Belmont building, points to the front door and turns to me, saying, 'We have an office up on the third floor. Do you want me to go in?'

I nod in the affirmative.

He turns again and, using a key card, opens the front door, moves through and holds it open for me. I stop once I have entered the doorframe, indicating he is to continue in front of me. A wry smile spreads across his face as he heads to the lifts.

Once the lift arrives, he again precedes me in, but I am tight behind him. Whilst precautionary, I am fairly confident he is legit and not a threat. I'm still alive because I don't assume!

The lift pings as it arrives on level three. Hunter exits, turns left and moves along the hall until he comes to suite 305. Without a word, I film the suite number with my phone, knowing Pig will have now seen it and know where we are. Hunter again uses a key card to open the door, holding it wide for me to enter.

As promised here is my old 'mate', Campbell McPherson, a former captain in the US Marines. He used to be Hunter's boss in the Marines. We had a few run-ins and more than a few beers. In the past. Now? Well, I'm about to find out.

2

As the door opens, Campbell raises his head from his computer screen, taking in the style of our entrance and immediately realising Hunter had been found out.

'Well, looks like it's your shout!' he says to Hunter with a smile, at the same time rising to come around to greet me.

'Hold up,' I say, raising my hand in the stop signal, causing Campbell to stop with a look of surprise. I continue, 'We have seen Hunter three times over the last few days. He, you, have made no effort to contact us, so as yet we don't know if you are friend or foe.'

After taking a couple of moments to digest this, Campbell says, 'May I?', indicating his coat pocket, which is hung over the back of his chair.

I nod. I have resumed my position half behind Hunter, again holding him around the neck. One squeeze and I cut off his windpipe and he collapses; he knows it.

Campbell digs his hand into the inside pocket, pulls out his FBI Shield, opens it and offers it to me.

I reach out and accept it. It shows his photo, name and title of 'Special Agent in Charge', so up the tree a little from Hunter whose badge only said a mere 'Special Agent'.

I nod and offer it back. He takes it, saying, 'Okay if we shake hands now?'

I smile and reach out and shake his hand and then Hunter's.

As I remove my Sea Hawks beanie, rubbing my hand through my short cropped (number one blade still) black hair, I say, 'Okay, let's make this short. Pig, Suzie and I are freezing to death. What the hell are you two doing monitoring us?'

'Where is Pig? Will he be joining us?'

Right on cue there is a knock on the door. Hunter goes over and opens it and Pig and Suzie walk in.

After greetings and after I have introduced Suzie to them both as my fiancée, I repeat, 'Okay what's going on? And make it quick. Suzie needs de-icing.'

Hunter makes a beeline for the thermostat, cranking the heating up, getting a wan smile from Suzie as a response.

Pig, meanwhile, has pulled his phone out and walks around the room, getting quizzical looks from Campbell, Hunter and even Suzie.

On getting no beeps, we know the room isn't bugged. He then taps another app on his phone and sets it on the table. He looks around, smiles and says, 'We can't be too careful.'

It's Suzie who asks, 'What's that doing?'

Pig replies, 'Blocking any signals, so if someone is trying to listen all they will receive is a humming noise.'

Campbell and Hunter nod in acceptance.

I turn to Campbell and say, 'Let's hear it from the beginning.'

He points to chairs for us to sit in, which Pig and I do, but Suzie takes up station next to the radiator, enjoying the chance to warm herself.

I'm looking expectantly at Campbell, who starts, 'Well, where to begin.' And pauses.

'I'm "Special Agent in Charge" of a special FBI taskforce targeting the Colombian Drug syndicates. Hunter is my 2IC and I report direct to an assistant director. We are a small, highly focused and well-resourced unit.

'The FBI is a big lumbering bureaucracy. It's impossible to be quick and nimble. You need a squadron of uniforms to do anything and with so many levels of approvals, we simply can't get anything effective done.

'The bigger issue is that the drug syndicates have so much money, they invariably know what we are going to do before we do it. Whether it's bribing or coercing our colleagues, they always know what buttons to press and what is going on.'

Here he pauses, fiddling with his pen before proceeding. 'When Hunter pointed out your names on the airline manifest showing you coming over for the games, and then apparently for an extended holiday, and knowing a little about some of your past endeavours, we came up with the idea of approaching you to see if you could give us a hand. Do us a favour, of sorts.'

Pig, Suzie and I have not yet said anything, waiting for the rest of the story.

Campbell continues, 'When I approached my boss with what I confess was a bit of a hair-brained "off-the-books" type scheme, she took me seriously and after she looked into your history a bit – she has the clearance to find out way more than Hunter or I – she gave me the green light to come up and at least chat to you. She even reached out to some major general of yours, as her routine inquiry came back denied. You clearly still work within the broader Australian Government structure to have such high-level security. This major general, once our boss explained what we had in mind, said something along the lines of, "They are contractors, not employees. I'm sure Mort and Pig will be happy to help if they think they can."'

We still remain silent. I am watching Suzie, hoping she is at least starting to thaw out.

'So,' he continues again, 'our hair-brained scheme was to ask if you two, knowing how successful you have been in the past, could get to Diego Garcia – he's the East Coast head of the Garcia mob. His brother Chico is based in LA and runs the West Coast. Whilst there isn't any love lost between them, they will always have each other's backs.

'Every time we think we are getting close to them, they find out about our undercover agent, or what we are planning, eliminate them, foil our plans and openly taunt us. We have honestly had a gut full and want to get them. To take them down. Hard.

'Our plan was to ask you two if you would be interested in trying to get a wire on them or some other way of getting some incriminating evidence.' He shrugs here, saying almost sheepishly, 'We have no idea how you might achieve this, but we are desperate to try and stop or at least limit the scourge of their drugs. Their drugs are destroying the fabric of our country, the one we fought so hard and proudly for.

'They are up to their eyeballs in underage prostitution these days as well. Bringing in young Mexican and South American girls, some as young as ten, who become addicted to drugs and a life as a prostitute. Sadly, these young girls only have a life expectancy of five to six years once they start down this track. Truly heart breaking.'

I look at Pig and get a small nod and then a questioning look from Suzie, so I say, 'Okay, that's enough for now. We are going back to our hotel now to thaw out. You can shout us all dinner tonight at the Harbour House Restaurant. It's reputed to be the best steakhouse in town. Make it for seven p.m. and book a private room so we can continue our conversation.'

With farewell handshakes, Pig grabs his phone and Suzie my hand as we exit the office, then the building.

I had managed to snag us two rooms at the Empress Hotel right here on the harbour foreshore, a majestic building in a beautiful location, for our last two nights in town, (they cost a pretty penny as well but hey, we are on holiday, right?) so we didn't have far to walk and not a word was said.

3

We arrive back at the Empress, a large imposing Victorian-era hotel right on the waterfront and head directly to the lifts, working our way through what seems like a busload of Japanese tourists.

In the lifts it's all dark wood panelling, like the hotel itself. The lifts seem as old as the hotel. I look at Pig and say, 'Why don't you come to our room around five-thirty, six? That should give us all time to thaw out and we can have a chat about Campbell's idea.'

He nods in the positive and exits the lift on level two, whilst Suzie and I head on up to our 'superior room with harbour view' on level four with its astonishing views over the waterfront.

As soon as we enter, I head to the bathroom and start running a hot bath for Suzie, then I come back and help her undress (well, for all you know, her fingers might be too numb to undo the buttons!)

I help her into the bath, now piping hot. I then return to the mini bar and pour her a whiskey. Suzie, like me, isn't a spirit drinker, but I'm having one too as I've always understood it helps beat the cold.

But after one sip, I realise whiskey isn't going to do it for me, so I dial up room service and order two pots of extra strong coffee. Yes, milk on the side for Suzie.

Surprisingly quickly, room service deliver our coffee and I pour a mug and bring it to Suzie, now comfortably reclining in the full hot tub.

Suzie sighs contentedly from the bath so I strip off and lie on the bed, awaiting my turn in the bathroom. Being an old hotel, the shower is over the bath, so I have to wait. Then again, patience is a virtue and I have plenty. Fifteen years in the Australian Army taught me many things – patience being one of them!

My mind wanders back over the last week or so…

Some of you might recall I am travelling with broken ribs after an escapade with a taxi.

Fortunately, the lie-flat bed in Qantas business class was as comfortable as promised so my ribs didn't create too big a drama for me. I am used to coping with pain anyway, so was never going to admit any!

My major concern was Suzie insisting on ensuring my ribs are better before unleashing her 'sexy nightie' on me. Me, I can't wait!

We arrived in Victoria after driving across from Vancouver and moved into a two-bedroom Airbnb cottage on the outskirts of Victoria. This was home for the duration of our stay here. An ideal, if not idyllic spot away from the crowds, just the way we like it!

Whilst Pig had lived with me for a few weeks previously, both Suzie and I were taken aback by the time and effort Pig had to put into caring for his leg and prosthesis. (Pig lost his left leg below the knee to an IED in Afghanistan). He never let on about any issue or hassles, climbing trees, ladders without even a grimace, but sharing the cottage we share and even help a little, as he bathed his stump, massaged it and then also had to care for the artificial joint, oiling and greasing it.

As always, never a word of complaint!

First morning, we discovered a nearby Tim Horton's, a proud Canadian coffee house. Yes, the coffee was as good as we had been told! Their donuts and timbits (the pieces out of the middle of the donut) were particularly yummy! Our first morning, we met a chatty local, Bill, a retired lawyer, who told us his morning walk was down to Tim Horton's with his faithful dog Rusty to get his morning coffee and half a dozen timbits!

The first couple of days of the Invictus Games was a real buzz. Pig's first event, the four hundred metres, wasn't until the morning of day three, so we all just enjoyed the atmosphere and camaraderie of the occasion. Pig and I ran into many former colleagues from all over whom we had served with, or met, in one corner of the globe or another. Mostly hell holes too!

Suzie even commented, 'It's like being with a couple of rockstars with you two. Everyone knows you and wants to say hello and shake your hands!'

We just smiled. It was pretty cool. Suzie often walked between us, holding both our hands. No, I'm not getting jealous or feeling threatened by Pig!

Back to the serious business of racing.

Well, in Pig's first race, it's fair to say he was flogged. The four hundred metres was one of the most popular races on the program, so heaps of competitors and forty-odd heats.

His next, the 1500 metres in the afternoon of day four, was a little better, but not by much. He was simply outclassed and swamped. Needless to say, he was disappointed; he had put in a lot of effort to get here and running disappointing times wasn't sitting well with him.

On day five, he had the day off and we all headed off to visit the Butchart Gardens, a marvellous man-made garden in an old quarry. My mum was a keen gardener and had heard or read about these gardens years ago. For many years, their annual calendar adorned our kitchen. In fact, as a teenager this was an easy Christmas present for me to buy for Mum, and I ended up having it on auto-buy each year.

Suddenly, I thought, I wonder if I'm still paying for it! Note to self, check the Visa statement!

Anyway, seeing it in person was great, made better by the nice sunny day, so casually wandering around these pretty gardens with Suzie and (to a lesser extent!) Pig was a delight. They even made a pretty good coffee, so we sat and enjoyed a 'High Tea'. Well, Suzie and I did; Pig wasn't eating any goodies, with what he hoped was his main event coming up the next day!

Next morning and Pig seemed a bit toey, edgy, so we gave him a bit of space. It's not like him to be this way. 'Mr Cool' is our Pig – a 'cool pig', heh heh!

We headed into town in plenty of time and as we let him off at the competitor's entrance, I got out of the car and gave him a hug – a 'man hug', that is – saying, 'Empty the tank!'

His reply, 'I aim to.' Pretty serious too.

Being this early, we were able to grab good seats near the finish line and we settled in, watching various field sports, javelin, discus and the like whilst we waited for the ten thousand metres to be called.

Here we go.

First heat was up. We knew from the program Pig was in heat five and with each heat taking about thirty to forty minutes, it was still going to be a while.

Time for a coffee, or two!

Heat five was up.

Twenty-five laps of the four hundred metre track – wonder they don't get dizzy, ah!

They are off. Most had a fancy-looking running blade, the same as Pig's.

Pig settled in the middle of the field, letting the competitors settle into their rhythm, like he was doing. I was timing him and he was running good lap times, better than he had ever done at training. I was also watching him closely and he was running tight, with good rhythm.

As they approached the bell with one lap to go, Pig was sitting in eighth place but nearly half a lap down from the third-placed runner, Edward, a Pom (Englishman), who Pig and I both know (but don't get on with!).

As he approached the bell, sounding one lap to go, Pig had stretched his stride and moved past the seventh-placed runner. I sensed something and said to Suzie, 'He's surging! Shit, there's a long way to go. Hope he can hold it together!'

I won't deny there was a catch in my voice either, as Pig continued to quicken his pace easily past the next runner, then another as they entered the back straight.

I was standing now, chanting, 'PIG PIG PIG,' and then Suzie was up joining me, also chanting 'PIG PIG PIG'. We weren't alone either I could hear quite a chant going around the crowd.

Out of the back straight into the final curve, Edward (it has never been Ed or Eddie – always Edward!) was now only forty metres ahead, coming out of the final bend.

But Pig was flying now. Yes, I know, Pigs don't fly, but this one was!

I had no idea where he had found this speed or energy, but he was reeling Edward in by the metre.

He too was now out of the final bend and hurtling down the final straight, finish line ahead.

Stride by stride, he was gaining on Edward, who had sensed something or someone was coming but was tiring quickly.

Twenty metres to go, fifteen, ten. Pig was striding out. I even admired how he had held his rhythm together – no question, he was going to hold it.

The chant went on, even louder if that was possible.

Five metres and he was two paces behind. Four, three, two – almost there.

They hit the line together!

Did he or didn't he? Neither we nor anyone else in the crowd could tell.

Suzie and I were still up, hugging each other and even some of the strangers around us. It was clear to all that we were friends of Pig in his loud yellow running strip as we were also adorned in our proud Aussie gold.

Of course, somewhere else in the crowd came another Aussie accent: 'AUSSIE, AUSSIE, AUSSIE! Oi, oi, oi!' Of course, we had to join in.

Pig was still on the track, having ended up halfway round the next bend before he stopped. He leaned down hands on his knees and stayed that way before having to move out of the way for other runners still finishing.

He headed to the inside of the track and started back toward the finish line. He knew where we were sitting so he looked up and gave us a smile and waved. We were still on our feet and yelled back to him, fist raised! We were pumped! AND proud!

Did he or didn't he?

We didn't know.

The final runners came in, in what seemed an eternity after Pig finished, and only then did they name first, second and third. Bugger, it was Edward's name they called.

Bugger!

They did note though that it was a tight photo finish and to use the horse racing parlance, Pig was beaten by a nose.

Bugger.

After such a barnstorming finish, he deserved a medal to have missed by 'that much' (remember Maxwell Smart saying that in Get Smart?!)

He was still getting a standing ovation as he moved along the side of the track, as Suzie and I tried to get through the crowd to join him. Not on the track, of course, but we knew he would be looking for us at the competitor's exit.

We found him standing there, beaming!

'Man,' I said to him, 'way to go!' and we high-fived and then fist bumped while Suzie grabbed him for a hug.

'Awesome job,' I said. 'Where did that speed come from?'

He smiled and shrugged his shoulders and said, 'Not sure. Didn't know I had that in me but as you said, didn't want to die wondering!' We high-five again.

He didn't even seem disappointed he missed getting the bronze medal by such a small margin, more just proud of his effort.

Awesome effort!

That night we avoided the games scene and headed into the suburbs for a quiet meal and a few beers. Pig was keen to catch up after two weeks of abstinence!

Then, after our meal, we decided to head back to 'Entertainment Central' to hang out. And hang out we did, into the wee small hours, but was good to let our hair down. I think all three of us enjoyed ourselves and with nothing planned for the next morning, why not!

***

I must have dozed off as I awaken with Suzie leaning over me in her fluffy hotel robe, her soft, silky blonde hair hanging down around her face. She has it cut shorter these days, off her shoulders.

But it is not her hair that has my interest. My hands are keen to know what she has underneath and she leans down further and kisses me as my fingers continue to explore. The kiss lingers as her hand too moves south.

Alas, she pushes my hand away and pulls out of the kiss before whispering, 'You still have broken ribs, remember?'

I reply, 'You won't hear me complaining!'

The moment has gone and she says, 'Off to the shower with you, otherwise Julien will be here and I need to talk to you before he gets here.' Suzie, as always, insists on calling Pig by his given name – even if Pig might prefer Pig! Except when we were chanting at the race!

I nod before adding, 'You can come and scrub my back if you like.'

As an answer, I get one of her wonderful smiles. (Yes, they still make my heart flutter – arh! Ah.)

My shower is, as always, quick and efficient. Army life teaches many things and quick and functional showers are one of them.

I'm quickly changed and pour another coffee and notice Suzie is now also fully dressed in her usual low-key, stylish way and is sitting on the lounge, checking her phone – of course!

She looks up as I sit down beside her, fresh coffee in hand. She puts her phone away and looks seriously at me before reaching for my hand.

'Mort,' she starts. 'I know you will want to help Campbell out. I know there is no way you will say no to trying to help stop these people. It would not be you to say no. More of your "Mortice" ah!' This is accompanied by a grin as she places her hand on top of mine.

'Frankly, I want you to help if you can. I just want you to be careful. And if we are going to help, then I'm in. No trying to sideline me. I want to help if I can. BUT I expect you to be careful – not just for me but for us and Julien as well.' She leans in for a quick kiss, adding, 'I have a wedding half planned so NO risks, please.'

Whilst I'm pleased there isn't going to be any argument from Suzie, as no way am I not going to try at least to help Campbell and Hunter out – not only because they too are 'good people' but simply because it is also the right thing to do.

These criminal gangs flaunt the law and seem to operate with impunity, like our outlaw bikie gangs in Australia. Police and law enforcement always have to comply with rules and regulations. The criminals, not so much. A very uneven playing field the world over.

As five-thirty p.m. approaches, I order another couple of pots of strong coffee so we have a fresh brew when Pig arrives. Those of you who have read the two previous books on our exploits will know we are addicted to coffee.

When Pig arrives, coincidentally at the same time as our coffee, we sit down but before I can say a word, it's Suzie who starts, 'Julien, I have already told Mort this, so just to be clear and so we are all on the same page. I have told Mort I'm keen to try and help Campbell and Hunter. If you can keep us safe. AND minimise all risks. I say "we" deliberately too, as if we are doing this, I'm in. All the way in. To help, not hinder or second guess, but I'm keen to help, even if only from the sidelines. I'm certainly not interested in getting in any firing line so to speak, but keen to contribute.'

Pig has watched her intently throughout her little speech, and then gives her a nod, saying, 'Fair enough.' He then looks at me and says, 'You okay with this?'

I nod. 'Yes. No way in the wide world I'll be putting Suzie, or you and I for that matter, in danger, and I'm happy for Suzie to contribute in any way she can.' I'm looking directly at Suzie when I add, 'We know from when she was kidnapped, she is cool under pressure and doesn't lose her head.'

I know from bitter experience Suzie doesn't like to be reminded of the events of her kidnapping. (I shot and killed her kidnapper whilst he held a gun to her head.)

Again, to her credit, she doesn't look away, merely nods acceptance of the point I've made.

Pig and I share another look and nod.

Sorted. Move on.

As Pig gets up and refreshes our coffees, I randomly think his bald head does suit him. He had surprised us, arriving at Brisbane airport for our trip having shaved his black hair all off. It had never been long, but now gone altogether. I had teased him about his new aerodynamic look.

I bring my thoughts to order.

'Okay, we all agree we will have a look-see and see if we can come up with a plan to nail this Diego Garcia. As I see it, that's all we can agree to for now.

'We will want them to provide all the video surveillance they can offer from the last, say, four weeks – a list of his known haunts, home, family set up, mistresses or boyfriends, whoever. Any and all confirmed routines. First and foremost, we have to be off the books totally. If they can't guarantee that, it's no deal.'

As I pause, Pig takes over. 'I will handle how they supply this data. Midge has introduced me to these dark web sites where you get a short window of time to upload data, then the site closes and no one can trace it.

'I have a few set up so we can put these to good use. I suggest we buy them throw-away phones, so they never use their official phones when talking or texting us. Ditto for us – we will need to turn our usual phones off and remove the battery. Maybe even let Maria and Jenny know not to call us to minimise all contact.'

I see Suzie pull a face at this. Jenny is her PA/para legal, and they have been talking frequently during our holiday so far. Not only about work, I hasten to add! A fair amount of idle chatter and of course plenty of gossip – they are women and good friends, after all!

Time to head off to dinner. I've checked and it's only an eight-minute walk, so an easy stroll, made more pleasurable by Suzie slipping her hand into mine as we walk.

Don't mind that!

4

We arrive at the restaurant and see Campbell and Hunter already at a table set for six in a small side room.

Hunter waves us over and we take our seats.

Pig once again wanders around the room, checking for bugs. Once he's finished, Hunter pipes up, saying, 'Don't worry, I have already done that too.'

We make small talk whilst we review the menu and order our drinks and food all at once to reduce the interruptions. However, it isn't long before Pig asks them both, 'How can you two proud soldiers work for your bloody government after the way they abdicated their responsibilities to the Afghan people and left them in the worst possible mess? It is a downright disaster and a smack in the face to all of us who served there. Even more so to those injured or who died.'

Phew, Pig, like me, isn't a talker, so this is a major speech for him. And a heartfelt one.

It is met with silence.

Then Campbell, after looking at Hunter, nods, saying, 'We essentially agree with you, Pig.' (Yes, he was only ever known as Pig during our army years.) 'But we also recognise the major battleground we face now at home. All this woke shit and soft government is meaning life for "normal Americans" is becoming tougher and harder. That is why Hunter and I both joined the FBI direct from the Marines. We need to make a difference. We need to do it within our country now as we have so many struggles within.'

Silence returns, with Pig and I separately acknowledging his message and accepting it.

Then it's Hunter who says to Pig, 'Man, that was some finish to your race yesterday. Can't believe how well you were running. And to miss by a nose. Man, you deserved the medal!'

Campbell then adds, 'Yes, I watched the race as well and we were both yelling and cheering you on with the "PIG PIG PIG" chant! Well done.'

Pig, in his usual calm manner, nods and says simply, 'Thanks. Was a great experience.'

I add in, 'Yes, it was an awesome effort. He has even been contacted by Paralympics Australia and been invited to trial for the Brisbane Paralympics in 2032.' Yes, our hometown will be turning it on for the Olympic games.

'You serious? Man, that's awesome. You're in, right?' is Hunter's response.

Pig smiles, saying, 'I'm certainly flattered they have reached out but it's still a few years away and I'm not sure I have the time or commitment for years of training and competing.'

Pig had admitted this to us himself earlier, making me wonder if he had another motive…

Hunter then says, 'Brisbane, isn't that the home of Ash Barty, your tennis player?'

I quickly step in, 'Well, technically, her hometown is Ipswich, same as mine. Ipswich is a city only forty-five minutes from Brisbane and has a rich history of being the hometown of numerous Australian sporting legends. Ash is simply the latest – and such a great ambassador for our state and country.'

Hunter nods before adding, 'My ten-year-old daughter Tegan is a BIG fan, has Ash's posters on the wall and trains so hard at her tennis, wanting to be able to play like Ash when she grows up.' This final statement is complemented by a big smile as he is clearly thinking of his daughter, and family in general, I suspect.

Once all orders are taken and first drinks delivered, I look at them both and say, 'We are here to listen. We will help if we can see a way to do that safely. First, some non-negotiables: one – we must remain "off the books" at all times. Not to be mentioned by real names in any documentation or phone or video calls, for example, any communication.

'Two – we will require you to provide clean passports for use whilst on assignment. Again, these names are not to be used within any files of communications.

'Three – the whole assignment is not to be mentioned, not to be given a code name.

'Four – guns. Pig and I will need "off the book" weapons. Preferably a Glock 19 or Sig Sauer P226. Not our first choices, but hey, we don't want to stand out from the crowd. These can't be traced back to you or us and we need permits in our new names to carry these. We will want these made available once we are across the border – for obvious reasons!

'Five – payment.'

Here, I write a number on the back of a coaster on the table and push it across to Campbell. He picks it up whilst Hunter leans over to look at the number as well.

Neither of them blink.

Shit, I think. I should have doubled it!

Campbell looks at me, saying, 'I'm authorised to go above that, so that is not an issue.'

I nod and say, 'As usual with these sorts of assignments, fifty per cent on agreement and fifty per cent upon delivery. Plus one hundred thousand dollars to cover expenses. All payable from and to an offshore account, so no US-domiciled bank transaction.' Here, I slip him a bank deposit slip of one of my 'offshore' Grand Cayman Island bank accounts (I have a couple!) saying, 'These are my bank account details, in case we proceed.'

Campbell takes it, giving me an 'I'm impressed' nod, clearly realising I'm ensuring I don't have to put bank account details into an email or text.

I also point out we have not yet agreed, 'but merely laying out our non-negotiables, so no money payable just yet.'

I let the silence linger as our first-course plates are cleared and they table our mains. An eight-ounce New York strip for Pig and I – mine medium, not rare like Pigs! Suzie went for the 'filet of Sole' whilst the other two both went for the steak and prawns.

We all settle in to enjoy the mains and it wasn't until we are all largely done that Campbell comes back, saying, 'Okay, we have no issues with any of that. My boss, as an assistant director, is well-versed with ways and means to beat the bean counters and the do-gooders. We have already agreed; in fact, we will only ever discuss this mission face-to-face. No phone, text or emails. No one will ever know your names or even the real purpose of our visit here. To be honest, Hunter and I are officially on leave, telling all colleagues we are up here supporting friends. Which is true in fact.

'New passports also won't be a problem. As you might appreciate, we provide quite a number of false passports – or in actual fact, real passports with false names! The guns also won't be an issue. There are plenty of confiscated firearms we can use.

'I will need to take a couple of photos of you each to make this happen but don't worry, I will be hand delivering these as well. Maybe we can detour back to the office after this so I can take your photos, in case you agree? No shortcuts. We want these bastards so bad; we will not jeopardise our chances, believe me.'

Hunter nods aggressively in agreement.

I look at Pig and Suzie in turn, getting a small nod from both before I continue, 'All right, we can come back to your office after dinner for the photos. What data can you provide on this Diego and his offsiders? What video surveillance can you provide – his routine, favourite haunts, mistresses, you name it. We will need access to the whole shooting box. We won't know our chance until we see it. No shortcuts here either.'

Hunter digs into his pocket and pulls out a USB stick and puts it on the table in front of us.

I let Pig take the floor. He knows I will and is ready, already shaking his head.

'No. We won't be taking that. Too easy for you or one of your techs to hide a spider on there so you can track us and see where we might be focusing our attention.'

He pulls a slip of paper out of his pocket and passes it to Hunter, saying, 'Upload all your data and videos onto this link. I activated it at six p.m., so it will close tonight at eleven p.m. You need to ensure you get everything you think we might need uploaded before then. We aren't taking any risks.'

Hunter has a bit of a grizzle, assuring us the USB stick is 'state of the art' and not compromised, but we hold firm. Pig answers him, looking at his watch. 'Two hours and fifty minutes now.'

Hunter accepts he has some work to do when we are finished.

'One other question, a rather important one for us to understand.

If we manage to plant a wire on him or source information some other way, this will not be legal and therefore not eligible in any court proceedings. So how will you overcome this?'

Campbell immediately replies, 'Glad you brought this up. We have so many court-approved wire intercept authorisations, it's not funny. We simply have never managed to set or install any. So, if you do manage a wire – great, no problems!'

I nod to them both, saying, 'Okay then, fair enough. We are out of here tomorrow, booked on the three p.m. ferry back to Vancouver for a few days' sightseeing. If we get the data tonight, this will give us this time to view it and see what we can find. Might be something, might not. If we see a shot at this, a safe, minimal-risk one, we will call you on these phones.'

Here, Suzie pulls the two new prepaid mobiles out of her handbag we had bought from a convenience store on the way to the restaurant. Pig had set them up in the store, so we already have the numbers in our own new phones as well. (We bought ours from a nearby service station as an added precaution.)

'But we will only be telling you we have a plan, so you can make payment of the expenses and the fifty per cent upfront payment. You won't know any of the details, not the when, or the where. We won't even tell you when we plan on entering the country, although I'm sure you will try to track us once we do. We ask you not to do this. No attention – any distraction will only jeopardise the "mission" as you call it. Hope that makes sense.'

Campbell and Hunter both nod acceptance and it's clear they are a little excited at having us come on board.

Our conversation continues as the four of us reminisce over our years in Afghanistan before Suzie asks Hunter and Campbell, 'So how did you meet these two?' She gives me a nudge and a nod toward Pig.

Hunter smiles and replies, 'Well, to be honest, if it wasn't for these two, I wouldn't be here today. They saved my skin and that of my platoon when a mission behind enemy lines went belly up. But that's classified, so I can't say any more. Needless to say, we shared a few beers once they got back to barracks, some weeks later.

'But a few weeks after that, my platoon was on standby in Kabul when a "spooky" mission was called. Just so you know, we called any CIA or spy-type mission a "spooky mission" because you never knew how they would pan out. These CIA and spy types seemed to live in a different world.

'Anyway, we were ordered to provide armed back up to this CIA mission early one morning. So we are on station, a fully armed team of six in our armoured Humvee, sitting a couple of blocks away from where the action was planned to take place.

'We didn't even know what was going down, only that if it went belly up, we were to go in "full force" – guns blazing. But they did provide satellite feed of the action, so we are sitting quietly – this is just after five in the morning – and we are watching two Afghan men walking down the road. The one in front was clearly out for his morning walk, the other seemed to be a bodyguard. But a pretty slack one as he simply followed along, watching something on his phone as he walked.

'Next minute this big guy we assumed was a local dressed as he was in the traditional "Tunban" appeared out of nowhere, hand around the neck of the bodyguard'– he used air quotes as he said this – 'whose head collapsed forward, and the big guy laid him on the ground. The front walker, who we now assumed was the target, hadn't heard a thing, not missing a step.

'As the big guy quickened his pace again and just as he reached out to repeat the process of cutting off the air supply by squeezing his throat of the front walker, a little motor bike silently pulled up beside him. The big guy simply lifted the unconscious walker, holding him upright by each arm pressed against his body, onto the bike between himself and the rider and away they went.

'It was so seamless and efficient. I looked at my crewmates and said, "Shit, did that just happen?" It was like the perfect abduction.

'It was only later as we were driving back through the barrack entry gates we noticed the same two Afghans, sitting on the back of a Hilux and bugger me, when they leapt out and removed their headgear, I recognised Pig and Mort here. Full black beards and all.

'I must say I shared this memory with our boss when we suggested trying to recruit you. I gather she looked it up as she commented later about the success of it and what they learned.'

Pig and I share a smile at the memory of this mission.

I then add, 'Dwight Brown. That was the name of the CIA agent who recruited us. Or at least that was the name he was using. Apparently, he saw us come back in from the field after one of our lengthier missions and couldn't believe we weren't Afghans. Before we were even allowed a shower or anything, we were escorted to his office, accompanied by our CO and recruited on the spot.'

I smile at Hunter and say, 'Yes, that mission did go smoothly but as you may know, that wasn't the end of it. His name was Abdul Amir. He was a mid-ranked Taliban leader. Working right under our noses in the middle of Kabul. Anyway, to finish off the story, once on the bike, we zig-zagged through the streets, not speeding but still pretty quickly until we got to our rendezvous point where we handed him over to a CIA team. We then rode on to a little shopfront, left the motorbike and jumped on the back of the ute – or Hilux, as you called it – to head back to base.

'I didn't know your team provided the backup; we were told there was a team nearby if the need to abort arose. Anyway, this Abdul, as soon as he was confronted, offered a full record of all his dealings. He promised if his wife and two young children could be rescued and they were all provided safe passage to the States, he would provide full disclosure of all his dealings, names, locations et cetera.

'The interesting thing was, none of it was written down, but his wife had a photographic memory or whatever they call it. Tell her something once and she will remember all the details. They believed it was only a matter of time until Abdul was captured and had planned for this eventuality. They had even been practising writing and speaking English in the privacy of their home. I know Dwight was shocked when he went in to start the interrogation, expecting to have to use all his usual resources of torture to get anything out of him. For Abdul to then greet him in English and request we recover his family and get him out of the country set in motion the second mission that day.'

Pig pipes up. 'It's called eidetic memory – total recall of any facts or figures or images.'

I nod, agreeing with him before continuing, 'Abdul had demanded that we be sent back in to get his family, apparently impressed by the way we managed to abduct him without him even, as he said, "Seeing, hearing or smelling us."'

Suzie interrupts me, asking, 'What did he mean, smell you?'

I smile and reply, 'Afghanis don't have much water. They certainly do not waste it on showers or baths, so you can imagine to Westerners their body odour can be rather ripe. So, whenever we went on a mission, we would not shower for four or five days, never used deodorant or other chemicals, even to wash our clothes because, even though we don't smell these, if you're not used to the aroma, these smells stand out and are one of the quickest ways for a mission to be compromised. Locals simply smell the imposters.'

Suzie wrinkles her nose at the thought of this!

I continue, 'He must have made a good argument because Dwight authorised the mission. A little after nine-thirty that night, we are dropped off a block from their apartment building, this time armed with our EF88 assault rifles hidden beneath our tunbans.

'Abdul has assured us his wife would be expecting us and their door would be unlocked. He also warned their team of three bodyguards shared the neighbouring apartment on the left and we would need to neutralise them to have any chance of making good our escape. Good to know.

'They lived on the second floor of the two-story walk up, so we quickly hustled up the stairs knowing someone would have reported two strangers entering the building. From Abdul's description we knew which was the bodyguard's apartment, so we quickly pick the lock, needing to surprise them to neutralise them quickly and quietly.

'We open the door and even though it squeaks, we take care of all three, quickly and easily. They clearly aren't the sharpest tools in the shed, not having learnt anything from that morning. Back out in the hallway and I push on Abdul's apartment door, and sure enough it opens silently. His wife Aalem is standing in the middle of the room, two young girls hugging her tight with their large, frightened eyes. Watching us, she says, "Welcome. Is Abdul safe?"

'I reply, "Yes. We are here to take you to him. Now." She nods and reaches behind her. Pig and I move quickly in opposite directions, not sure what she is reaching for, but it is only three large bags she has gathered all their necessary belongings into.

'She gives one to the older girl and at my nod they start following me to the door. I peer out, looking for any signs of danger whilst Aalem whispers, "Turn right, it is quicker."

'As we enter the hallway, Pig reaches past the youngest girl holding a stuffed toy, a rabbit by the looks. The older girl grabs it with a muffled sob. Aalem turns and nods her thanks to Pig. Ever thoughtful is our Pig!

'We quickly make our way back down the stairs before having to move along the hallway on the ground floor. Here, we come across a large woman standing in her doorway, arms crossed, clearly understanding what is going on. She spits at our feet. Her way of expressing her disgust, I guess. No matter to me.

'Out into the street, our getaway van is parked waiting for us, the driver at the ready. In we get, all five of us. It's a bit tight but we quickly head off. Not making a beeline for the base to attract too much attention, but we get there in one piece and as per our instructions, we head straight to the airport and stop outside a designated hanger. I noticed a Gulfstream jet sitting there already waiting.

'Abdul comes out of the hanger and runs toward his family. But before anything else can be done, Dwight takes the family inside the hangar. Pig and I follow, keen to see what happens next. Clearly, this has been agreed between Abdul and Dwight as Abdul is quickly chatting to his wife, the CIA interpreter listening in.

'She starts nodding. "Yes, yes," she says. They all sit down with Abdul taking care of the kids. Aalem composes herself in a chair, still in the full Hijab, then nods.

'What follows is Dwight hammering out dates and names. Each time, Aalem quickly replies with events or activities relating to the date. The CIA interpreter translated both questions and answers. All of course is being recorded as well.

'Dwight and his colleague mark these off. Clearly, some had been trick questions but she seemed to have answered everything correctly. Dwight is smiling, obviously very pleased with this outcome as he confirms this to both Abdul and Aalem, shaking their hands and having the interpreter tell them to get ready, they will be flying out in ten minutes.

'Dwight then comes over to us, shaking both our hands, saying, "Thanks, you did a marvellous job – both parts of it, so thank you. You will be hearing from me again shortly."

'With that, he leads the family out of the hangar and directly onto the Gulfstream Jet. Door closes, stairway removed and they are wheels up, bound for USA!'

We all sit quietly, having all been absorbed in the story and in Pig's and my case, reliving it.

I then add, 'You know, Dwight came back about ten days later. We again met with him with our CO and we agreed to a six-month secondment to the CIA. This was later extended, twice. They flew us back to Quantico and a couple of other bases Stateside where they taught us "Spycraft". Some of these skills have come in real handy too, I must say. We eventually did a few other missions for them as well, but not in Afghanistan. They too are classified.'

Campbell, who has been silent through the whole storytelling, then adds, 'You know Aalem is now a college professor somewhere in Connecticut, so has done very well for herself.'

It's Pig that asks, 'What about Abdul?'

Campbell pulls a face, saying, 'He was killed in a hit and run a couple of years ago. We suspect it was a Taliban hit.'

This seemed an appropriate time to end the evening. We leave the table, shaking hands all round, with Hunter footing the bill and paying in cash, I note, so another marker indicating they are not on the FBI dime.

Good to see!

As we leave the restaurant, I ask them, 'So how come our names came up on the airline manifest? I thought that was only for undesirables?'

It's Hunter that replies, 'No need to worry, you were both flagged as allies, so a green flag not a red one!'

'Okay,' I respond, 'but how did you know Suzie's name?'

Hunter looks at me as if thinking, That's a dumb question, before replying, 'Wasn't hard. She was flying with you, seated next to you. It was all there on the manifest.' I nod in acceptance and think, I agree with him. It was a dumb question!

After our detour back to their office, where we take turns offering an unsmiling face against the blank white office wall, we three head back to the hotel, Suzie's hand once again firmly in mine. We discuss the basics as we walk but hadn't learnt anything other than they and the FBI seem genuinely desperate to catch this drug mob and stop them.

Once back in our room, Suzie is equally excited and apprehensive. The excitement at this little adventure, apprehensive, as I had made it clear, the risk we would all be taking if we got into this and stuff it up. The reach of these gangs knows no bounds.

I again assure her we won't be taking any risks. It's not in mine or Pig's nature to be 'gung-ho' about any such operation or assignment.

As we snuggle in for the night, she again repels my amorous advances by saying, 'You will need your ribs to be fully healed if you take on this assignment.'

Bugger, I can't argue with that, but I do assure her I'm close to being back to full fitness, now doing most of the same training routine in the gym that I was doing prior to being hit by the bloody Prius. Bloody electric cars – I hadn't heard it coming.

Alas all to no avail!

5

Next morning, we meet Pig down for breakfast, served in the 'Q at the Empress' restaurant. It is the usual large hotel buffet, so Pig and I help ourselves.

Suzie comments dryly, 'Well, we won't need to stop for lunch, will we!'

Around a mouthful, Pig confirmed he had received 'a whole pile of shit' from Hunter and whilst he had started to look through it, it was going to be a slow process.

He detailed that he had received:

- Four weeks of daily surveillance tapes, commenting, 'I haven't seen him taking a shit yet, but it seems like they watch every public step he takes.'
- His home and office addresses along with one suspected to belong to a mistress. Apparently, he only ever stayed there for one to two hours, normally only once a week or so. The woman's name was listed with a note neither the FBI nor the police had any record of her, so a true clean skin.
- A list of close associates and enemies along with their addresses and photos.
- Likewise, his usual three-man security detail plus chauffeur are also listed along with 'mug shots'. They aren't pretty boys

but look big, mean sons of bitches, as I'm sure they need to be.

I then tell them both I want to change rental cars once back in Vancouver before heading off to Lake Louise. Not because of anything in particular but I don't want to make it easy for them to track us, if they have a mind. I point out they would have had ample time to affix a tracker to our car whilst we had been here, and I'm sure they can track us through hotel bookings and use of credit cards et cetera, if they wanted to. I tell them I will start using a prepaid Visa now, not my usual Amex card, again just to make it a little harder. It's Suzie who points out we have hotels booked at Lake Louise and Calgary already, to which I reply, 'Yes, but I'm going to extend our stay at the Fairmont in Vancouver, so they won't be looking for any other bookings. They won't think they need to look any further.'

She nods, looking impressed by my forward thinking! Even Pig is giving me a nod of approval!

Plan in place, we spend a few hours sightseeing around Victoria, stopping for lunch at Oak Bay beach before heading to the ferry terminal.

Next stop, Vancouver.

We're booked into the Fairmont at the airport – not because we're flying out, but because it saves the drive in and out of the city centre as we want to hit the road early in the morning for our road trip to Lake Louise.

And as an added bonus, we had managed to get tickets to the Canucks, Vancouver's ice hockey team's home game tonight against their archrivals from Calgary – the Calgary Flames.

Violence on ice – I love it!

Once we have checked in, I head over to the airport, drop off the Suburban at Thrifty, wander along the row of booths and find Avis has a Chevy Tahoe on special, so I snare this and use a prepaid Visa to pay.

Not foolproof but again it will make it just that much more difficult if Campbell and Hunter (or any other FBI types) do try and track us. Someone else will be driving the Suburban around Vancouver, leading them on a wild goose chase!

Next morning, we are up early and on the road. Not surprisingly Suzie holds her hand out for the key, saying with a sweet smile, 'I'll drive if you like!' As if we had an option.

Pig makes himself comfortable in the back 'captain's seat', pulling his laptop onto his knees and earphones at the ready. He had told us he was planning on reviewing the videos as we drove, content to not do any driving. Knowing Suzie's opinion about my driving, claiming in the past 'I drove like a grandfather', I'm in no doubt she will be wanting to do most of the driving.

We head out along the Trans-Canadian Highway through the Fraser Valley, to Hope, which becomes our first coffee and pee stop, where we veer off highway one and onto highway three.

We stop at Princeton for lunch and surprisingly I'm allowed to drive from here to our evening destination of Vernon on Okanagan Lake.

That night over dinner at the Blue Heron, which seems to be a popular spot with the locals, Pig confirms he has watched three weeks of video so far, but nothing has 'hit him' yet.

Next morning, we are again on the road early, not because we have long distances to travel but because we are keen to get to Lake Louise, it being one of the destinations we had spoken about most and an expected highlight of our holiday.

A couple of hours in – yes, Suzie has again taken the wheel – and Pig says, 'I might have something.'

I turn in my seat, eyebrow raised, and he continues, 'Would be easier to show you rather than try and explain it.'

Suzie responds, 'We are twenty minutes out of Revelstoke and I need a pee so why don't we stop there for coffee and you can show us?'

Pig and I nod our agreement.

Suzie then adds, 'There is a café called "Village Idiot" that gets good reviews on TripAdvisor so I thought we could stop there.'

I reply, 'With a name like that, perhaps we should!'

6

A short time later, we are all settled in the oddly named restaurant, an early lunch of burgers and coffee ordered.

Pig opens his laptop and Suzie and I lean over to see what he wants to show us.

He has the video already to start so explains, 'Every morning Diego walks his son Juan to school at The Dalton School. Looks pretty swanky too, by the way. They always leave between eight a.m. and 8.15 a.m. and it takes them roughly fifteen to eighteen minutes depending on lights, et cetera.

'They live on 5th Avenue overlooking Central Park, as you do, and they walk the same route every morning. He has his usual three-man security detail with him. Then his car picks them up from the school and they are off for the day. But watch this.' He pauses here and presses play.

We watch the five of them exit a stylish apartment building, turn right and at the first corner turn right again into East 86th Street. With construction on the right side of the road, they immediately jaywalk across the road and continue on down 86th until Park Avenue, turning left for three blocks before turning right, crossing over Park Ave at the lights and then on down East 89th to The Dalton School.

I note they walk in a spear shape, one of the security detail in the lead, Diego and Juan side by side behind and two out-flankers – one either side of them, so they take the whole of the sidewalk as they walk along.

The bodyguard on the inside of the sidewalk is always one step back behind Diego, so protecting his back as well as the side.

Being the bodyguards are all big burly men. All other pedestrians get out of their way. Not that they have a choice.

This is a common method of protecting a person whilst walking in public. The only thing they could do extra would be a fourth guard walking at the back. But I'm sure they are confident they have it covered.

So, I'm intrigued to see what Pig has in mind!

We are still waiting on our burgers, as the video only took ten odd minutes, so he presses play again, saying, 'This is the next day.'

It is an exact replica of the day before and just before they reach the school, the waitress arrives with our burgers, then refreshes our coffees and leaves us to it.

Pig stops the recording and we all tuck in.

Enjoyable burgers but I'm keen to know what Pig has seen as I haven't seen any opening yet.

Once Suzie has finished her chicken burger, licking her fingers and saying, 'That was "finger licking good"!' (heh heh), Pig restarts the video and lets it play till the end. He then starts the third day and as soon as they turn into East 86th Street, he says, 'Watch this.' He then slows the video down as they walk along the street, now pausing it before saying, 'See this little gate.' (There is a little gate covering a small laneway between two buildings, which he points to on the screen.) 'See how the little garden around the kerbside tree acts as a natural funnel, forcing the back, inside guard to slow down with Diego, who always walks on the inside, forced over close to the building or in this case the gateway?'

I nod, seeing what he is suggesting, but still not sensing why this is important, so he continues, 'So, if I remove my prosthetic and dress the part of a street bum – a one-legged beggar if you like – and position myself in this gateway, Diego will almost have to step over me. I would have a good shot at getting a small mic onto him.

'Midge was showing me online some of these newer mics the other week. Called mini spiders because they have six little feet – they are designed to attach to any sort of fabric. They are all plastic, so not detectible by metal detectors and are 5G enabled, so everything recorded will go straight to our cloud storage base.'

He quickly switches screens pulling up a website selling these little spider mics.

I'm impressed, but…

'Okay, I can see the potential, but how do you feel about becoming a one-legged beggar, to use your words?'

Suzie nods as if she shares my concern.

Pig simply shrugs his shoulders, saying, 'Doesn't bother me. Use what we've got. In this case, I reckon I could make a good hobo!'

With the waitress hovering, waiting to clear our table, Pig shuts the laptop. We ask for fresh coffees to go and head back to the Tahoe. Pig and I fist bump on the walk over to it.

I hold my hand out for the keys but Suzie is having none of it, saying, 'It's okay, I have this,' but gives me a lovely smile – knowing damn well that gets her whatever she wants!

Once settled in the SUV, Pig and I discuss the scenario he has just shown us, but our conversation lapses as we head deeper into the Rocky Mountains.

The scenery is what we have come for, so our discussions can wait! Also, all three of us are hoping to see a bear in the wild up here in the Canadian Rockies! Our eyes are glued!

No such luck seeing a bear, but we do marvel at the scenery – such a contrast to our Australian countryside, the steep mountains all covered in cedar trees – such a deep green with raging rivers in every gorge.

We eventually wind our way through the little village of Lake Louise before heading up to Chateau Lake Louise, right on the shore of the lake.

An absolutely stunning view – or it would be if we hadn't had low cloud and drizzle for the last few miles.

After checking in, we agreed to meet Pig down in the ground floor bar for a quick drink before dinner.

Of course, I had booked high-level lake view rooms so we have marvellous views – or will do if it stops raining and clears up. We can only hope. Summer Canadian style, I guess.

Suzie and I unpack as we are staying three nights and coming out of the bathroom, I notice this slinky sexy number lying on the end of the bed. I definitely haven't seen this before, so I hold it up against myself and ask, 'Nice. Did you buy this for me?'

Suzie snatches it off me before saying with a smirky (or is that sexy?) smile, 'That depends on if you behave yourself or not.'

I pull her in for a kiss, which sizzles before she pulls away, saying, 'We don't want to be late; we don't want to see another smirking Pig!'

I lean in again and whisper, 'I can't wait to see you wearing that – but not for too long! We might have to make it an early night!'

She pushes me away and heads for the door. I take a moment to compose myself – well, it has been nearly three weeks of deprivation, you know!

We head out to the outdoor bar but shit, it's cold out, at least to us thin-blooded Queenslanders, so we head back inside and join the queue for the restaurant for dinner.

Once seated, a perky young waitress comes over, to take our order, then starts chatting away. She introduces herself as Helen from Seven Hills in Sydney – you hear more Aussie accents in the Rockies than you do Canadians!

Later, as she is clearing away our plates, she comments that the rain and cloud have lifted, and it is now a lovely evening. She then asks if we have been to Moraine Lake, about a twenty-minute drive away. She goes on to explain, 'It's so crowded through the day, you would be lucky to even get on the shuttle bus, so if you want to see it, and you have to, I suggest you go now. The evening light on the lake is magical.'

We three look at each other. Pig shrugs his shoulders as if to say, 'Fine by me,' and I know without looking that Suzie has a smile hovering around her mouth as she sees me reconciling to not getting my desired early night. Ah, well, the night is young and we are here to see the beauty of the Rockies. So, it's off to Moraine Lake after collecting the SUV from the Valet.

Helen is right – we are able to drive right up to the head of the lake, park and wander around the lake shore, Suzie taking heaps of photos and yes, including plenty of the obligatory selfies. Fortunately, she hasn't bought herself a selfie pole; she would be walking around on her own if she had!

7

Next morning finds us out the front of the hotel, awaiting Pig's arrival. We had agreed on the drive back last night we would take an early morning walk to the head of Lake Louise this morning if it wasn't raining, so off we go.

Yes, if you do want to know, Suzie and I had a lovely evening 'reconnecting' and yes, she did wear her slinky, sexy nightie – but not for long, if you get my drift!

Pig arrives, giving us a smirky smile, and I suspect a little surprised to find us already here waiting for him.

It is a clear morning, if a little cool for us Queenslanders, but nothing a brisk pace doesn't take care of.

There are plenty of photo stops; it is amazingly beautiful, Suzie particularly stopping regularly and turning around and taking photos of the Chateau from these various angles. In the end, I suggest she will have a better view of the chateau on our way back when we are walking toward the hotel.

She admits, 'I guess,' then starts taking more photos of the mountains and glacier at the end of the lake!

By the time we get to the far end, Pig is becoming toey, so of course I start dragging the photoshoots out, posing with Suzie until it all gets too much for him and he says, 'Okay, I'm going to leave you two love birds to it and head back. I'll grab us all a coffee and come back and meet you.'

I smile, grab Suzie's hand and say, 'Love birds. I don't know what he means, do you?'

She hams it up, comes into my arms and we have a snuggle while it's my turn to smirk at Pig. We then wish him goodbye and he heads off at a much quicker pace than Suzie and I.

Fortunately, I resigned myself to a slow trip back, even more photos being taken, some I was even forced into, and more bloody selfies too.

As we get back near the hotel grounds, I spy Pig sitting up on a picnic table above the track, three coffees on the table.

We wander up to him and he growls, 'Coffee's bloody cold, you took so long.'

Suzie gives him a sweet smile and Pig can't stop himself from smiling back.

The coffee isn't totally cold and I've certainly drunk my share of lukewarm coffee, so no bother to me.

After a few minutes of contemplative silence, I say, 'Okay, we have all had a bit of time to churn over Pig's idea of where and how to get a mic onto Diego, so what are your thoughts now?'

Suzie beats Pig to it, saying, 'Well, my first concern is Julien having to use his disability to our advantage. I'm not comfortable about that. It doesn't seem right to me.' I nod my head in agreement, Suzie and I had discussed this privately and I share her concern.

After a pause, Pig replies, 'I have no issue doing it. Use the best resources you have, I reckon. Anyway, there's a bit of "there but for the grace of God am I" about it for me. Who knows what or where I would have ended up if I hadn't had George to hold my hand, figuratively speaking, through my rehabilitation? And, I must add, if you' – he nods at me – 'hadn't come along when you did and treated me same as always, like an equal, I'm not sure what the future would have been like. Being George's "maid", now looking back on it, was demeaning and I can truly say I was deeply unhappy. When Mort cashed out and moved to Brisbane, I was pretty desperate to see him but also apprehensive, not knowing how our relationship may have changed. So, my relief was tangible when you treated me same as always. Allowed me to regain some self-confidence and self-belief.'

Pig is a bit emotional, having laid bare his inner thoughts and Suzie reaches over and gives him a consoling hug.

Me, I say, 'Shit, mate, bit early in the morning for all this psychological shit!' I smile as I say it and I too lean in and give him a hug. A man hug, that is.

I let the companionable silence linger before saying, 'Okay, we'– I nod at Suzie – 'wanted to have our say and if you're comfortable with doing it, let's make a plan. We will need to visit a Salvo's store or some such to get clothing for a hobo and we certainly don't have anything suitable to wear either.'

Suzie pipes up, saying, 'I'll be fine. I brought plenty of gear.'

I smile, shaking my head thinking, Yeah, I know, I'm the one lugging your suitcases (yes, plural!) in and out of the hotels, and say, 'You don't even own anything suitable to fit in with a New York working crowd. If you notice in all the videos, everyone is wearing black jeans and black reefer or padded jackets and boots. No, you will be coming to the Salvo's too.'

'Okay, but I will dress and make Julien up. Always fancied being a makeup artist!'

I nod. Pig shrugs his shoulders.

I continue, 'We don't know how they may react to having a hobo half blocking their path, so that's the first thing. I'm thinking we need to do a few trial runs, just be there in place for a few days letting them become accustomed to seeing you in place, rattling your tin.'

Pig nods at this, his face creasing in a slight smile.

I continue, 'We also need a distraction, a diversion, something that will make them react and take their attention away, just at the right instant. Not sure what or how though.'

Into the silence, Pig says, 'You mean something like a firecracker?'

'Yes,' I reply. 'That's the sort of effect we need, but a firecracker in downtown New York isn't going to work.'

It's Suzie who then says, 'Why not a car backfiring?'

'Shit, you don't hear a backfire very often these days. Can't recall the last time I heard one. Do cars still backfire?'

Suzie's in her element, cars! 'Well, no, it's pretty hard these days to make an electronically managed engine backfire. You need one of the older engines with carburettor, points, et cetera.'

Pig and I look at her blankly, then I say, 'So something like the old man's Patrol?' (My father still drives a 1990 Nissan Patrol, as big and basic as they come.)

Suzie smiles and says, 'Yes, we won't get a Patrol over here, but it will need to be something of that vintage.'

We ponder in silence before I ask, 'Okay, there are still heaps of old delivery vans on the road over here. So, if we can find one with the older type engine, you could then provide a diversion?'

'Sure. It's not hard to make a car or van backfire if they have the old engine. You just turn the key off and on quickly. Simple. Used to do it all the time growing up – even on the track when the racing was tight, I would do it to put the boys off!'

I smile, thinking, That's my Suzie!

I smile at Suzie (can't stop myself!) and say, 'Okay, you're in charge of finding a suitable van. Needs to look nondescript so no one will even notice it.'

She seems happy to have something to focus on and asks, 'How much can I spend?'

I shrug. 'If we say yes, they will be paying us a hundred K to cover expenses, so the cost won't really matter. It should only be a few K I would have thought, anyway.'

Suzie already has her phone out, looking up vans in New York, I guess, so I say, 'See if you can find one in New Jersey, around Newark preferably.'

'Why?'

I smile without answering, getting a puzzled look from her.

I look around from our possie on the picnic table, situated as it is overlooking beautiful Lake Louise. I pause to watch a group of joggers heading off down the edge of the lake. Then a couple look like they are heading up to the tea house, high above the lake.

Pig interrupts my reverie. 'This is going to need to be tightly controlled. Timing is going to be crucial.'

We continue to sit there thinking this through before I say, 'Okay, the way I see it, Pig is in place and Suzie will have her van further down the road, needs to be about a block away I reckon, and I will follow them along the sidewalk from the corner of 5th Avenue, as back up if Pig gets into trouble and as a plan B if Pig fails to land a mic.

'We need to spend a few days beforehand timing their walk from their apartment to the corner of East 68th, then the timing for each block down to Park Ave. Then, I will be the coordinator, giving you both the "go" when the time is right. I'm also right on hand if Pig gets into trouble and once they have passed him, Suzie, you can circle back and pick Pig up. I will meet you after a couple of blocks.'

Suzie has to ask, 'How will you place a mic if Julien fails?'

'I will wander up behind them, maybe make a bit of a nuisance of myself at the next set of lights and see what happens.'

I smile at her, knowing she won't like the bit about me 'making a nuisance of myself' (Mort talk for a disturbance!)

'But if we get the plan A right and execute it, it won't come to that.'

Silence as we all contemplate what we have discussed.

'All right then, are we agreed we will give this a go?'

Pig looks at me and says, 'I'm in.' we fist bump.

Suzie then nods her head and says, 'Okay, but I'm relying on you two. This is what you're supposed to be good at, so I'll do my bit but you two have to ensure we remain safe.'

Pig and I nod, so she holds her fist out for a fist bump with a smile playing around her mouth! We do a three-way fist bump. She wants to be 'one of the boys!'

'Okay, I will give Campbell a call and tell him it's in play and to make payment of the expenses and fifty per cent of the fee. Come on, we better head in for a quick shower otherwise we will miss breakfast.'

I help Suzie down from the tabletop. She keeps hold of my hand as we head back to the hotel.

8

A little later we are in the Tahoe. I'm driving for a change as we head to the Lake Louise gondola for a bit more sightseeing.

As our chatty Aussie waitress had recommended a stop there, we detour via the Lake Louise bakery for fresh coffees and muffins for our drive up the Icefield Parkway.

Anyway, we choose an enclosed gondola rather than an open chair; there is a 'cool' (their standards, not ours!) breeze, so it feels better to be enclosed.

Bugger me, only a few minutes from the terminal and we are looking down open-mouthed as a mother brown bear with two cubs in tow wanders along directly beneath the gondola. We are not the only ones watching her as you can see others in the gondolas going both up and down, pointing, smiling and of course, taking photos. And, yes, all three of us take photos as well!

Pig even says, 'How cool is that!' I'm sure the photo has been sent straight to Stacey as I hear his phone ping a couple of minutes later. He reads the message and smiles. Yes, a love-struck pig. Still, better than a smirking pig!

Once at the top, we admire the view back toward Lake Louise with the chateau sitting proudly on its shores.

Still, no time to waste as we have booked a trip on the Colombia Icefield, about an hour up the highway from Lake Louise.

On the down trip, we decide on an open ski lift, hoping to see the bear again and yes, she and the two cubs are still meandering around, nibbling the bushes as she goes. Being in the open enables us to get much better photos than through the glass of the gondola. We all agree, pretty cool seeing our first bear!

I even manage to keep the keys and rather enjoy the drive. We arrive at the tour depot and join the queue for our tour. It is a bit of an anticlimax to firstly be herded onto a conventional bus for the short journey to the head of the glacier, then we are again herded onto one of these massive 6WD buses.

We simply crawl along going up and then down again some rather serious angles. Enough for Suzie to grab my hand!

Once on the glacier, we exit the bus with the guides warning that the ice is slippery. Boy, he isn't wrong. Worse still, it is bitterly cold with a strong wind blowing, so not pleasant at all. Still an awesome experience and again many photos are taken. As big as Pig and I are, we still look small next to the wheels of these huge buses!

Even though we are wearing our warmest coats, all three of us are shivering when we return to the bus. Summer Canadian style, ah!

On the drive back to Lake Louise, our conversation again turns to New York and Suzie – who, yes, you guessed it, is once again driving – asks, 'So why should I look for a van near Newark, New Jersey and not New York?'

I reply, 'Well, we are booked on Air Canada from Toronto to LaGuardia in New York, so if anyone is watching us, they will know this. There's a smaller airline, Porter Airlines, that leaves Toronto for Newark an hour before our flight and I'm planning on getting on it at the last minute. We will then be through customs and out in Newark before anyone will realise it. They won't be able to track us so easily, if in fact anyone is trying to.'

Pig and Suzie both pull a face, clearly thinking this is a good idea.

I continue, saying, 'I spoke to Campbell earlier also. Hunter will meet our flight in Toronto with our new passports. Doing it in person, again minimising outside contact – another tick for them! He also confirmed they would make payment today so I will check to confirm payment has been received once back at the hotel.'

Of course, Suzie can't resist. 'So how much do I get?'

'You get to shoe and handbag shop to your heart's content,' I tell her with a smile.

'Not so fast, Mister,' she replies. 'I was doing that anyway – and all at your expense.'

'Bugger,' I say, smiling as well, 'thought I might get away with that one.'

'Not a chance, Mister. You owe me.' She continues, 'I meant to ask; how come you have bank accounts in the Caymen Islands?'

I look at Pig as if to say, do I tell her? He shrugs, so he's no help.

After considering my answer, I decide on the truth. 'I mentioned the other day we were seconded by the CIA – well, it was agreed the services we were expected to provide were way above the paygrade of a mere army grunt, so Dwight helped us set up a couple of accounts each over there in the Caymans. We even went over there for a weekend. Swam with stingrays whilst we were there. That was awesome. We reckoned it was safer than dealing with the bankers, who all seemed like sharks to us! The CIA paid well!'

Pig pipes up, 'But we bloody earnt it too.'

I nod in agreement with that.

Suddenly, we are back at the Chateau; it never seems to take long when Suzie is driving.

With few handy options for dinner, we decide to stick with the Poppy Brasserie again in the hotel.

Another fine meal, different waitress this time. A Kiwi for a change!

It turns into an early night, not that I'm complaining.

9

The next day, the last of our Rocky Mountain sojourn sees Suzie and I once again go for an early morning walk along the lake shore. The weather isn't as kind to us as yesterday, so no photos and we walk at a brisker pace. Halfway along, lo and behold here comes Pig, already heading back to the Chateau and jogging not walking. We don't slow him down merely smile and wave to him as he passes.

We then meet up for breakfast, check out and head toward Banff on our way to the airport in Calgary.

But not before another visit to Starbucks in the chateau basement!

Coffee, you can never have too much!

Banff is another delightful, picturesque town, surrounded as it is by mountain peaks and ski fields, with the Bow River flowing through it.

After stopping in town for a quick bite, we head up on the Sulphur Mountain gondola ride. The day has cleared just for us, and we are lucky with some spectacular views, least of all the Banff Springs Hotel, which looks far more imposing from a distance than it does up close.

Alas, with time ticking away, we need to hit the road to Calgary to make our onward flight to Toronto. Another of our eagerly anticipated highlights, Niagara Falls, awaiting us tomorrow. After, we meet with Hunter on arrival in Toronto.

***

It's a few hours later as we exit the flight from Calgary and there waiting for us at the gate is Hunter. As promised.

We shake hands all round and move away to a quieter corner. He hands over the envelope with our new American passports. I slide them out; the first one is for Suzie with the name Suzie Duncan, same age and date of birth but showing she was born in Iowa!

For Pig and I, they have actually changed our names, Hunter pointing out that as our names are known within certain circles, they decided to use entirely false names. So I'm Russell Crosby for the duration and Pig is Bryce Smith.

After collecting our bags, we adjourn to the bar so Hunter can buy us a drink. Pig gives him another link to upload new data, with it again closing tonight at midnight. I also give him the name and address of the Lincoln Tunnel motel and instruct him to have our weaponry delivered there before Sunday.

Hunter is back off to New York in another hour, simply coming up to meet us and handing over the passports. Of course, he can't resist asking how the planning was going and Pig jumps in saying, 'So far so good,' shutting the conversation down.

After a couple of beers, we pick up our rental – another Suburban – and head off to our hotel, leaving Hunter to await his flight home.

Unbeknown to me, Pig slipped a mini spider onto the collar of his jacket. He had ordered twenty of the mini spiders whilst we were in Lake Louise and with express delivery, they were delivered the next day. Some service!

When I asked him why, he answered, 'You can never be too careful.'

The only thing we heard through the night was Hunter calling his wife to confirm what time he would be home and then saying good night to his daughter Tegan – and asking her how her tennis training had gone.

In the evening, we decide on Italian and head off to the Old Spaghetti Factory downtown. As we park in the open area city car park, we notice a couple of older ladies alighting from their small Toyota Corolla and then as they get to the back of their car, a young teenager on a bike rides by, grabbing the older lady's handbag.

'Stop, thief,' both ladies cry out.

He's off, peddling madly.

Unbeknown to him, so am I. But on foot. As I give chase, I randomly think, Glad I'm wearing shorts and sneakers, not thongs. Then just as randomly, As if Suzie would allow me to wear thongs to dinner!

As he is unaware I'm chasing him, he quickly slows down. He hasn't even changed direction. Then from behind me, I hear another voice yelling, 'Look out, Arnie, he's chasing you.'

Arnie, the thief, apparently, looks over his shoulder and starts peddling fast, suddenly veering left between two parked cars. No matter, I veer left a couple of cars before him, making it harder for him to see me or know where I am.

I'm now only three-four car lengths behind Arnie, not that he knows it as he has slowed down again.

He is now back on the main driveway of the car park, clearly thinking he has avoided my attention. I turn back onto the main drive also.

Then through my earpiece (as is habit, I had put it in as soon as trouble started, knowing Pig would be watching my back), I hear Pig say, 'Second bike following you, catching up quickly.'

I don't turn around, knowing Pig will give me warning and more likely instructions to eliminate any threat.

'He has pulled a knife in his right hand. Standby.'

I keep pounding away, now only a couple of car lengths behind and start to make my plans to take Arnie down. He still has the old lady's handbag hanging off his handlebars.

Then Pig is back. 'Be ready to swerve right in three… two… one.'

On cue, I swerve sharply to my right and sense rather than see my assailant lunging for me as he rides past. His lunge having missed its mark – he is off balance so a quick step back to my left and I have his wrist in my hand and squeeze. Hard. Likely breaking a bone or two.

He howls in pain and drops the knife.

I then yank him hard by the wrist toward me, pulling him off his bike, which clatters to the ground. I let him drag along the road on his knees as I keep running. No harm in a little extra pain. Then I grab him around the throat with my right hand and squeeze his neck, stopping him from breathing.

It only takes a few seconds and he lapses into unconsciousness. I drop him on the edge of the drive, behind a small car. None too gently either.

All the while I continue to run, still chasing Arnie. But with all the commotion of his mate's unsuccessful attack, he has again ducked left and as I too turn left see he is again peddling furiously.

Bugger. Need to bring this to a head or someone else might get injured. Besides, I'm getting hungry!

I stretch out now, full stride, knowing he is likely again needing to slow down and rest. I'm one car over from him, so hard for him to know where I am. I see the edge of the car park is now approaching, lined with shrubs and trees between the car park and what appears to be a major road.

I again lengthen stride; I'm not letting this little shit get away.

I see a couple of small trucks parked ahead so I take advantage of these and surge past him whilst he can't see me. I'm one lane over and once sufficiently ahead of him I turn back toward him and wait between two cars.

As he goes past me looking over his left shoulder, I rip him off his bike by the neck.

A simple one-handed yank and he is struggling up in the air, feet kicking wildly. His bike clatters down just ahead.

Without letting his feet touch the ground, I pull his face to mine and say, 'Next time, pick on someone your own size and age.'

I then squeeze his larynx sufficient to send him too into la-la land, drop him none too gently onto the asphalt, retrieve the lady's handbag off his handlebars and turn around and jog back to the car, passing his accomplice, still out to it, on the driveway.

A small group has now gathered around the two older ladies and when they see me jogging back holding the bag, they start applauding. Naturally, the lady is overcome with relief, starting to cry again saying it had all her monthly cash in it along with her personal information and credit cards.

As quickly as possible we make a quiet exit, wanting to be nowhere in sight when the police – or the Mounties, as they are known in Canada – turn up. One of the crowd had said they had called it in.

We three quietly exit the crowd and head off for, what we hope at least, would be a quiet dinner. But I did reckon I had earned an extra beer! Even Suzie agreed!

After a pleasant dinner, we are walking back through the car park and as we approach our car, I pause, having noticed an unmarked police cruiser parked behind our SUV. Too late, both doors on the cruiser, a black Ford Crown Victoria, crack. We have been spotted. Suzie's hand slips into mine. I'm sure she is not used to being approached by police. To be honest, neither am I.

I sense rather than see Pig drift backwards into the thinning crowd, leaving Suzie and I front and centre as the two Mounties exit their Crown Vic. The driver, a small, dark-haired woman, accompanied by a tall, older male, approach us as we continue toward our car.

'Excuse me, sir, madam,' the woman says as she approached us from the side, already holding out her credentials. 'I'm Detective Carmichael and this is my colleague Detective Paterson. Can we have a quick word?'

No choice really.

I smile and say, 'Sure.' They are both looking around, looking, I suspect, for Pig, which tells me the crowd or someone within it had given sufficient details for them to know there were two males.

Detective Carmichael continues, 'I understand there was an incident here in the car park earlier?'

I nod affirmative. 'Yes, a young guy' – I decide not to describe him how I thought of him! – 'on a bike stole an old lady's handbag. I gave chase, recovered it and gave it back to her.'

She seems to be reading from her notebook but a little surprisingly, neither are writing notes. Interesting.

She continues, 'When the first patrol car arrived, they found two young guys' – she deliberately uses the term I used – 'both unconscious and one with a broken wrist. You only mentioned one?'

Mmmm. 'Well, yes, a second young guy also on one of those little BMX bikes attacked me as I chased after the thief and tried to slice me as I ran. I defended myself, disarmed him and I guess he hit his head on the road when he fell off his bike.'

This time her colleague Detective Paterson speaks for the first time. 'How did he break his wrist then?'

'I crushed it.'

'Crushed it?'

As an answer, I hold my left hand up in a crab shape. I do have large hands; they have been described as the size of baseball mitts in the past.

Both of them are looking at me closely, so I elaborate: 'I am always going to defend myself and I do know how to do that. Well.' I have decided to let them know I'm not an ordinary citizen; I can take care of myself.

Detective Carmichael again. 'Our report says there were two large males.' As she says this, she again looks around looking for the missing 'large male'.

She is clearly trying to keep me off balance by switching the focus of their questions.

'Yes, our friend Julien went to the bathroom, so should be here anytime.' Pig will have heard this as we both automatically put our phones on our special communication app at the first sign of anything unusual. I'm sure he has been listening and, I suspect, ensuring there is no back up parked out of sight. He hasn't given me a warning, so for now I'm assuming not.

Detective Paterson. 'So, one-handed, you broke his wrist?'

I look him in the eye and say, 'Yes. I was holding him off the ground by his wrist at the same time, so physics had a fair bit to do with it as well.'

He's giving me an appraising look now.

Now Detective Carmichael says, 'Okay, can I have your names and some form of identification please?'

Bugger.

I dig out my license from my wallet and hand it over silently. Suzie is digging through her handbag for her ID, still not having said a thing.

Detective Carmichael looks up from studying my Queensland license and says, 'So, Australian?'

Clever. No wonder she's a detective!

'Yes. We are just visiting, so don't want any trouble. All I did was help an old lady in trouble and hopefully helped you to arrest a couple of likely suspects.'

At this Detective Paterson scoffs before saying, 'Sure, arrest them, into the revolving doors of our youth justice system they go, then they are back out on the streets before we can finish the paperwork.'

I nod in agreement, saying, 'Yes, we have the same problems at home, young teenage gangs creating havoc, good hard-working police being abused and ridiculed and the courts let them off scott-free. Must be so frustrating for you all.'

Both detectives are nodding. Good.

Detective Carmichael is still holding my license with a puzzled look on her face. 'Moreton Island. My sister lives in Brisbane and is always raving about Moreton Island being her favourite camping spot for her and her family. Is this for real?' This last sentence is spoken firmly as she shakes my license in front of me, giving me a hard, suspicious look.

I laugh, saying, 'Yes. My father has a warped sense of humour. It was his favourite fishing spot, and, as the story goes, my mum told him when I was born his time going away fishing was going to be somewhat curtailed. So, he called me Morton in memory!'

This gets a snort from Detective Paterson, obviously enjoying the story. It's true, by the way!

Detective Carmichael seems to accept this and records my details in her notepad before looking at Suzie who hands her passport over. 'So, what brings you both to Canada?'

I nod to Suzie, letting her know she can answer. (I'm sure as a lawyer she knows this it is best to tell the truth – well, mostly!)

Suzie replies, 'Our friend Julien competed in the Invictus Games over in Victoria and since then we have been sightseeing. You have a beautiful country.'

Right on cue, Pig arrives, looking around as if surprised at what is going on.

I introduce him to the detectives, explaining they have a few questions about the incident earlier.

It is Detective Paterson who gets in the first question, looking from Pig to me, saying, 'Military, both of you?'

I nod, saying, 'Former.'

He nods as if something has clicked for him. 'And I'm guessing not mere "grunts"?'

Pig and I both smile back and I add, 'No, not "mere grunts",' adding air quote marks as I say this.

Detective Carmichael has now recorded Suzie's details in her notepad, handing her passport back before saying to Pig, 'Can I have your identification as well please, sir?'

Pig digs it out of his bum bag. Boy, haven't I teased him about wearing a bum bag – mercilessly! But I have to be honest, it is a sensible way to carry critical personal documents. I'm just not going to concede that to Pig!

He hands over his passport and his details are duly recorded. She nods her acknowledgement as she hands it back.

She then looks back to me, saying, 'May I also see your passport, sir, just to keep our records straight.' Not sure if she was still suspicious of my license, but no problem.

No bum bag for me as Suzie fishes my passport out of her handbag and hands it over! Pig adds a sly comment, 'My bum bag is cheaper than yours!'

'But mine has far more uses,' is my quick retort as I give Suzie a smile and shoulder hug.

Pig, Suzie and I have a laugh and our interchange also getting smiles from the two detectives, even if they didn't know the back story.

Once Detective Carmichael has finished recording my passport details, the two detectives share a look before she looks at us all, saying, 'We do not expect to be taking this matter further. We have the two juveniles in custody – we have plenty of local witness descriptions and statements. We thank you for your cooperation in taking the initiative and recovering poor Mrs Olsen's handbag for her. She will be eternally grateful, I am sure. However, we do have to caution you on taking the law into your own hands, no matter how capable you may be, as this can be fraught with danger.'

We all nod and it's Detective Paterson who then leans in, shaking my hand, Suzie's and Pig's, which his partner then does likewise, saying to me, 'Thank you.'

'Well, that could have been a lot worse,' I comment as we get into our rental to head back to our hotel.

Next morning, again no urgency as we have learnt nothing gets going until after ten a.m., so with only a little over an hour's drive, we head off, looking forward to seeing one of the five great waterfalls of the world, Niagara Falls.

I'm driving so it does take an hour to get there and we quickly realise this is a popular spot with car parking at a premium.

We decide we might as well pay up rather than cruise the streets looking for a parking spot and we head down to the river to go on the famed 'Maid of the Mist' boat tour. Fortunately, we pass a Starbucks on the way, so we do get some sustenance!

We join the queue and shuffle along, gathering a distinct blue poncho along the way. They make no secret we are going to get wet, and, well, that is part of the excitement of it!

Sure enough, once we are on board and heading closer and closer to the falls, the noise is thunderous the closer we get.

Yes, we get drenched, but we are smiling. It is a great experience.

Afterward, we remove our ponchos and wander along the gardens fronting the river, taking plenty of photos and yes, hamming it up for the selfies. Pig rolls his eyes at us, which just makes us act a little more silly!

Afterward, we head off to the tranquil and picturesque village of Niagara-on-the-Lake for a late and leisurely lunch.

Without any of us verbalising it, we all seem to understand the next few days are likely to be rather more intense than our last week or so.

Tomorrow, New York.

10

We are wheels down over New Jersey. Suzie, in the window seat, is peering out at the vast metropolis – it seems to go on forever. A massive sprawl of urban-ville interspersed with patches of green.

She turns to see me watching her, her face lighting up in a smile and she clutches my hand, her excitement palpable. Yes, New York is certainly always the highlight of her trip, I even suspect her main purpose in coming. Sure, no question she wanted to support Pig at the Invictus Games, even (I like to think anyway!) spend this time with me, but no doubt I come a long second to shopping on 5th Avenue! I guess many a girl's dream! (I have even tried the line she 'isn't a girl any longer' but that was never going to work!)

She rattles off the names of the big stores she 'can't wait' to visit.
- Saks
- Bloomingdales
- Macy's
- Tiffany's
- Nordstrom
- Prada
- Chanel

There are more but their names are lost on me!

Having cleared immigration and customs before leaving Toronto, its straight through to the baggage carousel to await our luggage, me collecting a trolley on the way. Yes, I have learnt the hard way Suzie's cases are large and heavy. I've even warned her she hasn't left much room for new purchases – her answer: 'Watch me.' Trouble is all this shopping is on me for a past indiscretion. So, in her mind, money is no object. Ouch, I know this is going to hurt.

Whilst waiting for the bags, I think back to our conversation over dinner last night, where I pointed out New York is a holiday too, so we can't become solely focused on our 'mission'. We have agreed we will allocate three to four hours each morning to the mission with trial runs, et cetera. Then the rest of the day is for sightseeing.

We all made a list of 'must dos' whilst here in New York which I'm sure reads like most other first-time visitors.

- Times Square.
- Central Park. Suzie suggested a rickshaw ride and Pig surprisingly wants to jog through it, so we all agreed we would do this maybe one evening as our mornings are likely to be our 'busy time'.
- We are staying at The Mandarin Oriental Hotel on Columbus Circle, so easy access to Central Park.
- We list the must-see museums. I get out-numbered here when Pig sides with Suzie on a couple. I'm seeing a new 'cultural' side to me old mate!
    - Metropolitan Museum of Art (The Met)
    - Museum of Modern Art (MoMA)
    - American Museum of Natural History
- Of course, the 9/11 Museum is a must-see as well.
- Brooklyn Bridge.
- Visit Staten Island.

- Statue of Liberty cruise & visit to Ellis Island.
- Broadway – we are booked to go to the Phantom of the Opera – the longest running show currently on Broadway. Yes, Suzie says I need a dose of culture, so this plus a few museums are 'nonnegotiable', I'm told!
- And of course, Suzie's must-do 'Shop 5th Avenue' and a list of high-end shops! Pig muttered he 'might be sick that day', giving me a consoling pat on the shoulder!

We have also arrived with a plan, with so much to achieve here in New York we can't waste any time.

With bags collected, it's straight off to the rental cars to sort out our transport.

I choose a Suburban (black, of course!) from SIXT, one of the smaller operators, using my Russell Crosby license and one of the prepaid Visas.

Luggage loaded, GPS engaged and off to our first stop.

We are out of the airport before our official flight from Toronto to Newark has even left, so if Campbell or Hunter or any of his FBI colleagues are trying to track us, hopefully this will slow them down a little more.

Susie has been busy and identified two suitable 'Salvo stores' where we plan on getting our New York workers' outfits. Well, used jeans for all three of us (I made Suzie agree nothing fashionable for her, making the point it is more critical she fits in and doesn't draw attention to herself, than how she looks.)

As there are three of us, particularly the size of Pig and I, we had agreed Pig and Suzie would go to one store and I would go on to the other on my own, so we don't stand out.

Suzie insisted she needs to help Pig to ensure he can get into the hobo theme.

Not for me to argue!

I'm in and out, shopping done, two pairs of well-worn black jeans, a couple of long sleeve t-shirts, a reversible green/black reefer jacket, safety boots, high-vis vest and hard hat plus a 'stylish' dark suit. Why do I need a stylish suit? Wait and see!

I also bought Suzie a black NYC cap, knowing her reluctance to wear one, complaining she would end up with 'helmet hair'. I don't care, I want her safe, and that means not standing out in a crowd and her blonde hair will do that.

I'm back sitting around the corner waiting patiently for Pig and Suzie and when they finally come out carrying three large shopping bags. I can't help wondering what the hell they have bought!

As they climb in, I ask, 'Are they closing for the day now you have bought them out?'

Pig snorts (yes, I know, I know) and Suzie pokes her tongue out before saying, 'When I'm finished with Julien, not even you will recognise him! We told the lady we were going to a fancy dress and he wanted to go as a hobo, so she was right in there helping us. Even got him a dreadlock hairpiece. Can't wait to dress him up. Don't forget we need to go to a chemist (pharmacy) so I can get some colouring, blush, et cetera for him.'

I can't resist. 'Pig wearing blush, ah – can't wait to see that!'

He raises his middle finger to me whilst we all smile.

Next stop is a Walgreens Pharmacy just up the road. I had looked it up whilst waiting; fortunately there is a Starbucks almost next door, so I know where I'll be whilst Suzie is in Walgreens. As I pull up, I ask, 'Do you need Pig to go with you so you can try the various colours on his complexion?'

Of course, I thought I was just stirring, but Suzie takes my question seriously before deciding, 'No I should be okay. Besides, these places are meant to have an awesome collection of makeup. I might be a while.'

Pig looks relieved when he adds, 'Okay, we will have two coffees before we come looking for you!'

We let Suzie off and head up the road to Starbucks.

We go in and order our coffees and toasted banana bread as a little treat!

Our conversation quickly turns to our mission. One of the challenges to me, at least, is keeping our two purposes in New York separate. As tourists, we are booked into the Mandarin Oriental on Columbus Circle but do not want to be traipsing in and out of there in our NY work gear.

We have found a small motel not far from the Lincoln Tunnel. Quick and easy access through to 5th Avenue. The Lincoln Tunnel Motel is an old-fashioned, single-story motel, park-outside-your-door type of place, so just what we need when trying to stay anonymous.

We aren't sure whether Pig and Suzie may have to sleep here yet. This will depend on travel time back from our hotel on Columbus Circle. They need to be able to get here for Suzie to make Pig up in the morning before driving him into position on East 86th.

Pig and I finish our coffee and order refills and decide to go back and wait for Suzie outside Walgreens so there is no delay.

Yes, yes, of course I get a coffee for Suzie as well. What do you take me for?

We are almost finished our second coffee before we see Suzie coming out of the pharmacy with not one bag but two. Seeing our faces, she asks, 'What, isn't a girl allowed to buy up large with makeup and the like?'

Neither Pig nor I are game to comment.

Once settled in her seat, I punch in the address of the Lincoln Tunnel Motel on the GPS and head there.

Pig goes in and registers – no need for them to see anyone else – and he gets a room in the middle of the complex, as requested. I move the Suburban along and park outside his room.

He comes out carrying a DHL carton. Our weaponry, we presume.

We unload just the bags from the Salvo stores and Walgreens, with our main luggage staying in the SUV. We will take this later when we go to the Mandarin Oriental.

Once inside, with the door locked, we open the DHL box, carefully inspecting it for hidden bugs or trackers but find none. Good thing too; we might have aborted the mission if they had tried to track us through these.

We find two Glock 19s inside, serial numbers removed, with two cartons of ammo, and also two KA-BAR knives as favoured by the US Marines – and coincidence or not, the knife Pig and I prefer. We hadn't asked for these and hopefully won't need them either, but still good and thoughtful that they have been provided.

Old habits die hard, and Pig and I dismantle our Glocks and clean them with the cleaning kit provided. Pig comments, 'Would much prefer to test fire these, in case we do need them for a fire fight.'

I nod in agreement before saying, 'Agreed, but that's one step we can't take.'

Pig nods his agreement, while Suzie silently watches this exchange.

We try on and adjust the shoulder holsters also thoughtfully included.

Once we have finished fiddling with our weapons, we slip these into our luggage, as certainly aren't going to leave these unattended here in the motel.

I now leave Pig and Suzie and head off to inspect a couple of old 1990s vintage delivery vans Suzie has identified at local Newark used car dealers.

Why only me?

Again, the van is a potential thread if anyone tries to trace us if it gets connected to what we plan in the coming days. Therefore, the fewer people that are connected to it the better.

I walk up the road to a Dunkin' Donuts and order up an Uber. Yes, I grab a coffee whilst waiting. And I decide their coffee is more than just okay – good to know.

The Uber arrives, driven by an Indian, just like many at home.

I give him the address of the first dealer with a van I want to check out. There are a number of suitable dealers along Broadway and nearby McCarter Hwy.

The first three I inspect don't suit. Too battered and bruised, all rusty and likely to stand out when we need it to be anonymous.

Walking along the road, I glance up a side street and see a rundown used car lot with a couple of older Ford Econovan vans for sale. I turn and wander in to have a look.

One looks ideal and Lyell the salesman comes out, extolling its virtues. I start it up and it seems to run okay and he tells me it had an engine rebuild 'only one hundred and fifty thousand miles ago'.

'Like new then,' I reply.

I take it for a spin around the block, testing how it runs at highway speed, wanting to ensure there are no vibration or transmission issues and decide she will do.

'How much?' I ask and he replies, 'Six thousand dollars.'

'Ah come on, I'm not paying that for this old heap. Make it five thousand and we have a deal.'

We to and fro a bit and finally agree on $5250, so we head back to the shop to sort out the paperwork.

This takes half an hour and I'm on my way back to the motel. I have no intention of transferring the ownership anyway and have used my

Russell Crosby ID and a fictitious address in Trenton NJ that I had worked out in advance.

Paid by prepaid Visa and next to no trail.

Just the way I like it!

I head back to the motel and park outside Pig's room.

Suzie and Pig have also been busy making a few changes to some of the clothes they had bought. Suzie had thoughtfully bought needle and thread at Walgreens and surprised us both by knowing how to use them!

As she explained, 'Growing up as the younger sister, I wore plenty of hand-me-downs, so often had to make adjustments that suited me!'

We live and learn!

We have ticked off everything on our 'to-do list' for today, so it's back in the Suburban, GPS set for the Mandarin Oriental on Columbus Circle.

Driving in New York. What an experience!

But we do get there, having missed a couple of turns but hey, we are driving on the wrong side of the road!

The valet takes our keys and we are whisked up to our rooms.

I open our door to our high-level 'Central Park-view room' and allow Suzie past me to have a look at the view first.

'Wow, look at that,' she exclaims as I join her at the window. She turns, smiling, puts her arms around my neck and pulls me in for a kiss, saying, 'I think I will leave all our honeymoon planning with you. You know how to find all the best rooms. We have stayed at some awesome hotels, Mort.'

The kiss lingers and who knows where it might have led if our baggage hadn't arrived when it did!

We freshen up and as agreed, we meet Pig for a drink and dinner in the Mo Lounge with its stunning New York views as a backdrop.

Even had to 'dress up' as it's a bit swanky – fresh jeans and polo for me, something a bit smarter for Suzie (of course!)

As Pig dryly comments as we settle over a beer a short time later, 'A bit different to my digs at the Lincoln Tunnel Motel!'

Over dinner, we agree that as it's Sunday tomorrow, we don't need an early start in the morning.

11

Next morning, Pig and I jump in a cab and get let off on 5th Avenue between East 84 and 85.

Suzie? Well, she has booked herself into the spa at the hotel, claiming she needs a bit of pampering!

We get out of the cab and walk back past Diego's apartment building, just to get a feel for it.

It's a flash joint with a uniformed doorman, but that's fine, we are not planning on going in.

Staying on the park side of 5th Avenue, as we wander along, we are looking for a good spot where I can watch Diego and his crew from.

There are benches along the wide sidewalk and plenty of cover amongst the trees inside the park but no immediate quick access from the sidewalk to the park – other than jumping the wall. And whilst that wouldn't be an issue, it would draw attention, which I'm not wanting to do.

We agree I can either take a seat on the benches or sit on the wall, which many others are doing. Either option will give me a clear view back to their apartment – I even identify where along the wall will give me the best view of the entrance to the apartment building, and still being close to the intersection with East 86th.

My biggest concern – especially on the first day Pig appears as a hobo on their route, which we are planning on making tomorrow, Monday – is their reaction. I want to be close, real close, in case they react aggressively or violently. Threaten Pig and they will know I'm around!

Once we are happy with this part of the plan, we head down 86th to inspect the little gate Pig had identified as his action station. We stop adjacent to it and I lean against the small tree on the kerb and pretend to talk on the phone. This gives Pig an excuse to stand there next to me and have a good close look. He gives me a small nod once he is satisfied and we walk across the road where there is construction going on. Not on Sunday though. They have traffic cones blocking the parking bays, having rubbish skips, et cetera sitting here. I comment to Pig that some days I will stand around here, hard hat and clipboard in hand, looking important. I certainly will be this close on the day we decide to put our plan into action. Up close and ready for action, aggressive action if need be!

We walk further down the road next to the closed-off sidewalk and I suggest at the end of the construction zone we could extend the traffic cones enabling Suzie to park the van there on the day of the 'takedown'!

At the intersection with Madison Avenue, we again cross East 86th and head back toward 5th. We are now walking in the opposite direction to where Diego and crew will be walking. That's fine, we are just sussing the street out. Obviously, we, as always, are keeping an eye out in case anyone is taking an interest in us, but everyone else around is bustling along, going about their busy lives.

We again slow down as we pass Pig's little gate and he says, 'Yeah, I'm happy this will work. I will need to keep my good leg bent at the knee, so it doesn't intrude too far into the sidewalk. But that's okay, not going to be an issue.'

We nod and head on toward 5th Avenue and grab a passing cab and I tell him, 'Columbus Circle but find us a Starbucks on the way.' We deserve it!

Once back at the hotel and with Suzie's spa session finished (she didn't look any different to me – but you won't hear me say that!), we decide on a quick lunch and we head off in tourist mode. I have been warned it will be a cultural afternoon!

Over dinner at a nearby restaurant later that evening, Pig asks if I can don my suit and come down to his room.

Yes, he knows why I bought the suit.

So, after dinner I go back to our room, change into the suit and with Suzie tagging along, we go down to Pig's room where we find him sitting on the floor. With his prosthesis removed, he sits how he will need to sit on the sidewalk. We then measure the distance to where we estimate Diego will be walking past him – 955 millimetres or thirty-eight inches, so only a short distance for him to be throwing the mini spider.

The purpose of the suit is to see how the spider attaches to this style of material. Now you know. We do try to think of everything!

From the videos, we had even timed Diego's walk and length of stride, so now I walk back and forth in front of Pig at the same pace and stride length as Diego. Thus, giving him plenty of opportunity to practice landing the spiders.

At one stage, we even debate whether Pig should aim at the trouser cuff (yes, apparently cuffed trousers are back in vogue – in some circles, anyway.) But after a dozen or so throws, we agree this would be a little too difficult and resume aiming just at the lower half of the leg, around the calf, ideally at the back of the calf.

After half an hour of solid practice, Pig is getting a one hundred per cent stick rate. Can't ask for better than that, so we call it a night.

12

Monday morning. Day one of our mission.

Needing to be set up in East 86th well before eight a.m. and with Suzie needing around forty-five minutes to make Pig up as a hobo and not knowing what sort of traffic delays we might encounter both ways, we decide on a five a.m. breakfast. Too early for the restaurant, so it's room service for all of us.

Then Pig and Suzie jump in an Uber and head back to the Lincoln Tunnel motel around five-thirty a.m.

Checking the weather forecast, it is meant to be a fine day, if a bit on the cool side for us Queenslanders.

Yes, Pig had decided he preferred the eight-hundred-thread Egyptian cotton sheets at the Mandarin Oriental over whatever the motel was offering, a decision Suzie was all in favour of as well. I tell Pig he is getting soft – too many years of comfort! This just means an earlier start is all. No big deal!

Whilst they are away playing dress up, I go over my tooling, clipboard and lanyard with pass key (it won't open anything, but it makes me look important!). High-vis and hard hat all stuffed in my backpack and I'm good to go. I add my work boots as well, not wanting to walk out of the hotel looking like a workman, it is a bit flash for that! Of course, I also slip on my shoulder holster and fit the Glock into place, then slide the sheathed knife into my right sock, using the small strap attached to the sheath and Velcro it around my lower leg.

I then do a few stretches and bends to ensure neither the holster nor knife are dislodged. Good to go.

My plan is to observe and time our targets along each section of their walk: from the apartment's entrance to the corner of East 86th; the corner to Pigs station; then to the corner of Madison Avenue and on to Park Avenue, along Park Ave to East 89th, then on to The Dalton School. Thus, ensuring these times matched what we worked out off the videos.

I'm restless. With Pig and Suzie away, I decide to head out early. Just after six-thirty a.m. I head out and head into Central Park, planning on walking across and coming out on 5th Ave near East 67th Street.

When I get there, I realise the traffic is going in the wrong direction to jump a cab to East 86th so I walk onto Madison Ave; this time, the traffic is going the right way. Cabs are plentiful this time of the morning and I find myself at East 87th Street in no time.

Pig has texted me to say they are on their way with an ETA of 7.32 (very precise is our Pig!) at the agreed drop off outside Brooks Brothers on Madison, giving Pig just a short 'walk' to his station, now minus his prosthetic and using crutches, bought along with everything else at the Salvo's store. With construction on the corner of East 86th and Madison, I take the opportunity to slip on my high-vis vest and hard hat and stand around with my clipboard in hand. I make a point of recording the trucks pulling into the parking zone for the construction site (four concrete trucks and one with steel reinforcing if you have to know!) No one takes any notice and once Pig is heading on down East 86th, I put my clipboard away and head down after him, remaining on the opposite sidewalk.

Pig reaches his station, pivots on his crutches and gets himself settled exactly how we had discussed and agreed.

Now he is in position and minus his prosthesis, he looks the real deal. Dreadlocked, scruffy black beard, long-sleeved tee under a battered black puffer jacket, ripped jeans and with a cardboard sign saying, 'Afghan vet – please help' and an old biscuit tin he found somewhere to rattle – he looks the real street hobo!

Of course, I have to text Suzie saying, 'Love your handiwork!', getting a red heart as a response! (Yes, I do like getting these from Suzie!)

We now have our phones on our own private messenger network through WhatsApp, so confident no one else will hear or see what we say.

We have agreed we won't talk to Pig whilst he's on station just in case someone hears and gets suspicious.

Suzie had suggested and we both agreed she would simply drive around the area, getting to know the van and our surroundings. Working out the best exit strategies in each direction. She too has her earpiece in so will know immediately if anything goes wrong and she has to come barrelling in to rescue us.

Coming in this morning, she had practised the backfire, even apparently doing one in the Lincoln Tunnel with the accompanying echo. I'm sure she had a smile making that sort of noise!

The plan is, she will be sitting just around the corner in 5th Avenue this morning from just after eight a.m. We simply don't know how our targets might react to a hobo intruding on their walk space. I will be directly across the road, Suzie in the van, both ready to rip into action should it go pear-shaped this morning.

Plan for the worst, hope for the best. Wise words I read somewhere!

As eight a.m. approaches, I move across to the park side of 5th Avenue and take my position on the wall, exactly where I decided on our reconnaissance yesterday.

At 8.08 a.m., I see the 'target' Diego Garcia, his son Juan and his three bodyguards exit their apartment building and head along 5th.

As agreed, I let both Pig and Suzie know by noting 'one'.

Then three minutes later, I intone 'two' as they reach the corner of East 86th and start to cross over.

I do the same, crossing from 5th Avenue to the right side of East 86th but behind them so they don't notice me.

With my high viz on, I don't look out of place on the construction site.

We are quickly approaching our first 'pinch point', as we have no way of knowing how they will react to having a begging hobo sitting in the way.

Time to find out.

Phew. All of them politely step over and around Pig, no one even glancing at him or his rattling tin, except the back bodyguard uses his left leg in a symbolic kicking gesture as he steps over Pig's semi-extended good leg. But there was no malice or intent in it as far as I could see.

I continue to follow them, still on the southern side until they get to Park Avenue.

They turn left as expected, heading along Park toward East 89th and The Dalton School.

I watch them go, and let Suzie know, deciding there is no reason to follow them any further.

As planned, Pig stays on station for another three-quarters of an hour, then returns back to Brooks Bros where he is picked up by Suzie.

I stay in the background, watching, making sure no one is taking any notice.

Nope, no one is taking the slightest interest in Pig using the crutches rather adeptly now as he heads back down East 86th.

I watch from the corner as Suzie pulls up in the van at the designated drop off/pick up point outside Brooks Bros on Madison Ave.

Pig clambers in the back side door and after a few minutes, whilst I assume Pig is getting settled in the rear seat, and off they go. Neither they nor I acknowledge the other.

As planned, Suzie, with Pig now as a passenger, makes multiple drives down East 86th from 5th Avenue to Madison, where she turns left and goes round again. I'm timing each one.

I'm also timing the light sequence on the corner of East 86th and Madison. This could be critical for the best timing of the backfire, which needs to happen just as Diego's entourage is one pace away from Pig.

Timing will be everything.

I ask her to stop by the construction zone. Then start off again. We have determined the best place for Suzie to be positioned for the backfire is approximately fifty metres before Madison Ave, so she can quickly then turn left on Madison and be gone from sight.

After half a dozen runs, I'm confident we can make it work, so they head back to the Lincoln Tunnel Motel so Pig can remove his hobo clobber.

I head back to the Mandarin to change into more casual, touristy clothes, knowing Suzie too will get changed at the motel.

We have agreed to then meet at Saks Fifth Ave store.

Yes, I know, not my choice, first cultural lessons at the famous (and impressive!) museums, now I have to endure an afternoon of shopping.

Later, after dumping the shopping back at the Mandarin, we jump a cab to the 9/11 memorial. This is an extraordinary museum dedicated as it is to the events of 11 September 2001. You can feel the pain and terror they must have experienced that day as you move through the place.

Then to cap the day off, it's another cab ride (it's New York, you have to use the yellow cabs – not Uber!) to Tom's Restaurant on Broadway, the diner depicted in the long-running Seinfeld TV series. Naturally, we go in for coffee and a slice of apple pie. Seinfeld was always on repeat in the mess on base in Afghanistan, so Pig and I are very familiar with most of the episodes, so we start discussing a couple of the scenes from the diner. Suzie has no idea what we are laughing about. Still, we enjoy it – and the apple pie is good too!

Day one down. We achieved our goal for the day, setting a scene that we hope they will accept over the next few days as a new norm, thus enabling us to carry out our 'hit'.

13

Next morning is a repeat of Monday, same early start with Pig once again settled in his spot by the gate on East 86th comfortably before eight a.m.

I am again sitting on the wall of Central Park with line sight to both their apartment building entrance and to the corner of 5th and East 86th. I have reversed my jacket to show the green colour and have a beany pulled down hard on my head to minimise anyone recognising me from yesterday.

Of course, these are small cosmetic changes as I can't change my size or build, so I stay seated to avoid making my size obvious.

Diego's security team are pretty blasé, hardly even monitoring their surroundings. Maybe they think they are above an attack. The lead, who I assume is Diego's head of security, rarely looks anywhere but where they are walking.

Suits me!

It's 8.03 a.m. this morning as they exit the apartment building – a few minutes earlier than yesterday. I note 'one' into the phone so they know they are on the move. Suzie is a block further away today, as we didn't want her to be noticed being parked in the same spot two days in a row. Today I stay in my spot sitting on the rock wall of Central

Park. Pig's station is only eighty-odd metres from where I'm sitting, and I can cover that distance very quickly if I need to. Mind you, Pig is rather adept at protecting himself anyway and we are both armed, so if the shit does hit the fan, they will suffer consequences.

'Two,' I say into the phone as they turn right off 5th Avenue and into East 86th.

Again, no reaction as they step over and around Pig, rattling his tin and begging, 'Can't you help me please, sir?'

None of them bat an eye or react at all.

We follow the same routine as yesterday, wait three-quarters of an hour and then Pig stands up grabs his crutches and heads back down East 86th to Madison to the pickup point.

Like yesterday, Pig only has a few dollars in his tin, including the three one-dollar notes and a few quarters we had put in so it rattled and the notes added authenticity, making it look like others had already given.

I don't follow, staying on the wall until I receive a text from Pig saying they are ready.

We have agreed yesterday we need to practice the timing of Suzie's backfire and ensure she is close enough for the backfire to be loud enough to ensure a quick reaction but far enough away she can quickly get out of sight.

We know the timing of their walk down East 86th so know that about ninety seconds after turning into East 86th they will be stepping over Pig, then it takes them a further three minutes to walk on down East 86th to the corner of Madison, where invariably they will need to wait on the lights before crossing.

This morning I have extended the traffic cones further on toward Madison outside the construction site on the right-hand side of East 86th, but past Pig from Diego's perspective.

Suzie and Pig go round the block and she pulls up in this extended area behind the traffic cones.

As she then takes off, I time her until she gets to the designated 'fire' position fifty metres before the turn onto Madison.

We repeat this three times, so we get a measure of how other traffic might impact on our timing. It takes her between forty-five and fifty-two seconds.

Mmm, that means she needs to start moving forty to forty-five seconds after Diego turns into East 86th, as it will take him ninety seconds to reach Pig and we need Suzie to be approaching the corner of Madison at the same time. The joker in the pack is of course the timing of the lights on East 86th and Madison. I do not want Suzie still sitting at the lights with Diego's crew catching up to her.

Still, that's enough for today, don't want anyone wondering why the same old van is stopping and starting in the same spot.

Suzie and Pig head off to get changed. I do likewise and we have agreed to meet at The View near the ferry terminal at the Battery, another unique New York location.

Today we are off on a cruise out to the Statue of Liberty and Ellis Island – the arrival point of immigrants in an earlier era. We follow this with another boat trip to Staten Island. We don't do much there, but it seems to be 'a must-do' whilst in New York.

As planned, we are back at the Mandarin Oriental in time for an early evening run through Central Park, another 'must do' we had all agreed to up front. We have our cab drive up Wall Street from the Battery, so we can get the prerequisite photo of the 'Bull' on Wall Street. Another box ticked!

We quickly get changed into our running gear and meet back down in the lobby and walk across to Central Park. Yes, we all do our stretching exercises!

We stay together, jogging leisurely along the main six-mile loop. This gives us another dimension of life in New York and we certainly aren't alone on the track with multiple cyclists, runners, skateboarders and, of course, walkers all out in the early evening sunshine. A pleasant and enjoyable experience and it's also good to burn up a bit of energy – haven't been doing too much lately.

To offset our exercise, we decide on 'Quality Italian' to dine out at tonight. The chicken Parmie served in a pizza dish gets our attention (well Pig's and mine, if not Suzie's!), but for a change she is outnumbered!

After an enjoyable dinner, we head back up to Pig's room for some final spider-throwing. Yes, I dressed up for dinner, wearing the suit I bought at the Salvo store.

There is nothing wrong with Pig's aim and he seems to give his wrist a flick as he throws them, which he reckons improves his success rate.

He gets three spiders away in the two to three second window of opportunity but we decide a max of two would be better, don't want him rushing the throw and missing or worse, being noticed.

Then again that's what the purpose of the backfire is – Diego, his son and all three bodyguards should all be distracted as they walk past Pig.

If we get the timing right!

14

Day three, Wednesday.

We had agreed that if all went according to plan on days one and two, we would attempt our 'hit' on day three.

Today.

Like Monday and Tuesday, Pig and Suzie head off over to the Lincoln Tunnel Motel to dress up.

Before they head out, I catch Pig's eye, we nod to each other, then fist bump and then we hug.

My way of acknowledging the dangerous position he will be in if Diego or his crew realise what he is doing.

Their response will be quick and vicious. No question.

Suzie watches this happen and then we too hug (a bit more tightly than Pig and I, I might add!) and I whisper 'stay safe.'

The day is drizzly, so we are unsure how that changes Diego and his crew's plans. It's not heavy rain, just misty drizzle so we are hoping they are hardy New Yorkers and don't let this bother them.

Fingers crossed.

I head out across Central Park as I have enjoyed these morning walks, observing New York awakening, getting ready for another day.

We are all on station just after seven-thirty this morning and whilst waiting for Pig and Suzie, I have again extended the traffic cones outside the construction site.

Suzie is sitting around the corner awaiting my call to come and park there. We don't want her sitting there too long and have a parking warden or cop come along and move her on.

At 7.55 a.m., I tell her to 'come on round' (yes, I do try to lighten the atmosphere by imitating the popular TV series catch cry 'come on down!' but I didn't get a reaction to my attempt to ease the tension.)

She comes around the corner and pulls up. She too has a clipboard with a list of 'deliveries' on it. It is just a prop in case anyone gets nosey!

8.05 a.m., no sign.

8.10 a.m., no sign. Bugger, don't tell me they are taking the car?

8.13 a.m. 'One,' I say into the phone. All five of them have come bustling out of the apartment building entrance, Diego and Juan still doing their coats up. I must say I am relieved. Being keyed up and focused on this little 'hit' it would be disappointing to have to delay a day – or more.

Today, I move off the wall ahead of them and into the construction zone opposite Pig. I'm ready.

'Two.' I have my stopwatch running, watching the time and Diego at the same time. After twenty seconds I hear Suzie start the van. It's not loud but she is now only a few metres up the road from me.

Thirty seconds.

Forty seconds. 'Three.'

The van eases out slowly into the traffic. She has two cars coming up East 86th behind her now. She doesn't hurry – keeps her pace slow and steady, according to the script.

I can't watch the van and Pig, so I focus on Diego and his crew approaching Pig, full faith in Suzie following through.

'Five.' I calculate they are five seconds away from Pig – five strides as he walks one stride per second – I know, we have timed him!

I'm no longer watching the stopwatch, fully focused on Pig and the approaching crew.

'Four.' Ignition time.

BOOM.

BOOM.

Not one but two backfires shatter the city bustle.

I'm watching the bodyguards closely and all three hands dart to their holstered weapons but none draw them. There is also a hesitation in their strides, including Diego and Juan. Juan even casts a glance at his dad, not sure if in fear or just looking for guidance.

Two seconds later, they are past Pig and I glance up to see if Suzie has got around the corner into Madison. No sign of her so clearly, she did.

Diego and his crew walk on toward Madison and judging by their body language, I suspect they are having a chuckle at their reactions to the car backfiring.

Certainly, they don't seem to be suspicious at all.

Good.

Pig whispers, 'Bingo. Two.'

I do an imaginary fist pump. He is telling us he reckons he hit the target with two spiders.

We will know soon enough.

We had agreed if we were successful, Pig would not stay on location after they reached Park Ave so a few minutes later he is up, bringing his crutches into play and heading back to Brooks Bros to be collected by Suzie.

Once Suzie has Pig on board, they swing around back onto 5th Avenue and collect me as well.

Pig is sitting in his seat, already laptop on his lap, headphones plugged in.

As I get into the passenger seat, he raises his eyes, smiling and giving me the thumbs up.

I fist pump the air. Suzie and I high-five – even whilst she is driving.

Bingo.

Job done.

After a couple of minutes, Pig again looks up and says, 'I can hear them talking, not very clearly but they are still walking along the road. I'm sure I got two spiders on Diego – one on each leg and also another one of the back bodyguard, just for the hell of it.'

'Boom,' I say, smiling.

We are all headed back toward the Lincoln Tunnel, with the plan to drop me off before the tunnel as I don't want to be seen back at their motel.

We head through Central Park on the 97th Street Traverse before heading back along Broadway. Suzie pulls into a servo with a Starbucks.

The plan is I'll leave them here and cab it back to the Mandarin. I jump out and go in and buy three coffees. When I get back to the van to hand them their coffee, Pig says, with excitement in his voice: 'You better listen to this' and pulls off his headphones and unplugs them so we can all hear the audio.

A voice I recognise as Diego says, apparently talking into a phone on speaker, 'Morning update, please.'

A second voice I don't recognise, and from the shake of Pig's head he doesn't either, replies, 'Sir, we brought Pedro in this morning. We are holding him at the East New York warehouse for you.'

Diego responds, 'Good, hold him there. Have you roughed him up?'

'No, sir.'

Silence for a few moments. 'Good. Santiago.' Addressing the driver, I think. 'Change of plans, we are going to the ENY warehouse first.

Seb, we will see you there shortly. I will teach him a lesson. One that everyone will know what happens if you cross a Garcia.'

A click sounds the end of the phone call.

Another voice pipes up. 'Sir, do you think it wise for you to be involved? Let me and the boys take care of Pedro for you.'

'No. This is personal. He was a friend. He has double-crossed me. I will teach him a lesson. One everyone else will know about.'

I glance at Suzie, who is turned looking back at Pig and I'm not sure how to read her expression – one of hope but also maybe concern for what she is hearing and the likely consequence of both our actions and what we have just heard.

Pig mutes the sound. It's being recorded and uploaded to our cloud base, so kept for eternity.

I ask, 'Have you shared this with Campbell and Hunter yet?'

Pig replies, 'No, not yet. This is a live conversation, but I'm uploading a link now so they and Midge can hear it. I'll send them all an urgent message. Sounds like the perfect time for Campbell to take this mob down.'

'Yes,' I reply, thinking as I sip my Starbucks.

'Maybe we sit tight for a few minutes to see how this evolves. This may necessitate a quick change of plans.' I look around, noting a small Safeway across the road. 'Suzie, can you drive us over there? Find an isolated parking spot so we can stay still for a little while if need be.'

She nods as I climb back in, buckle up and she takes us across and parks in the Safeway car park.

I watch as Pig pulls his prepaid phone out of his pocket and sends Campbell and Hunter a text including the link and says, 'Hurry up, here is your chance.'

It's literally seconds and his phone starts ringing. Pig looks at it, smiles hands it to me, saying, 'Shit, that was quick!'

I answer the call without identifying myself.

It's Campbell and he is pretty excited.

'Man, how did you get this? Man. Awesome! We are on it. We know they have a warehouse in Linwood Street, East New York. We are mobilising now. THANK YOU.' And he hangs up.

Pig and I smile at each other. I take another sip of coffee – make that two.

'Okay,' I start. 'I think this calls for a change of plans. I suggest we skedaddle, now. Leave New York today and head to Washington. Whether Campbell and co are successful today or not, Diego's mob are going to be backtracking trying to see how a mic got onto him. We need to make ourselves scarce.'

Pig is nodding his head, whilst continuing to listen to the conversation from Diego's car through his headphones.

Suzie looks from Pig to me, catches my eye, smiles and says, 'Just as well I got my shopping done then! Mind you, I never did buy the extra suitcase I need for my new clothes, handbags and shoes.' All said with a smile just for me – just rubbing in how much of my money she has spent. My penance.

I smile back and then turn to serious mode.

'Okay, you two head back to the motel, get changed and sanitise the room before leaving. You will need to find a skip bin or big rubbish bin and throw all the clothes and props into it. Then find a small strip mall or maybe even a Dunkin' Donuts to leave the van, leave the keys in it so it's easier to steal, thereby making it harder to trace back to us. Then jump a cab or two to ensure you don't leave a trail back to the Mandarin. How long do you think it will take you and how long to pack your gear up at the Mandarin?'

I then add, 'I'll stop at a Walmart and pick up another suitcase to throw all your new shopping in.' This time, it's me smiling at Suzie and using the words 'throwing' expecting her to react, but her response is, 'Well, not sure you will get a suitcase at Walmart suitable for our usual accommodation standards.'

Mmm, fair point, I decide (without conceding it!)

Pig's phone buzzes and he looks at it and smiles, reading the text aloud. 'You boys have been busy. Awesome! From Midge,' he adds.

Pig looks at Suzie and says, 'What are we, ten, fifteen minutes from the motel?'

Suzie replies, 'More like twenty, twenty-five.'

Still looking at Suzie, he then says, 'Okay, say thirty, ninety minutes to change and sanitise the room, dump the van and thirty to forty back to the hotel so two to two and a half hours all up?'

Suzie nods her agreement, adding, 'Sanitising the room and the van shouldn't take too long, as we have always worn gloves.'

Pig nods his agreement.

'Okay, I'll look at Amtrak services to Washington leaving in three to three and a half hours from now.' They both nod. We fist bump all round.

I get out of the van and head to the road to find myself a cab. Mind you, I'm not going to take a cab from here direct to Mandarin – that would stand out in the cabby's mind. When I find one, I tell him to take me to the Lincoln Center for Performing Arts. I had seen a sign for it a few minutes ago just before we stopped.

Suzie and Pig pull out of the car park and head off behind me. No wave, no acknowledgement.

15

The train trip down to Washington is uneventful but not until after a bit of rush to make it.

Pig and Suzie get held up in traffic, only making it back to the Mandarin as it's time to head to Penn Station for our Amtrak Acela service. But all good, I have packed both Suzie's and Pig's clothes and gear, so I am waiting for them when they arrive.

We jump one final New York yellow cab and we're off to Washington.

We have not yet heard any further from Campbell or Hunter, so unsure what the outcome had been for the FBI out in East New York.

Then just as the train is pulling into the station in Washington, Pig gets an encrypted message from Midge saying, 'We got them! Got them all. Caught in the act. Hallelujah! GREAT JOB, boys! Drinks are ALL on me this week now.'

Pig and I smile and fist bump, which wakes Suzie who had been dozing, so she was all smiles too as we exited the train, looking for a cab, in Washington now though.

I decide, with our job well done, to upgrade our accommodation in Washington from a mere Marriott to the JW Marriott, located right in the heart of Washington.

Once we check in it's time for a feed, so we ask the concierge for directions to the local Ruth Chris Steakhouse, knowing you always get a good steak there.

It's only a mile and as it's a pleasant evening, we agree to walk there, oohing and ahhing at sites we have seen in movies or on TV.

Pig and I have been to Washington a couple of times previously; the last time we had even been was to the White House to receive our Presidential Medal of Freedom medals, but of course that was in secret – no one saw us go in or out. We did have a day of sightseeing though so at least this time we have a better understanding of what's worth seeing. But being soldiers, there is a lot. They do memorials well here in Washington DC! The previous time we had mostly been holed up at 'The Farm', CIA headquarters in Langley Virginia. No sightseeing on that trip!

We arrive at Ruth Chris and after checking our reservation, the young waiter leads us off to show us to our table.

As always, I study the restaurant, just in case. Always on the lookout, never be taken by surprise.

Bugger me, what's he doing here? I'm suddenly thinking to myself as I immediately take a detour from following the waiter and I sense rather than see Pig and Suzie hesitate and then follow me.

I head over to a table against the back wall and as I approach, I notice the younger woman watching me alertly and even placing her right hand under the table, close to, I suspect, a weapon. I also notice Pig veers to his left, extending the angle between us, thus making any attack on us more difficult, obviously also having seen her hand movement.

'Uncle Albert?' I say, addressing my mum's older brother, sitting at the table with a smartly dressed middle-aged woman and the other younger woman more casually dressed in jeans and a top.

Uncle Albert, who had been speaking, stopped mid-sentence and just looked at me, non-plussed I guess, then bellowed, 'Boy, what the hell are you doing here?' He stands up and comes around the end of the table to shake hands, then we even hug. I don't recall ever hugging him previously but shit, I have hardly seen him for fifteen years, other than family weddings or in fact, mainly funerals.

After we finish our greeting, he turns to the table and says, 'Mary, this is Mort, my nephew.' He points at the younger woman. 'And that's Hannah, Mary's daughter.' Then, lowering his voice into a conspiratorial whisper, he says, 'She's a Secret Service agent, so don't upset her, she might shoot you.' Hannah gives him an eye roll as if she is over his jokes.

I introduce Suzie as my fiancée. I haven't had too many opportunities to do this but I still like the sound of it! And then Pig as well, with Suzie quickly adding, 'You can call him Julien, his given name,' added with a smile.

Uncle Albert, says, 'Are you just arriving?'

'Yes,' I reply. 'We were just heading to our table when I couldn't believe my eyes, but there you were.'

He then addresses the waiter who has been hovering, not sure what to do and asks, or is that demands? 'Grab a spare table and add it here onto ours please.'

He nods and moves away. I say to Mary and Hannah, 'You sure you don't mind?'

They both smile and say, 'Happy for you to join us.'

We just chit-chat whilst the wait staff rearrange the table until they have made it into a table for six. I notice they still have their menus, so they haven't ordered yet, but their drinks are delivered whilst the table is being sorted.

Once settled, Uncle Albert looks at me, saying, 'I heard you were out, boy.' (He has always called me 'boy'; I've never really known why but I guess it is because I am his only nephew and he only has two daughters himself. Even more incongruous now, considering my size and him being more medium build.) 'What did they let you out for, good behaviour?' He laughs at his own joke.

I smile and say to Mary and Hannah, 'He means the army not prison!'

Uncle Albert leans in and again with the conspiratorial whisper, says, 'Mary is a major in the Marines, so you better be careful around her too!'

I look at her and nod, showing her the respect that position deserves.

'But what are you all doing here in Washington?' Uncle Albert asks.

I decide on the full explanation. 'Pig, here, competed in the Invictus Games up in Canada a couple of weeks ago and Suzie and I came over as his cheer squad and since then, we have been on holiday, visiting Lake Louise, Niagara Falls, New York and now Washington.'

It's Hannah who asks Pig, 'Wow, I hadn't even noticed a disability?'

Pig smiles and says, 'Yes, I lost my left leg at the knee to an IED on patrol in Afghanistan, so now have a prosthetic.'

'Wow, sorry for being so insensitive.' She smiles before Mary adds, 'How did you go; did you enjoy the games?'

Pig smiles and looks at Suzie and says, 'Yes, we had a blast. Ran into plenty of former colleagues, drank plenty of beer. Well, after my events finished, that is. Great time.'

Suzie, who has been playing with her phone, now proffers it over to Mary and Hannah, saying, 'Here, watch this. It's Julien running the final lap of his ten thousand metre race.'

Silence as the three of them watch Suzie's iPhone, with Uncle Albert leaning over as well.

Well, to be honest, it isn't really silence as you can hear me and Suzie yelling and screaming!

After they watch the end of the race, it's Hannah who asks Pig, 'Did you make it?'

Pig smiles and shakes his head in the negative. 'No, lost by a nose was the official decision.'

As she retrieves her phone, Suzie adds, 'It was like accompanying two rockstars there at the games, these two' – indicating Pig and I – 'were so popular. It seemed everyone wanted to chat to them!'

Suzie then asks the obvious question, 'So, Albert – is it okay if I call you Albert?' As he nods, she continues, 'What are you doing over here?'

'Well, dear,' he replies, 'I'm basically retired these days and my two hobbies are landscape photography and long-distance swimming, so I wander around the world doing a bit of both.'

'Okay, so how did you meet Mary then?'

Uncle Albert laughs, saying, 'Now, isn't that a story? Let's order first and I will tell you.'

With the waiter again hovering, we take turns to order steaks all round – it is Ruth Chris, after all!

Then with glasses refilled, he starts off his tale.

'I was driving from San Francisco to Lake Tahoe – ah, this was, what? Three, four weeks ago?' Mary nods in agreement. 'And not sure if you know the road but it's a nice driving road, so I was enjoying the drive. I only drive a little Subaru XV so nothing flash but it gets along, and after a little while I caught up with a Golden Wing – you know the Honda motorbike tourer, the Golden Wing? Anyway, this rider was a real pain in the arse, riding in the middle of the road and every time we got to a bit of straight road, she – yes, I had guessed it was a woman from her posture and the long hair helped.' He laughed self-depreciatingly. 'So she was slowing me down. After a little while when it was obvious she wasn't going to let me pass, I backed off and let her go, thinking I'll give her a head start and hopefully won't see her again.

'Anyway, a few minutes later I come to a scenic lookout, so pull in to see what the view was like and bugger me, there was the Golden Wing with her' – he points at Mary – 'standing beside it. So, I parked next to her and we shared a couple of words.'

Here, Hannah pipes up, saying, 'Come on, tell them what you said,' with a hint of amusement.

'Oh okay, it was a hot day and Mary had pulled the zipper on her leathers down a little, so I said to her, 'Always wondered what you bikers wore under your leathers.'

This brought a few sniggers from around the table before he continued, 'She replied, "Wouldn't you like to know?" So I looked her in the eye and said, "Yes I would!"'

This brought more laughter from the table and Mary was colouring a little.

'Anyway,' he continued, 'we chatted for a few minutes then I went off to take a few photos for my library and when I turned around, she was there taking photos with her phone so I offered to take one of her with the view in the background, like the old days before all you young folk started taking selfies all the time.

Nearby, a table of teenagers break out into loud laughter, interrupting Uncle Albert's flow. He waves a hand in annoyance before leaning in.

'Back at the bike, I told her I would give her a ten-minute start and she promised me if I caught up, she would let me pass this time. That was it – I didn't even see the bike and I must say I started to push the Subie to try and catch her. Then when I pulled into the Ritz Carlton there at Lake Tahoe, I was a little disappointed we hadn't got to continue our battle. But then, bugger me, there was her bike sitting outside the hotel lobby and when I went through to check in, she was just finishing her check in so I asked if she would like a drink later. She agreed. Then a drink became dinner and, well, we became friends!'

Mary then chimes in, saying, 'Yes, there I was. I had scraped all my Marriott Bonvoy points together so I could enjoy a night of luxury and be pampered at the spa and he walks in, being escorted by the concierge and then has the manager come out to welcome him as a "hotel ambassador", no less.'

'How do you become an ambassador for the Ritz Carlton anyway?' This time it was Hannah asking.

'By spending a lot of money,' I guess out loud.

'Well, there is that, although I do get a fair discount. I do use them wherever I can, so all through Europe and the UK as well as here in America. But the main reason is I became friends with one of their senior managers a few years back and with my swimming profile, I do have a large following and surprisingly most serious open water swimmers are comfortably off. So, an attractive demographic for the Ritz Carlton to target.'

Our first courses are now being served and before he tucks into his prawns, Uncle Albert continues, 'Anyway, if you think how I met Mary was funny, wait until I tell you how Hannah and I met – it's a real hoot!'

Hannah gives another eye roll.

We eat in silence enjoying our entrees.

As soon as he's wiped his hands after finishing his prawns, Uncle Albert continues, 'After I left Lake Tahoe – I was there to do their annual lake swim – I headed up to Coeur d'Alene up in Utah for another annual lake swim, then headed here to Washington as Mary had invited me to stay if I was "passing through", so here I am.

'The first morning after arriving, I'm sitting there working on my photos when the front door opens and bugger me there's Hannah, gun drawn down in that shooter's stance you see on TV, yelling at me to put my hands up. I'm guessing it's Hannah but I had never met her, so I say, "It's okay. I'm staying with your mum." Then she threatens to shoot me if I don't put my hands up. But I'm in the middle of editing an image and if I stop, I'll stuff it up, so I suggest she ring her mum who will confirm I'm staying with her.

'I finished editing the image so I put my hands up and she managed to call Mary one-handed, the gun never waiving from pointing at me. Mary, of course, didn't pick up and so she left a message saying, "Hi Mum, I called in to your place for a change of clothes and found some stranger here, saying he's staying with you. You need to call before I shoot him."'

Uncle Albert has a way of telling a story, mining it for everything, and we were all spellbound, wondering how Mum was going to explain a strange man staying with her.

He continues, 'When that didn't work, I suggested she check the bedroom for my luggage and of course, when she headed toward to spare bedroom, I had to tell her wrong room. So, you can imagine the steam was nearly coming out her ears by now!

'Then her phone rang and I heard her say, "Talk to me, Mum, his luggage is even in YOUR room." Being the gentleman I am, I moved away so I couldn't hear the rest of the conversation. Needless to say, she had put her gun away when I saw her next. I even made her a cup of coffee as a peace offering! And I thought I would shout them both dinner as a "get to know you" thing, and then you all walked in!'

We had all had a few laughs through the telling and I hear Suzie and Hannah start chatting, then Mary leans over to me, saying, 'Australian Army?'

'Yes,' I reply, indicating Pig as well. 'Both fifteen years each.'

'Did you see any action?'

'Yes.' I smile, as does Pig, watching the conversation and knowing where it's headed. 'East Timor in the early days, Iraq and lately

Afghanistan. Two tours, five years in the country in total. So, a lot more time than the usual.'

'So, what battalion?'

'1RAR,' I reply and then having thought through my answers, she comes back with, 'You must have had some special skills to do extended tours like that?'

'You might say that,' I add with a smile. Now the others at the table are all listening.

'I've been there, did my share, in the early days, I admit, but got to experience it the hard way,' Mary responds.

'With the Marines?'

She nods yes and Pig pipes up, 'Do you know Campbell McPherson or Hunter Buchanan? They were both in the Marines.'

'Yes, I know them. They are both in the FBI now – I still know them, in fact. Deal with Campbell quite a bit. I'm on a joint task force with his boss. I was also his CO for a little while when he first went to Afghanistan.'

I let the silence lengthen then say, 'We have just done Campbell a little favour up in New York.'

'A favour?' she asks, then it dawns on her. 'The Colombians?' she says, almost to herself with a shocked look on her face or is that astonishment?

'Sorry, what did you say your surnames were?'

'Ireland and Le Tonge,' I reply.

Another incredulous look passes over her face, not missed by Hannah or Suzie or I guess by anyone. She stands up, putting her hand out to me, saying, 'Sergeant Ireland, I am truly honoured to meet you and thank you for your service.' She then quickly moves down the table to Pig, doing the same. Now it's Hannah, Uncle Albert and Suzie whose mouths are hanging open.

Once she is back in her seat, she addresses the others. 'I can't say too much about our guests but believe me, they have gone way beyond in providing service to their country and ours.' Looking at me, she continues, 'Didn't you get awarded the Presidential Medal of Freedom?'

'Yes, we both did, by the President himself. But that is meant to be top secret,' I reply, giving her an appraising look. I'm also wondering how a mere Marine major would know anything about the FBI actions today in New York, know our names and that we had been awarded our Presidential Medals of Freedom, which is highly confidential. There is more to this lady than meets the eye. I do need to get clarity here, just not in front of civilians.

As she sits down again, I lean over and say quietly and firmly, but also loud enough for Hannah and Uncle Albert to hear, 'Our involvement in New York was strictly off the books. No names mentioned. Anywhere. Please respect that.' The look that accompanied my words clearly makes an impression as her expression changes as she nods and says, 'Certainly. Understood.'

Good, I can still intimidate a Marine major, I think!

Our meals appear so it's a good place to stop. I don't like being the topic of conversation and everyone seems to think it was a good idea to let things settle and tuck in.

Ruth Chris doesn't let us down either, another good steak.

When Uncle Albert had finished his steak, he leans over and asks, 'So, Mort, what are you doing now you have left the army?'

I finish my last mouthful and reply, 'I have my own business. Digital Data Solutions. Pig and I work together doing data security audits and have had a fair success in recovering stolen data – you know when a company loses their data through a hacking attack or other means? We go in and recover it. One hundred per cent record on full recovery so far. Touch wood,' I add, tapping my own head.

Uncle Albert nods and then asks, 'What about you dear?' addressing Suzie.

'I have my own family law practice.'

It's Mary who comes back saying, 'Ah, that must be heartbreaking at times.'

'Yes,' is Suzie's reply, not wanting to get into the hurt and heartbreak that some of her clients suffer.

A little later, I hear Pig ask Hannah, 'So, that's why you are carrying – being Secret Service?'

'How did you know I'm armed?' she responds, rather defensively.

'It was your reaction when Mort first approached the table. Your hand went down near your gun.'

'Oh,' is her reply, then a few moments later, 'so is that why you are sitting next to me and Mort opposite?'

'Yep, we have you boxed.' He smiles!

Once he finishes his meal, Pig asks Mary, 'Have you ever heard Campbell being called "Sunshine"?'

'Yes, it's a curious nickname – for him,' she replies.

Pig points his fork my way, saying, 'He has him to blame for that.'

'How come?' This question comes from Hannah.

Pig smiles – he likes telling this story and doesn't get the opportunity very often.

'You know the mission to grab Abdul Ahmadi?'

Mary nods, saying, 'It was after my time, but yes, I know the details.'

Pig continues. 'We' – again, pointing his fork at me – 'were in deep, monitoring radios and movements way behind enemy lines. We cracked the local code, so we knew some highflyer was coming to the area, then when we heard and passed on his name, they decided to send in a team of Marines to capture Ahmadi. Hunter was the team leader.

'But we had a funny feeling about it so we "borrowed" a local Toyota and drove twenty kilometres in total darkness, I might add, and took up positions about seven hundred metres outside the village. We hadn't been in position long when the shit hit the fan. One of the guards turned, suddenly seeing one of the team and opened fire. It went downhill from there. Fortunately, we both had our "long guns" so started evening the odds.'

'What, from seven hundred metres away?' This question comes from Hannah, who is looking at us both.

We both nod affirmative, before Mary adds, 'Yes, they' – indicating us both – 'are world-class snipers, amongst other things.'

Pig continues, 'We were able to help extract the team, rounding them up in our beat-up old Hilux and Hunter calls in, declaring the raid a failure, although we, or at least Mort, had witnessed Ahmadi being killed.'

Mary looks at me and I nod affirmative.

'Anyway, there are eight of us in the Hilux, Mort driving, Hunter squeezed in the middle and me riding shotgun, the rest in the back hanging on for dear life with Hunter calling for the extraction helicopter. We didn't know then, but Campbell was the duty officer and as far as he was concerned, the extraction point was as per the plan. He expected them to retreat back there. Mort grabs Hunter's lapel mic and earpiece and says, "Listen, Sunshine, we have just saved your team's arse. I don't have time to do it again. I have somewhere to be well before dawn, so the retrieval point is…" And he repeats the coordinates of the backup retrieval point. "Clear? Have them there in six minutes. Don't be late. Clear?"

'Campbell was silent for a moment then responded, "Clear. But this is not the end of this."

'"Sure, Sunshine," was Mort's response! Then the chopper turned up two minutes early so they got another earful for bringing the friendlies out before we even got there, dumb bastards. Anyway, they got their lift and we made it safely back to our hidey hole before dawn. Not a great success but with Ahmadi dead, it was certainly a big plus at the time.

'It was a couple of weeks before we were extracted. We were on station well behind enemy lines for six weeks straight, so we were glad to get back to base. Campbell was one of the first to greet us when we disembarked, starting to get into Mort. Of course, Mort wasn't taking a backward step either but a passing colonel gave Campbell a sharp reprimand and that shut him up. To be fair, he came to the mess the next night and bought us a beer. Well, make that three or four,' Pig finishes with a laugh.

Before anyone else can ask questions, I pipe up, saying, 'I think that's enough tales for one night. I do fancy the apple pie though, anyone else?'

This got the conversation back onto an even keel, then as the evening draws to a close, Mary asks if we would like to come over to her place the next evening for a barbeque.

'Sure,' we say in unison. We haven't had a home-cooked meal in nearly three weeks, so we promise to bring dessert and head back to our hotel, after paying our bill, of course.

The fresh air is good for our heads after the warm atmosphere of the restaurant. Suzie seems very clingy walking back, so I guess she didn't like hearing the war stories, or at least those about me.

As we walk into the JW Marriott's lobby, there is a surprise for Pig.

He, like me, is always scanning what's around us, and I notice his gaze stop and his head turn to me with a slight smile and then he is lengthening his stride; at about the same time, as Stacey sees us coming, jumps up and whilst not running, it's clear she too is keen to see him.

Suzie takes my hand and whispers, 'This is your doing, isn't it?'

I smile and give her a nod and she squeezes my fingers.

Pig and Stacey have disengaged themselves now, although still holding each other tight – I'm reminded of when I had met Suzie at Sydney Airport on another occasion…

As we head up in the elevator, chatting mainly about Stacey's flight over, Stacey is reaching up, rubbing her hand over Pig's newly bald head, making me think maybe this had been her idea.

I remind them, 'Don't forget, the bus picks us up at eight-thirty in the morning for our tour. So don't be late!'

As we get close to their room, Stacey disengages herself from Pig and comes over to me, giving me a big hug and whispers, 'Thank you, Mort,' and pecks me on the cheek.

Pig gives me a nod. We are blokes, after all – no need to fuss!

As we enter our room, Suzie asks, 'Didn't you tell me Stacey had been convicted of prostitution?'

I nod.

'But that means she can't get a visa to the States? How does that work?' she continues, looking at me inquisitively.

My face creases in a smile as I reply, 'What's the use of having both the Queensland Police Commissioner and the Prime Minister's chief of staff on speed dial if you can't do a friend a favour! They agreed to wipe her and Christi's records clean. They did help us bring down the corrupt State Government, after all!'

This gets me a smile, her arms going around my neck as she whispers, 'Mort Ireland, you are a good man!' She kisses me, pulling me toward the bed.

I like where this is going!

A bit later, Suzie admits she is always scared when she hears what I have done in the army.

I tell her, 'I am well-trained and "bloody good" at it, so you don't need to worry, especially now I am retired.'

'Yes,' she replies, 'until MGC calls you up.'

'Yes, but that's different. We are up against rank amateurs these days.'

'Well, don't get too cocky, Mister. One of those amateurs might surprise you.'

I take her in my arms again and say, 'I have too much to lose these days to be taking any chances.'

She replies as she snuggles in, 'Yes, you do!'

16

After a day of sightseeing around Washington the next day, taking in all the sights including all the memorials for the various wars – World War II memorial, Korean War, Vietnam War and of course add in the Lincoln, Roosevelt (including his little dog, Fala!), the Thomas Jefferson memorials, the White House, Congress, the Hoover building and the Pentagon – it was a busy day!

My personal favourite (if favourite is the right word) is the Korean War memorial. Something eerie and haunting about it. It certainly resonated with me.

Stacey had settled in comfortably, chatting away to all and sundry, a bit less reserved than Pig and I. It also brought Suzie out of her shell, having someone other than Pig and I to talk to. I enjoyed the peace!

Well, sort of.

Pig and I had a quiet chat together where I broached how surprised I am that Mary, as a major, knows so much about us and even the FBI actions in New York, and we agree we need to have a quiet chat to her tonight. No, I don't mean in a threatening way!

We had received a phone call from Campbell and Hunter, ecstatic that they had arrested Diego and five of his gang on the strength of the mic we had landed. They couldn't thank us enough with Campbell concluding with, 'Our boss carries a lot of weight and she said to tell you thank you, very well done.'

Pig and I fist bump, then Suzie insists on joining us with a three-way fist bump.

The tour bus drops us off just after five p.m. It was a long day, but a worthwhile one.

The four of us agree to meet in the lobby at six-thirty p.m. to jump an Uber to Mary's place for our keenly awaited barbeque.

It's a balmy night so a chance to put the shorts on instead of jeans!

Whilst waiting for our Uber, I note Pig has not worn his bum bag all day, so putting my arms around Suzie's shoulder, I lean over to him and say, 'I see you have upgraded to my model of bum bag, ah?'

Of course, I am smiling, as is Suzie. Pig gives me the middle finger, whilst Stacey is looking puzzled, causing Pig to explain what I mean!

Our Uber duly arrives and we head off to Mary's home in Chevy Chase, an outer suburb that is actually in Maryland, an adjoining state.

We take a quick stop at a convenient Safeway supermarket to pick up not one but two key lime pies and fresh cream, plus two packs of cold beer and two bottles of Oyster Bay, the Kiwi Sauv Blanc, Suzie's favourite.

We arrive in a lovely tree-lined street and pull up outside a nicely kept detached home. In the driveway sits a lime green Subaru XV and an older VW Golf GTi.

Suzie quickly notes, 'That must be Albert's Subaru and I wonder whose Golf that is? They obviously like to get where they are going. They get along!'

We three just nod. None of us know as much about cars as my Suzie!

We ring the door chime and it's Hannah who opens the door and ushers us through to the back lawn with a barbeque set up under a pergola.

Mary and Albert are bustling about getting salads, et cetera ready.

Mary turns and wiping her hands on her apron, smiles and says, 'Sorry, I was late home so still getting sorted.'

We all smile and Suzie answers for us, saying, 'No worries, happy to help if you like.' Then introduces Stacey to them all.

Uncle Albert, as blunt as I remember and digesting that Stacey is Pig's partner, looks at Pig and says, 'I thought you were gay?'

Oops.

It's Mary who beats Hannah with a quick reprimand, saying, 'Albert, you can't say that!'

Uncle Albert, looking a little sheepish at the reaction his words have evoked, adds, 'Sorry, didn't mean to be inappropriate, but I remember Mort's good mate as being gay.'

Pig (or Julien as everyone else is calling him) smiles, saying, 'No problems. For the record, I deem myself to be bisexual, or I did until Stacey and I teamed up.' With this, he smiles and gives Stacey a squeeze around the waist, getting a smile from her in exchange.

Uncle Albert then says, 'I didn't get a chance to pick up some wine for Mary, so I will just shoot down to the bottle shop to pick some up.'

Hannah adds, 'I'll come with you. Might stop someone shooting you if you say something else inappropriate in public!'

Pig opens a couple of beers for us, the ever-popular Budweiser, whilst I open a bottle of Oyster Bay for the girls. When offering Mary a glass, she pauses, then says, 'Why not. I usually drink a red, which is what Albert's gone to get, but I'll join you. Thanks.'

The girls then chat quietly whilst giving Mary a hand, explaining that Oyster Bay is a New Zealand wine and a favourite of theirs.

Pig and I gravitate to the barbeque, drinking our beers, noting it's a Weber brand, same as many at home.

A few minutes later, we hear the Subaru return and even I note the light rumble the engine makes.

Uncle Albert and Hannah come in, carrying a box of red wine, opening one and when going to pour a glass for Mary, he realises she has a glass of white and pauses, saying, 'Okay, you happy with that?'

Mary smiles at him and nods. 'Yes, the girls have offered me this New Zealand Sauv Blanc so I'll stick with this for now.'

Hannah comments, 'New Zealand must be a beautiful country from all the movies and pictures I've seen.'

The Aussies amongst us all agree it is a pretty and pleasant place to visit, Pig sharing the old joke about more sheep than people!

In a lull in the conversation, Suzie asks Uncle Albert, 'So your Subie is tuned, is it?' I quickly glance at Suzie and the slight smile on her face reinforces my suspicion that she is expecting a reaction to this, following Uncle Albert's story of last night.

Uncle Albert nods, saying, 'Yes, it's chipped so gets along all right.'

Suzie then adds, 'With it being lowered, it will also improve the handling, wouldn't it?' Again, an innocent question. As Uncle Albert nods agreement, Mary suddenly exclaims, addressing Uncle Albert, 'Hold on, are you telling me your car is hotted up or something?'

Suzie quickly chimes in, smiling now, 'And lowered to improve the handling!'

Mary again, 'So, all the time you have been telling people I was holding you up on the ride to Lake Tahoe, you were driving a modified car – and didn't say so?'

With this, she cuffs him around the ear and none too gently!

Uncle Albert's feeble comeback is, 'Well, you didn't ask.' Then, I think, realising he had been found out, he puts his arm around Mary's waist and says, 'Besides, if it hadn't been, we would never have met, would we?' He gets an 'umph' as a reply from Mary.

Suzie and Hannah seem to be enjoying Uncle Albert's discomfort – girl power at work, I guess. Poor Stacey, having not been with us last night, doesn't know the back story, so Pig is quietly filling her in.

Uncle Albert wanders back to the barbeque, glass of red in hand, so with Mary momentarily on her own, I slip over next to her and say, 'Can we have a word?'

She nods and we take our drinks off over to the back corner of the lawn and a few moments later, Pig joins us.

Before I can say anything, Mary jumps in. 'You know I had to watch the video five times this morning to see how you managed to place the mic. So bloody clever and smooth. No wonder you are so highly regarded. The only way I worked it out was when I realised the backfire had to be a distraction and focused on what was happening to Diego at that point in time. Then I realised that had to be you, Julien. To be honest, even though I knew that had to be the moment the mic was planted, I could not work out how you did it. Couldn't work out how it was done!

'I don't know who did your make up and wardrobe but they should get a job in Hollywood. Very, very professional job all round. Out of curiosity, who created the backfire?'

I nod toward Suzie and say, 'That was Suzie's idea and she was the driver. She also did up Pig. She was a complete member of the team.'

Mary is still shaking her head in amazement at our achievement.

I start, 'Mary, with due respect, you are obviously a very well-informed major. To have access to our records, know we received the Presidential Medal of Honour and to be able to watch video of yesterday's FBI action in New York, you very clearly are not "just" a Marine major. And, sorry we don't know your surname.'

Mary smiles and says, 'Mary Cutler' and we shake hands again formally and I acknowledge, saying, 'Major Cutler?'

She nods in agreement.

I glance back to see that Suzie is watching us intently and, I suspect, dying to come over and join us but refrains herself. No doubt I will be given a grilling later!

Mary smiles and says, 'Well, yes, whilst I am a major and will never progress above that rank because of a black mark on my record, for many years I have been recognised for my expertise in "urban warfare" and have dedicated myself to eliminating our enemies within, such as crime gangs, drug cartels, militia groups and the like.

'For the last five years I have been seconded to various joint taskforces with FBI, Homeland Security and other organisations I can't share with you, being tasked with identifying internal enemies and eliminating them.'

She pauses and Pig asks, 'So why from within the military and not from Homeland Security or the FBI?'

Mary nods, saying, 'I am happy to remain a member of the military. I retain an office in the Pentagon so I'm not readily recognised as part of other agencies. Believe me, senior members of both FBI and Homeland Security are monitored by the larger gangs, always looking for a point of leverage. But by remaining within the military, even meeting the other agencies, I am largely ignored. Which suits me.'

Pig and I nod our heads as we digest this and see the sense of it. But I can't resist asking, 'So what is the blemish on your record that prevents you being promoted?'

Mary smiles wistfully and says, 'Many years ago, when I had just made Major, my CO at the time, a colonel, thought having just promoted me would entitle him to fondle me and I suspect a lot more. He got a right surprise when I backhanded him and made a formal complaint against him.

'Sadly, the Marines – the overall military, in fact – back then was very much a man's world. Us mere females were merely tolerated, in what they hoped was a passing fad. My complaint got buried, but the colonel was forced to take early retirement, but my record was marked for eternity.

'My replacement CO knew the full story and became my mentor and with his background in the espionage and intelligence gathering fields, he steered me in that direction, where rank is not as critical as skill and ability. It's worked for me ever since!'

Our quiet word is being noticed with Stacey, Suzie and Uncle Albert giving us the eye, so I wrap it up quickly and say, 'That's fine, Mary, pleased for you, but I reiterate what I said yesterday, our deal with Campbell is and remains NO mention of names in any communications, so trust that is still being followed?'

Mary nods her head, saying, 'It certainly is. I certainly haven't mentioned your names whatsoever. Nor have I seen any mention of you or your involvement. I sit on an "oversight" taskforce with Campbell's boss so am privy to most of what is coming up or going down. There is no explanation being given on how they got the mic on him. I noticed also the recording doesn't start immediately, which put me off for a while.'

It's Pig that answers, smiling, 'Not long enough, obviously!'

She lays her hand on his arm in a friendly gesture, saying, 'Julien and Mort, please understand I am very skilled at interpreting furtive actions. It's one of my core skills, so please don't be concerned others too might be able to watch the video and pick up how it happened. I know for a fact Campbell and Hunter and his team have not worked it out.'

'Good,' Pig and I say almost in unison.

Right then Uncle Albert calls out, 'Come and get it. Chow time – dinner's up!'

We break up and head over to load up our plates. I suddenly realise how hungry I am.

17

'A SHELBY?!' I'm not going to say my Suzie squawks but that one word certainly carries a high level of excitement!

Even I know a Shelby is a high-performance Mustang, and I look over to see Suzie is almost hopping from one foot to the other excitedly as she talks with Uncle Albert. I'm keen to know where this conversation is heading so I amble over to find out. I'm not the only one as everyone else is paying attention and moving over toward them.

Suzie turns as I approach, saying, 'Albert is going to lend us his Shelby Mustang to drive from San Fran to LA – isn't that awesome!

Before I can point out it wouldn't be feasible for four adults plus luggage to fit into a Mustang, Uncle Albert takes up the story.

'I have a little business based in LA and Chicago renting Mustangs, Camaros and even Harleys and Golden Wings for anyone who wants to ride or drive the old Route 66. I keep a Shelby for special occasions or special clients.

'My LA agent Carlos would love to drive it up to San Francisco – he loves driving it anywhere. He can meet you at the airport and then fly home. You will still need your other rental but Suzie and whoever else wants can take turns burning up the highway. She is a beast to drive,' he adds with a smile.

Hannah is first to respond, clearly astonished by this declaration, saying to Mary, 'Did you know he has a business here in the States?'

Mary nods. 'Yes, he had told me he owns half a dozen Harleys and Golden Wings but has never ridden either. He mentioned the cars as well but it was the bikes I was interested in.'

Suzie is hugging me, saying, 'I can't wait to tell Dad, he will be sooo jealous!' I think I haven't seen Suzie this excited since I proposed to her. She did dance a little jig then!

We then confirm with Uncle Albert we are due to fly to San Francisco in four days' time, next Monday. Suzie pulls her phone out and lets Uncle Albert know our flight number and ETA so he can organise Carlos to meet us at the airport in San Francisco.

Works for me, no doubt I will have a drive for the sake of it but clearly it will be another highlight for Suzie.

Once the excitement settles down, Mary asks, 'I assume you two are going to visit Arlington National Cemetery?'

Pig and I nod in unison with Pig adding, 'We have a few fallen comrades we want to pay our respects to.'

Suzie adds, 'They even brought their slouch hats to wear when they go there.' (A slouch hat is a traditional hat worn by the Australian Army. These are distinctly Australian and recognised in the armed forces the world over.)

Mary nods, asking, 'When are you going? I will arrange for a private guide for you.'

Pig answers, 'Tomorrow actually, plan on being there at ten a.m. The girls plan on going shopping.'

'Shopping?' This time it's Hannah, who adds, 'Geez, I haven't had a good girly shop for ages. Care if I tag along with you?' addressing Suzie and Stacey.

'Sure,' they both reply.

'Cool. I will have to swap shifts, but that shouldn't be a problem. What say I pick up at your hotel at ten so we can make the day of it?'

'Great. You can show us all the best stores and hopefully a few little trendy, boutique-type stores as well.'

'Sure,' replies Hannah, 'I will also take you to a couple of artisan jewellers that make truly awesome stuff.'

Suzie smiles at me before adding, 'Further payback!' with Hannah, Mary and even Stacey giving her quizzical looks, but she doesn't elaborate.

Hannah then asks, 'Where are you staying?'

It's Stacey who says, 'The JW Marriott downtown.'

Hannah raises her eyes from her phone and says, 'These fancy hotels must run in the family! Any other nephews out there, Albert?'

This gets a few laughs and Suzie pipes up, 'Yes, we are being spoilt. First the Empress Hotel in Victoria, Chateau Lake Louise, then the Mandarin Oriental on Columbus Circle in New York and now the JW downtown!' blithely ignoring how uppity this sounds.

I'm getting an interesting and appraising look from Uncle Albert. Wondering, I'm guessing, how we can afford to be staying at all these fancy joints. Well, hey, we have earned it!

With the shopping now out of the way, Mary says to Pig and I, 'Present yourselves to the Welcome Center when you get there tomorrow. You will be expected. I will arrange a personal guide to show you the graves you want, plus the usual highlights.'

'Great. Thanks, that's very kind of you,' I reply whilst Pig gives her a nod of appreciation.

She replies, 'How many graves do you want to visit?'

Pig replies, 'Five. Two we were on patrol with when they died, two more we both knew who died in action and one Mort knew who has died since returning.'

This solemn statement has stopped the other conversations as everyone looks at Pig and me as if suddenly remembering what we did for a living, until recently at least. And the risks we had to take day to day simply just to stay alive.

By now we are all sitting under the pergola as the evening chill is coming in, when I remember… 'Uncle Albert, didn't Judy' – Uncle Albert's youngest daughter who tries to keep the broader family in touch with news, et cetera – 'send out a newspaper article about you rescuing a lady in Scotland? Off some mountainside or something?'

Uncle Albert breaks out in a smile, saying, 'Yes, that's right, it happened a couple of years ago. I was staying near Fort William at a castle hotel – an actual castle converted to a hotel.' It's Hannah who chips in, 'As you do!' but Uncle Albert ignores her, continuing, 'I was keen to do a bit of "wild swimming" where you swim in the lochs up there. Amazing feeling but bitterly, bitterly cold water, especially for thin-blooded Queenslanders!'

Suzie, as curious as ever, asks, 'What is wild swimming then?'

'Just that – you go swimming in any of the Scottish Lochs, no wet or dry suit, no protection at all. As I said, bloody cold but there are people over there that thrive on it!

'Anyway, I had done a couple of wild swims so to break it up, I decided to hike to the summit of Ben Nevis, the highest mountain in the UK. Trouble is, it was raining, cloud way down, a miserable day. It's a four-hour hike up on the best of days plus another two or three hours to come back down. But I enjoy hiking, or rambling as they call it over there, and truthfully, Ben Nevis is not really a mountain. It is high but not rugged. The track is pretty cruisey compared to some I have walked. Well, it was going up.

'I wasn't going to wait for a nice day, it is Scotland after all, so you have no way of knowing when the next fine day might be. In fact, Ben

Nevis is renowned for seeing all the seasons in one day, so maybe it would be sunny at the top! I had all the right wet weather hiking gear, so away I went!

'I told the hotel where I was going just in case and yes, they thought I was crazy, but away I went. Of course, there were no other cars in the car park. I swung my backpack on, adjusted my walking poles and off I went. I always go fully prepared when I hike – "prepare for the worst, hope for the best" being my motto!

'I was getting close to the top, three and half hours in and puffing a bit, to be honest, when suddenly I heard a dog barking. Odd, I thought, I wonder what he's doing up here. Next thing, a Border Collie came bounding down the track toward me, barking agitatedly, seemingly wanting me to follow him. I upped the pace a bit and then as I crested the next rise, I saw a lady lying on the side of the track.

'I headed toward her urgently. Her head was moving as she watched me approach, so I said, "Strange place to take a rest." She burst into tears, so I had to go into sympathy mode, not that I'm very good at it.'

(Suzie gives me a look as if to say, 'Must run in the family!')

'Once she composed herself, I introduced myself and found out her name was Annie and her dog was Mac, a black and white border collie, a bedraggled one at that, but friendly enough now I had found them.

'It turned out she was a local, known throughout the county as she and Mac walked everywhere. She loved the solitude of rambling and had summited Ben Nevis numerous times, even in the deep of winter, so thought nothing of it heading up in yesterday's rain. Then she had tripped. She still didn't understand how or why but she had broken her tibia. I didn't know then, but that's the big bone connecting the knee to the ankle.

'It turned out she had retired two years ago as the Head of Nursing at Belford Hospital in Fort William. So, she did know the extent of her injuries. As she said, "Knowing what I need to do and being able to do it are two completely different things. I know I need to make a splint but it's not possible to do this to yourself when laying on the ground and in the pouring rain."

'The first thing I did was dig out the small tarp I always carried along with the four little telescopic poles and erected a shelter over her, so she wouldn't get any wetter. There was tangible relief for her in my doing this. I also crawled under the tarp, with Mac beating me in there as well! It was only about a metre and a half off the ground and I followed her instructions. Using one of my walking poles, I made a splint. My poles telescoped down to a smaller size than hers, then using some cable ties I always carry, along with duct tape – you never know when these might come in handy!

'Splint in place, I helped her to a sitting position and sat down beside her. This was the first time she had been able to move in over twenty-four hours, so there were a few groans as she did this. We then sat quietly as I let her get her bearings, whilst I checked my phone for coverage.

'No coverage. Bugger. She started to cry again, admitting it was a relief as until I showed up, she was thinking she might die up there, not believing anyone else would be silly enough to want to summit Ben Nevis in such conditions. I replied, "Well, clearly, I am as mad as you are!"

'Once Annie calmed down again, I posed the question: "What do we do now?" I floated the first option: "Leave you here whilst I head down and alert the authorities." Trouble was it was now after two in the afternoon, so by the time I got down, and knowing there was still no phone reception in the car park (I had noticed that when I checked my phone before getting out of the Subaru), I would have to drive to wherever to get reception. Alert the authorities but by that time it would be dark. Would they attempt a climb in the dark in the continuing rain? Not likely. Would they try to evacuate Annie by helicopter? Again, not likely due to the dark and lousy conditions.

'Annie's immediate response was: "I do not want to spend another hour up here alone, let alone another night." We then pondered this in silence for a few moments before I raised the prospect of carrying her down. Clearly, she has been thinking the same thing.

'We looked at each other for what seemed an eternity before almost in unison we both nodded and I said, "Let's do this." Just to be sure neither of us was under any illusions of how difficult and likely painful this would be, we took turns spelling out the dangers before Annie said, "If you are willing to try, I'm willing to put up with the pain."

'I nod. We then discuss how best for me to carry her and she stresses in some spots she will be able to walk (make that hobble!) with the aid of her walking poles. I nod in agreement but I know this is not going to be very often – footing had been wet and slippery on the way up, so going downhill carrying a weight would be doubly difficult. We agree I will need the poles when I'm carrying her as balance is going to be critical to avoid falling down.

'We decided we would try different techniques as the conditions allowed. It sounded good at the time! We sorted through both backpacks, pulling out anything we wouldn't need and packed it into Annie's pack and agreed to leave it under the tarp, hoping someone might return it to her in the coming days or weeks.'

As I have said, Uncle Albert has a way of telling a tale and we are all silent, entrapped in his story.

He continues, 'Once sorted, I helped Annie to her feet, as she was determined to try walking to start with. I knew better than to argue with a stubborn woman, so I helped her up and with Mac barking and trotting off down the track, we shuffled after him. Round the first bend and oops, Annie took a tumble. Her walking pole slipped off a rock and down she went. Fortunately, she got her hand down to stop face-planting in the mud. I had thought to tie a quick-drying hand towel to the strap of my backpack, so we used this to wipe the worst of the mud off her. We ended up using the towel many, many times!

'Next, we tried a fireman's lift. Annie wasn't a big lady so I was okay carrying her weight, but I couldn't see the ground so this was very slow going. Of course, I had to put her down regularly for rests but we did make some progress. No face plants on this section, just slid into a couple of trees!

'Time flies but we didn't. It was slow, painstaking progress and when I looked at my watch, I realised we had already been going nearly two hours and thought, Not sure how far we have come. But we plodded on. We alternated between fireman's lift, piggy-backing and Annie walking, depending on the grade and terrain.

'Eventually, we came to a fairly open hillside where the track zig-zagged up or in our case, down. As usual in these conditions, someone had blazed a path straight up and down. I stopped and looked at this and saw how far down it went before saying to Annie, "What say we strap you on top of me and we slide down on my arse – or more likely on my back?"

'We discussed this for a few minutes whilst we gathered our breath. By now we had been going nearly four hours and remembering when I had climbed this ridge coming up, I hazarded a guess that it was about an hour from the car park. Annie nodded her agreement, saving her breath.

'It was already getting dark and the rain had not abated. Despite both having full weatherproof clothing we were wet through, bedraggled and absolutely buggered. We didn't stand any more to catch our breath and we sought a tree stump or large rock to sit down on.

'I pulled out a couple of bungy cords out of my backpack. Yes, I was prepared – I was always a good boy scout, following their motto of "be prepared"!

'I sat down at the top of the vertical track and waved Annie over. She sat down in my lap and I then leaned back, lying down. Annie then laid down on top of me, whimpering when she banged her broken leg – for about the hundredth time, I might add! – then with much difficulty, we tied ourselves together.

'The moment of truth. I pushed off down the hill. But whilst it was steep enough, the mud wasn't slippery, so I was pushing with my elbows. Remember, I'm lying on my back, with Annie tied on top. Hard work.

'Anyway, Annie used her hands to help get us some momentum, then suddenly we were off, gathering speed. Mac, tail wagging furiously and barking excitedly as if it's some type of game, followed us down the hill. Shit, it was rough. I felt every stone, let alone rock, boulder and tree root. Still, it was the best progress we had made, I was not going to stop because it hurt. Annie was getting noticeably weaker to the extent I was really starting to worry about her. All speed is needed.

'Our speed increased the further we went and I remember going over one of the zig-zags and actually getting air! Seemed great for maybe a milli-second before we came back down to earth with a thump! Ouch. And another moan from Annie.

'Eventually and whilst it was no doubt only maybe a minute at best – it seemed like five or ten – we hit the bottom, ploughing into the scrub on the other side of the main track. A sudden and another painful stop.

'We untied ourselves; we didn't bother talking anymore by this stage, just got on with it. I lifted Annie up into another fireman's hoist and headed off down the track. Whilst the track was now levelling out as we got closer to the bottom, I didn't have the energy to carry her for more than a few minutes at a time.

'We finally caught a break, with the rain easing, but the fog was thicker down here as we near the valley floor and we both now have our head-mounted lights on to help keep us on the track. We plodded on then suddenly in the periphery of the torchlight, I saw my car in the car park. Shit, we made it.

'We staggered the last hundred metres to my car and leaned against it in much relief. We leaned our heads together in silent thanks. I lifted the rear door and positioned Annie under it, out of the rain and now cold wind. She was shivering nonstop now, teeth chattering. I started the car, turning the heating up to full blast.

'I opened the passenger door, then went and got Annie, who had removed her heavy raincoat. We slowly and carefully sat her on the seat and swivelled her legs in. Even though I was trying to be extra careful, I must have hit her leg on something as she gave out a loud scream. Sorry!

'Once she was leaning back in the seat, I lowered it down until she was comfortable. I checked the splint again. I had to redo it three times through our descent and did not have any more cable ties, so this time I tied it on with my hanky. Don't worry, it was clean, but of course sopping wet!

'Going back to the back of the car, I enticed Mac in, where he immediately had a big shake – hair mud and rain flying everywhere, even up on the roof. Great. I removed my raincoat, shut the back tailgate and jumped in the driver's seat. That's a figure of speech, as I sure as hell did not have the energy for jumping into anything.

'I started the Subie up, leaned back in the seat, took a deep breath, opened my eyes, looked down at Annie and said, "We did it!"

'She smiled back and we instinctively high-fived, but not with much energy. I then checked the heater was cranked up to max as it wasn't only Annie who was shivering, I was now as well. Could be a reaction as well as cold, of course.

'I backed out and headed out of the car park, saying, "Okay, you're the local, what's the quickest way to the nearest hospital?"

'Annie replied, "Belford in Fort William is the only option we have. It's about twelve miles, so not sure how long that will take in a car."

'"Fifteen to twenty minutes on these roads in these conditions," I thought aloud. As we came around a bend down the road a little way, Annie pointed out a nice tidy little stone cottage on the left of the road, saying, "That's my place there." I just nodded. I had pulled my phone out and was watching to see when I would get reception.

'Not for another ten minutes, so we were already halfway there. I glanced down at Annie again; she had gone quiet and her eyes were closed. Shit, I was thinking. I hoped she was just resting. When I finally got three bars of reception, I asked Annie if she knew the hospital phone number. She rattled off the number without opening her eyes.

'I punched the number in and as soon as it was answered, I explained the situation. When I gave Annie's name, the level of concern and consternation rose with the receptionist saying, "You mean our Annie?" To which I replied, "I guess." Annie, still with her eyes closed, called out, "Hi Bernadette, can you get Dr Strahan out as my leg is badly broken and I want him to set it properly."

'We could hear Bernadette yelling to colleagues in the background. "Annie has broken her leg and had to be rescued from up on Ben Nevis." Someone replied, "What today, in this rain?" Another voice said, "We are talking about Annie, you realise."

'Bernadette replied, 'Certainly, Annie. Are you okay?" The reply: "I will be when we get there but I've been up on the mountain over twenty-four hours, so no doubt suffering from hypothermia plus numerous aches, pains and bruises." I chipped in, saying, "ETA six minutes." Bernadette responded, "I will have a full A&E team waiting for you. Pull into the ambulance bay."

"'Will do," I replied. We heard a chorus of "Hi Annie, hang in there" before I hung up. I put my hand down and gently held Annie's hand as I saw she was now crying quietly. Relief, I guessed.'

He pauses here and it's Stacey who asks, 'Was she okay?'

Uncle Albert. 'Well, yes, they put her leg in plaster, found plenty of bruises and scratches and she had also strained her right shoulder. Not that we could recall how she had done that.'

Mary then asks, putting her arm around Uncle Albert's shoulders, 'What about you? Were you injured?'

Uncle Albert smiles at her, saying, 'They wanted to admit me too, but I waved them off, telling them my hotel bed would be more comfortable than theirs and I would come back in the morning so they could check me out. The doctor wasn't too happy with that but I was sopping wet, absolutely buggered and told him I'm not bleeding – well, not too much – and I would come back in the morning. Once I was sure Annie was settled and there was no doubt the staff were taking good care of her, I headed off to the hotel.'

He pauses here but we all stay quiet as it's clear he is remembering the events and reliving them.

He then continues, 'It was funny. When I got to the hotel, the doorman came out to greet me, quite astonished at my condition, then when I opened the hatch to let Mac out, he grabbed the lead from me, saying, "This is Mac. What are you doing with Annie's Mac?"

'So, surrounded by the hotel staff, but fortunately now in the fire warmed lobby, I had to explain the whole story to them all. At the end of the story and once they were assured Annie was now safe in hospital, they couldn't have been more helpful. One of the housemaids insisted on coming up with me to help "clean me up". An older lady, she wouldn't take no for an answer, saying, "Annie is a dear friend, so helping you after all you have done today is the least I can do. And don't worry, I won't look when you're getting changed." This got a smile from me and a few giggles from other staff. The doorman had already taken Mac to dry him and feed him. It was a dog-friendly hotel, so this wasn't an issue.

'Once up in my room, Maude, Annie's friend, called up the first aid kit and cleansed and dressed the worst of my cuts and abrasions. My back was littered with them, with Maude telling me a couple of them would need stitching. "Tomorrow," I muttered as sleep closed in.'

18

'Next morning I'm awoken by the hotel phone ringing. I groggily answer it to hear, "Mr Richardson, this is Constable McTavish of Police Scotland. Sorry to disturb you, sir, but we need to ask you a few questions about yesterday's events."

'"What time is it?" I ask, not yet having looked at my watch. "Nine-twenty a.m., sir," is the reply.

'"You just woke me. Can you wait thirty minutes for me to shower and change then you can ask your questions whilst I have my breakfast. Would that be okay?"

'He is silent for a moment before he says, "That's fine, sir. I will wait for you in the dining room."

'When I get down there, he is putting away the last of a full breakfast and seeing that, I suddenly realise how hungry I am, not having eaten anything except a couple of protein bars since breakfast yesterday. Makes my decision on breakfast easy and I order a full breakfast and a large pot of tea. Of course, they serve Scottish breakfast, not English breakfast! I sit down at his table and the first thing he does is shake my hand, telling me, "It is an honour to meet you, sir. It was a heroic thing you did yesterday."

'And as the day wore on, I heard this more and more, people calling me a hero and all. I certainly didn't see it as heroic; I just did what had to be done, nothing more than I would hope someone would have done for me in similar circumstances.'

It's Mary, still with her arm across his shoulders, who replies, 'Albert, what you did is certainly courageous and heroic. You should be very proud to have brought Annie down safely. I am.' Here, she leans in and gives him a kiss.

Then it's Hannah who agrees, saying, 'Gee, Albert, that is an amazing story. I'm glad I didn't shoot you the other day now!'

Uncle Albert smiles and says, 'You couldn't shoot this friendly face anyway!'

Hannah smiles and says, 'It was the thought of all the paperwork I would have had to complete if I had shot you that stopped me, not your friendly face! Besides, Mum only redecorated last year and she would have been really pissed with all the blood splatter!' She does smile though, taking the edge off her words.

Mmm, I'm thinking, Hannah is letting Uncle Albert know whilst she admires what he did, she still isn't too happy with his burgeoning romance with her mum!

I reach out and shake Uncle Albert's hand whilst Suzie and Stacey get up and give him a hug, followed by Pig giving him a fist bump.

He then adds, 'Yes, it was a bit surreal and a bit of fun being a celebrity for a couple of days. They even had me on the BBC News.' Here, he digs out his phone and fiddles with it before giving it to Mary, saying, 'Here, watch this. This is my TV interview on BBC a couple of days after.'

We all crowd around, watching and smiling.

Uncle Albert is clearly quite chuffed at the admiration we are all showing him.

After he puts his phone away, he adds, 'They are going to make a telemovie of it now too. I have to go back next year. Annie and I are both "executive producers",' using air quote marks to highlight this.

'Wow, that's cool. What does an executive producer have to do?' Hannah asks.

Uncle Albert shrugs his shoulders, saying, 'Not much, from what I can understand. I assume guide them through what actually happened, I guess.'

'So do they pay you?' Again, Hannah gets in before anyone else.

'Yeah, we get one hundred grand each,' he replies.

'Shit, dollars?' Stacey asks.

'No, pounds,' Uncle Albert replies.

I look around and can see everyone is doing the maths.

Stacey gets there quickest, saying, 'That's $180k Australian. Wow, I'll have to get a gig as an executive producer!'

Pig smiles at her and says, 'You can rescue me anytime!' This gets groans all round!

Hannah adds, 'Maybe I can be your executive assistant; you know, executive assistant to the executive producer!'

But Mary has the final word, saying, 'I've never been to Scotland.'

She and Uncle Albert share a look, smiling at each other and he replies, 'Maybe we should change that!' both under the watchful eye of Hannah!

On that note, we decide it's time to call it a night. We all had a fun night with good company.

Tomorrow, Pig and I are off to Arlington Cemetery, something important to us both. And now the girls have a local guide to assist with their shopping!

19

Ten a.m. sharp next morning.

Pig and I exit our Uber. We line up, side by side, slouch hats firmly and proudly in place.

A nod and we are off.

Full parade ground march, arms swinging, full stride, shoulder to shoulder, fully in sync, stride for stride. We do have fifteen years of practice!

It is about one hundred metres to the entrance to the Welcome Center.

We are being noticed, people are stopping and watching us, everyone keeping out of our way.

A group of younger children, no doubt on a school outing, all stop and start clapping. Others watching join in.

We don't stop or slow down as we cross the car park. Cars stop, we don't.

Shoulder to shoulder, a big imposing, intimidating sight as we march toward the Welcome Center.

We know it and so does everyone else around us.

Approaching the entrance, a man leaving sees us coming and holds the doors wide.

Without missing a step, we enter side by side, just squeezing through the door (we agreed later we were lucky, we both grazed the door frame!)

We approach the front counter and come to a full parade ground halt. Double step and all.

Pity we are in joggers as it doesn't have the same sound effects as our military boots. Still best we could do.

Silence. All conversations have stopped. We are the centre of attention, no doubt.

A young black lady in full US Marine lieutenant's dress uniform steps up to the counter and addresses us. 'Sergeants Ireland and Le Tonge?'

'Yes, Ma'am,' we reply as one, smartly executing snappy salutes. She responds with her own salute, accompanied by a wry smile. I suspect finding it a little ironic we, two battle-hardened sergeants, having to salute a lieutenant as young as her.

Nevertheless, she replies, 'I am Lieutenant Monica Smith. I am honoured to meet you both. I will be your guide today.' Here, she extends her gloved hand for us to shake.

We stand easy.

Silence continues; the other servers at the counter are still watching us and all other visitors are also watching us, some even taking photos.

I'm not so keen on this but we did deliberately make an entrance. Our way of showing how important today's visit is to us both.

Mourning a lost comrade is not something you take lightly. Today we are mourning five of them. And in a very special place. No one other than US military veterans are permitted to be buried at Arlington, making everyone here a hero in our book.

Lieutenant Smith then asks, 'I understand you have a list of graves you would like to visit?'

Pig replies, 'Yes, Lieutenant,' and pulls out the folder paper with their names on it, handing it over.

The lieutenant takes the page, looks at it and replies, 'Please, call me Monica. Why don't you go grab yourselves a coffee over there whilst I locate these graves? I assume you want to see all the usual highlights as well?' She points to a café in the foyer of the Welcome Centre.

Pig and I nod in the affirmative and I reply, 'Okay, we will do that and wait for you outside. Would you like a coffee as well? And we are Mort and Pig.'

She smiles, saying, 'Yes, a long black would be good!'

'Soldiers brew!' Pig tells her as we all smile.

We walk over to get the coffee before going outside to wait. I comment to Pig, 'Monica looks like she is still in school!' (Geez, I sound old, don't I!) Pig nods in agreement, so I'm not the only one!

***

Our visit takes most of the day. Monica makes a great guide, showing us not only the graves of our fallen comrades but also many other famous people as well as the tomb of the unknown soldier and providing VIP seating for the Changing of the Guard.

We quiz Monica on Major Cutler. The name puzzles her for a bit then she says, 'Oh, you mean Major Mary? Everyone calls her Major Mary! She is a legend, a mentor to all us young ones learning the ropes, not only us girls but the guys as well. Helps them stay on the straight and narrow. She always has time for everyone and the higher-ups also. She told me you two are living legends, brave and courageous and highly decorated soldiers and I had to make sure you get everything you need!'

Pig and I look at each other with raised eyebrows. Living legends, ah? Got to like that! I think and I suspect Pig is having similar thoughts.

I send a text to Suzie around lunchtime to see how the shopping is going, getting a quick reply. 'Awesome, having lots of fun!'

So I reply, 'How many extra suitcases now?' but I only get a smiley face as a reply.

Pig had told me earlier he had given Stacey his Visa and told her to have fun and enjoy herself, admitting later she seemed to have taken him at his word and was spending up big too!

Then mid-afternoon, Suzie texts me saying the three of them have decided to do dinner as well, with Hannah taking them to The Cheesecake Factory, a chain of restaurants renowned not only for their fabulous cheesecakes but also their amazing menu and awesome food.

Pig gets a similar text from Stacey, so we shrug our shoulders and 'soldier on'. (Heh heh!)

Then whilst in the taxi back to our hotel, Pig's phone starts ringing with Keith Urban's Wild Hearts tune. We look at each other, smiling, and say, 'Midge!'

We have long planned to meet Midge for dinner whilst here in the USA but in his words, 'Not sure when or where but will let you know.'

Sure enough, Midge is on the line, suggesting we meet for dinner and a 'few beers' tomorrow night.

He suggests 'District Chophouse', a popular chop house (steakhouse in Australian!) and brewery right in the heart of downtown Washington.

'Deal,' we say, telling him we will bring the girls for dinner then us three will carry on for our 'few beers'!

Deal done, I text Suzie to tell her tomorrow night's plan and she replies, 'Cool, I'm keen to meet Midge!'

'Cool,' I reply. Becoming real social butterflies here in Washington, aren't we?

Back at the JW Marriott, Pig and I decide to order in pizza – good old Uber Eats! – plus a six-pack of beer from room service.

As we enjoy our pizza and beer, we review the day, recalling stories of the five former comrades we had visited the graves of.

Two had been killed whilst we were on patrol with them. Both rather heroically providing covering fire with minimal cover whilst a few of us, Pig and I included, recovered other injured members of the patrol, following another IED attack and ambush. A bitter memory for us.

Other than these sad memories, it is a nice relaxing evening – until the girls and all their shopping turn up, that is!

They redeem themselves, however, by bringing Pig and I a couple of slices of cheesecake from The Cheesecake Factory. We can confirm they are as yummy as they are renowned to be, too!

They also announce we are going to Hannah's for dinner on our last night. She is inviting Mary and Albert as well.

'Cool,' Pig and I chorus.

'Another home-cooked meal,' I add.

'Yes, she says she is renowned for her lasagna and we offered to bring desert and drinks,' replies Stacey.

Being a little nosey, I then ask, 'Did Hannah have much to say about Mary and Albert?'

Suzie and Stacey look at each other and Suzie then replies, 'Well, yes. She said she is still coming to terms with her mother seemingly developing quite an attraction to Albert. Whilst she is really, really happy to see her mum so happy, she is also concerned Albert will disappear back to Australia and leave Mary hurt and alone again. She added her mum hasn't had a relationship for years – that she knows of at least – so Albert has certainly come out of the blue, so to speak.'

I nod in understanding before saying, 'Monica, our guide today, says everyone knows her as Major Mary. She is "Mum" to the whole armed forces, it seems. A shoulder for many to cry on. Everyone loves her. So, Albert better be careful if he dumps her – he might not get out of the country alive!'

Later, once we are alone, Suzie tells me she had shared with Stacey and Hannah why she was spending so freely and they had then encouraged her – not, as she admitted herself, that she needed any encouragement!

She had even bought a new suitcase to load all the shopping into!

20

Next day was set aside for a couple of museums including a visit to both the Smithsonian Museum of Natural History and the Smithsonian National Air and Space Museum – both a 'must-see' here in Washington.

We finished the day with a hop-on hop-off trolley tour.

So, a leisurely day before dinner with Midge.

Whilst Suzie had a fair idea of how important Midge was to us, Pig had had to explain to Stacey some of the background.

We arrive at District Chophouse at seven-thirty p.m. as agreed and there, sitting in the back corner, is Midge. Man, it's been a few years since we have last seen him but he hasn't changed too much.

A tall white man, as skinny as a rake, with a large afro hair-do. For someone who lives his life in the shadows, he certainly stands out in person!

His smile is as infectious as ever, splitting his face in two!

Man, it's good to see him. We embrace as brothers before introducing the girls.

We sit down at his table and Suzie, looking around, says, 'This looks a cool place. You must have been lucky to get a reservation at such short notice!'

Pig and I smile at Midge, who smiles back.

Suzie, clearly put out by us having a secret, asks, 'What?' and it is Pig who replies, 'Midge would have just added his booking into their reservation system himself!'

Suzie and Stacey are a little non-plussed by this.

But not Pig or I – we know and respect what Midge is capable of doing digitally!

Once we have ordered and settled into our first drinks, Suzie asks Midge, 'So how do you know these two?' giving me a dig in the ribs and a wave to include Pig.

'Well, I wouldn't be here today if it wasn't for these boys!'

Again, the three of us share a smile as we remember.

Suzie again. 'Do tell!'

Midge smiles again and takes a good sip of beer before saying, 'Well, why not. It is top secret, so you ladies can't go sharing this story, please, or I might get shot!

'A few years ago, not long after I was recruited into the CIA as a "communications specialist" – their name for their in-house hackers! – I was sent to Cairo in Egypt to support a major operation over there.

'Being dumb and naive and without thinking, I decided to go out exploring around the time of the operation I was there to support. I didn't have any part in the operation. I was there to monitor phone and radio messages leading up to the op, and hopefully access data afterward, so wasn't needed once the op started.

'Anyway, we are in the old town in Cairo, plenty of narrow cobblestoned winding lanes, beggars and street vendors everywhere. I seemed to take a wrong turn somewhere and suddenly found myself with a dagger to my throat and this local with his harsh and heavily accented English demanding my wallet and phone. I was shit scared, I can tell you.' Here, he pauses and points to the right side of his throat where there is a black mole or something and says, 'I still carry the scar to this day.'

Pig takes up the story. Looking at Suzie, he starts, 'As you might remember, we – Mort and I – had been recruited by Dwight Brown of the CIA in Afghanistan and after they gave us spook training here in the States. They asked us to assist with an urgent and of course critical operation to bring down a major terrorist funding kingpin. They never told us where we were heading but once we agreed, it was a private jet across to Germany and then onto a scheduled flight from Frankfurt to Cairo on Lufthansa.

'When we landed, we were whisked away by the support crew, some locals or "assets" to a safe house in a pretty flash suburb there in Cairo. We weren't allowed out the whole time we were there and we were wearing only the traditional Tunban and our long bushy beards. They provided local soap and shampoo and of course, we weren't allowed to use deodorant.'

'Why?' This comes from Stacey, wrinkling her nose at the thought!

Here, I chime in explaining exactly what I had told Suzie back in Victoria when having dinner with Campbell and Hunter that locals don't have much water and don't waste it on personal hygiene.

Stacey nods her head in understanding.

Pig continues, 'Anyway, after being there for two days, the timing and planning started to come together. The target was a Mr Woo, a Chinese national who had been on Interpol and everyone's most wanted list for years. He had been identified flying into Cairo a week prior but had disappeared once he cleared customs and immigration.

'The local CIA team had been frantically twisting arms and bribing their informants to try and get a handle on him. Then suddenly they get an address where he will be tomorrow afternoon. Is it true or is it a trap? This question is debated by the spooks for what seemed hours. So much talk and not much else from our perspective.

'In the end, we walked out of the meeting and engaged with a couple of the lower-level local guys, grabbed maps of the area and started making our own plans. Eventually, Dwight came looking for us, saw what we were doing and asked us to walk through the plan. We did that, he made a couple of suggestions, improving the plan, then we said, "Let's do this."

'He looked at us and asked, "You sure?" We nodded, saying, "Yep."'

I take over the tale-telling, continuing, 'Next morning, the timing of Mr Woo's visit was confirmed with an expected ETA at a small apartment in the old town at one p.m. It was agreed we needed to be in the area by around twelve-thirty to be available if anything changes.

'We were transported to within a couple of blocks of the address on the back of little mopeds, with a small van promised as our getaway vehicle. The CIA had a lookout posted at the approach of the apartment building who confirmed Mr Woo and his bodyguard had arrived as scheduled at one p.m. Knowing why he was there, we then waited another fifteen minutes so he would be fully engaged by the time of our arrival so after fifteen minutes, we give the nod and Dwight instructs the start of the "diversion", as we had suggested.

'Somewhere within the apartment building and within earshot of the bodyguard, they had organised a domestic dispute with raised voices, banging of pots, lots of loud voices and noise, in what we understood is a fairly normal Egyptian domestic dispute, something to distract the bodyguard, who we knew to be a big bear of a man, with a long list of suspected killings. A seriously vicious individual from all accounts.

'As planned, with Pig leading and both walking quickly, coming at him from the front, whilst looking at our phones, we brushed past him and went around the adjoining corner. We too could now hear the domestic still going loud and strong! The bodyguard had not even looked up, too immersed in his phone.

'Once around the corner, we stopped. I nodded to Pig and then silently went back around the corner, now behind the bodyguard. I grabbed him around the throat and being the large man he was, I had to use both hands to throttle him. As you have noticed, I have abnormally large hands – as someone once said, they are the size of a baseball glove. Usually, I can throttle anyone one-handed – not this bloke. His reflex was instantaneous as he tried to pull my hands free.

'No chance as I dug my fingers in deeper, squeezing his windpipe. His struggles became more and more feeble as I strangled the life out of him. Pig had now joined me, waiting for him to expire. Whilst it was only seconds, it seemed a lot longer. Once we were sure he was dead, I grabbed the apartment key out of his pocket and moved to the door. I paused here, letting myself settle whilst Pig checked for any reaction to the bit of noise the bodyguard had made during his struggle. This had largely been covered by the ongoing domestic anyway.

'I quietly opened the door and as expected, there in the bed was Mr Woo, totally focused on what he was up to. We knew why he was there. I quickly and quietly moved to the side of the bed and grabbed him around the throat. I only needed one hand, using my left to cover his mouth so he couldn't make a noise. Very quickly, he stopped wriggling as life left his body too. Then from underneath him, a small boy, about ten years old, wriggled out, pulling his shorts up and looking very scared.

'I put my hands up, so he knew I was not a threat to him and he quickly ran out of the apartment, passing Pig on the way. Mr Woo was now history, but that was only part of the op – he was known to always carry his laptop with him, wherever he went. The spooks wanted it. Badly.

'Sure enough, even whilst shagging the poor kid, he had his briefcase handcuffed to his left wrist. No matter, we came prepared, so I pulled the miniature battery-powered grinder out of my backpack and quickly separated the briefcase from his body, stuffing this into my backpack. We looked round. All done, no clues left anywhere, as we are of course wearing disposable gloves.'

Pig then takes up the story. We haven't ever recounted this story to anyone other than the official operational debrief but we seem to make a good story-telling team as Midge, Stacey and Suzie are all entranced.

'We left the apartment, followed the planned exit and then around the first corner, we encountered Midge here being held at knifepoint. I didn't know who Midge was but had seen him at the safe house and at a couple of briefing sessions, so I knew he was part of the team. I disarmed the assailant without slowing down, the knife rattling to the ground. Behind me, Mort grabbed Midge and literally lifted him up over the collapsing body of his assailant and put him between us, growling, "Move it, Mister."'

Midge then butts in, saying, 'Yes, I'm standing there shitting myself with this large knife held at my throat, then Pig here comes from nowhere and karate chops this bloke in the neck, just like you see in old kung foo movies. My attacker collapses, dropping the knife. I'm lifted off my feet by my collar by Mort and one-handed, he lifts me up and swings me between him and Pig and we move very quickly out into the street. Not another word was said. I'm not aware of any of the operational details and I guess still in shock from my encounter, I blindly follow Pig, taking procs in the back from Mort to keep me moving at pace.

'We quickly move through a few of the narrow winding laneways, dodging locals and street vendors alike, out onto a bigger street, dodging between other pedestrians, around one or two corners, I'm not sure, I'm now puffing at the pace they are setting. Around another corner, Mort again grabs me by the collar and pulls me to the road verge where there is one of these little European vans sitting there idling. I'm forced in one side followed by Mort with Pig getting in the other side. I can tell you it was real squeezy sitting in that little van between these two!'

Pig again. 'Once in the van, the driver reported to Dwight we had a third person with us, so Dwight was immediately concerned – who and why? As the driver sped us away from the scene, he handed his two-way radio to Mort for an explanation.

'As planned after about a kilometre, the backpack was handed over to a moped rider so we wouldn't be caught with it. All without stopping, plenty of practice at it, I reckon, in those sorts of countries. We didn't even know Midge's name so mid-explanation, he had to ask Midge's name. Even Dwight had to double-check who he was. Then the question to Midge. "What the fuck?"'

Midge chimes in. 'Yes, I got a real bollocking about putting the whole operation at risk with my dumb actions. They even threatened to terminate my contract. But when we were reunited with the laptop, I proved my worth by being able to open it and access all the records. Then again, I can't take credit for being able to open it. It was thumbprint protected but Mort knew that. When he said before he separated the briefcase from the body, he failed to mention he cut the hand off the body with the briefcase attached.'

'Ooh,' both Suzie and Stacey respond to this comment and shudder at the thought, Suzie giving me a dubious look.

Mmm, I'm thinking, not a good subject to be discussing just as we are about to eat a steak for dinner! Not sure how Suzie will react to this story either.

I decide to finish the story off by adding, 'The op was an overwhelming success and Midge forged his reputation that day on the information he was able to extract not only from the laptop but by "following the money" and identifying banks involved in money laundering and clearing funds for the various terrorist groups Mr Woo was funding. He was even able to prove most of the funds originated from Chinese Government organisations, proving to the Western world what had been long suspected.

'We were flown back out of Cairo that same night, back to Frankfurt in Germany. But not before Midge found us and thanked us for saving his life. This is only the second time we have met him in person since that op. We had a few beers the time we came for our Presidential Medals as well. But we do chat and email regularly.'

Right on cue, the waiter places our meals in front of us. I'm tempted to mention the hand again, just for the reaction, but common sense prevails!

It's after dinner when Midge says, 'You know Dwight is still MIA.'

Pig beats me to it: 'How come?'

Midge explains, 'After you finished working with him, he was promoted to a desk job here Stateside, overseeing a range of agents and assets particularly in Afghanistan, then when the shit hit the fan and it was obvious what a cluster fuck the withdrawal from Kabul was going to be, he went back in there to try and get all his contacts and informants visas, as they would be real targets under the Taliban. He wasn't too successful and last word was that he and twelve of his main informants were trying to make it out by road via Pakistan. There hasn't been any word on any of them now for months.

'He was one of the good guys, always looking to help the locals and protect them. I know he was really bloody angry at the way the whole withdrawal was handled. He put it in writing too, through official channels, so in today's arse-covering world he wouldn't have much of a future with CIA or any other organisations.'

'Shit. I guess there are many stories like that coming out of Afghanistan these days,' I conclude.

The dinner went well, no more war stories and Midge and the girls all got on well.

After we finished our meals, Suzie and Stacey excused themselves and Midge, Pig and I adjourned to the brewery side of the restaurant.

It was a late night!

21

It's the next morning. And a slow start.

I can say it has been many years since I felt this 'dusty', 'fuzzy', 'woozy' – use any word you like to define hungover, heavily hungover.

It was a late night and all four of us are now sitting in the Avenue Grill, enjoying a late breakfast.

Pig and I are wolving down a big breakfast each, needing, wanting the grease to absorb the alcohol. Well, that's the theory and it's worth a try. The two Panadols earlier hadn't helped, I can tell you!

Suzie has also been 'mean' all morning, talking extra loud, banging doors and always with that smirky smile of hers.

Now, she is claiming to Pig and Stacey I was snoring!

I mean, really?

Like any red-blooded male, I am hotly denying it. The mere thought of being a snorer was inconceivable. I mean only old people snore. Right?

'No,' comes back Suzie, 'overweight people are also known to snore.' Again, with the smirky smile. Clearly enjoying winding me up!

And it's working.

Now as well as accusing me of being a snorer, I'm overweight as well.

I mean, I know I'm a big unit but I'm also bloody proud of my fitness level.

I respond, 'I'll take the pinch test anytime you like. I'm not bloody overweight.'

Everyone else is enjoying my discomfort, Pig more than the girls if anything.

I pull up my polo, grab my waist and do a pinch test. Mmm. Maybe I have been eating a bit much on this trip. Not the result I was expecting. No one said anything, but the smiles all round showed I was losing the argument.

Then to cap it all, Suzie, again with the sweetest of smiles, pulls her phone over, pulls up the voice memo app and presses play.

Shit. No doubt that's me and I'm snoring. Loudly.

I'm crestfallen, humiliated (not really but hey, got to let her have her fun!). Pig, in particular, is laughing loudly, so Suzie leans over, puts her head on my shoulder and whispers, 'I still love you though!'

I'm getting desperate, wanting someone to share this humiliation with me so I turn to Stacey and ask, 'What about Pig? Was he snoring too?'

Stacey seems to blush before saying, 'Well, we didn't get much sleep but it wasn't because of his snoring!'

Now it's my turn to laugh out loud, turning to Pig to see he is colouring a little too!

I don't have an answer for that, so I do the next best thing, get up and head back to the buffet – best to feed a hangover or so I heard somewhere!

Pig seems to have heard the same theory as he joins me at the buffet. I give him a dig in the ribs, teasing him about his efforts last night and calling him a 'horny Pig'!

When I get back to the table, I see Stacey playing with the photos on her phone.

After a few mouthfuls, I ask, 'What are you doing with your photos?'

'I'm uploading them to the cloud.'

Suzie jumps in. 'The photo app does that automatically.'

Stacey smiles and says, 'Yes, it does but I have the auto upload turned off, so it doesn't use up my free data. Something I have had to do, scraping through week by week, day by day as I had to.'

Pig leans over smiling, saying, 'You know you don't need to worry about that now, don't you?'

Stacey smiles at him, saying, 'Sure but old habits die hard. For years I have always used public Wi-Fi to upload all my photos, it's just second nature now.'

Clunk.

I mean, at any other time it would have been 'click' – you know, when an idea hits home.

But this morning it is a definite clunk.

I ask Stacey again, just so it's clear in my head, as fuzzy as it is. 'So, you can turn the auto upload function off and only do it manually when you want to, is that right?'

This of course is getting quizzical looks from all three but Stacey humours me by replying, 'Yes, that's right.'

A moment's pause and I respond, 'So if you have the auto function turned off, you need to manually download the photos back from the cloud to your phone then?'

Suddenly my second plateful isn't so urgent.

Stacey gives me a look that says 'well, duh' before nodding and saying, 'Yes, that's right.'

I ponder this in silence with both Suzie and Stacey watching me closely whilst Pig seems to have picked up on my thoughts, as he adds, 'Liz's photos. That's why there were no photos on her phone.'

I look at him and nod.

Before the girls can butt in, he adds, 'But why would she have the auto function turned off? I doubt many even know you can.'

I purse my lips, thinking the same thing. Remember, my head is fuzzy so I'm not as sharp as I should be this morning. I eventually respond, 'Well, I always told her she had had to have Scottish blood in her as she was always skimping and would buy a different brand if it saved her five cents.'

I look at Suzie as I say this, not willing to add, 'Not like someone else I know and love dearly.'

I'm hungover, not suicidal!

I continue, 'Well, I will be putting that at the top of my "to-do" list when we get home, check to see if I can download her photos. Trouble is, it's been a few years now so not sure how long Apple or Optus or whoever handles the cloud storage will hold info for. Might have to ask Midge!'

It's Stacey who turns to Pig, asking, 'Why do you need to access Liz's old photos?'

I let him explain.

'As you know, Liz was Mort's first wife and our investigations show she wasn't killed in an accident as is public record. Well, she was, but what we have found is that Liz was actually targeted by someone unknown but in cahoots with your mate Joe Lancaster and his clique. We were hoping that finding and looking through the photos on her phone might help in some way. But her phone had no photos on it. None, nada, zip. Most unusual.'

It's Suzie who now chimes in. 'What do you hope to find in her photos?'

Me this time. 'We don't know but for someone to have put a hit on Liz, a primary school teacher for heaven's sake, not a drug dealing bikie, we hope one of her photos might explain the why. You know, if she has accidentally taken a photo of something or someone that someone didn't want to be seen so they killed her. Bloody extreme but we can't explain her being targeted any other way.'

Not a happy tone to end breakfast but Stacey points at her watch before saying, 'Our tour bus picks us up in fifteen minutes. We better get going.'

Yes, we are being tourists again today, our last in Washington.

After our sightseeing, we get back in time to refresh before heading out to Hannah's townhouse in Alexandria, a separate city but still effectively a Washington suburb.

Stopping at a Safeway's, we decide on traditional apple pie (what's more American than apple pie?), some Aussie wine and a six-pack of Samuel Adams. (Pig is feeling adventurous!)

We exit our Uber at the given address, recognising Hannah's Golf in the driveway, then Uncle Albert pulls up beside us with Mary in his Subaru. So, we all knock on Hannah's front door together.

She opens the door wearing a chef's apron.

A bit fancy, I think!

Hannah's townhouse is nicely decorated and the girls are ooh and ahhing over some of her furniture, paintings and other nick knacks. As she proudly shows them around, she makes the comment, 'Well, I only have me to please so I do spend a bit much on anything I like, I guess.'

Pig, Uncle Albert and I? Well, we head outside to sit in the fresh air and crack a coldie.

The evening is another pleasant experience – superb lasagne and I didn't do myself any favours by suggesting Suzie learn to cook like it!

Over dinner, Hannah addresses Stacy and Suzie. 'How was your dinner last night?'

Suzie replies, 'Great. We met Midge, a bit of a mythical figure Mort and Julien often talk about, so that was great. The three of them went on and made a night of it! Then Mort snored like a trouper for the rest of the night!'

Nice, I think, dobbing me in like that. But of course, she gave me a sweet smile as she said it, knowing that gets her out of trouble. Always!

From the other side of the room, Mary says, 'Hold on, did you say Midge? THE Midge?' She might have been addressing Suzie but it was me getting the full stare.

I hold her gaze and nod as Suzie says, 'I guess, doubt whether there would be two like Midge!'

Mary again. 'You actually met him? I've known Midge for, I don't know, five or six years. Never met him in person. In fact, sometimes I think it is more than one person just using the same name.' This time, still looking at me, she adds, 'How did you meet him?'

Suzie again. 'I can tell you that! Midge told us the story last night.'

She then recounts the story of how we saved Midge and the Mr Woo mission.

Mary's eyes never leave me through Suzie's telling of the story, except for the occasional quick glance at Pig when his name is mentioned during the telling.

At the end, Mary is clearly astonished and responds by saying, 'You know the "Mr Woo" mission is part of CIA folklore now. No mention ever of the agents who carried it out though. Should have guessed it was you two!'

I quickly reply, 'Let's keep it that way. The mission is still classified as top secret and so is our involvement in it.'

This time it's me giving her a firm stare, which I broaden to include Hannah and Uncle Albert.

After a moment's silence, normal dinner chatter resumes as the girls continue to discuss today's sightseeing. But I catch Mary looking at me more than once with a new kind of awe or fascination. Or so I tell myself!

A little later, whilst Pig and I are talking together, Hannah comes over and asks us more about our sniper shooting, what guns we favour and why.

We don't say too much but I tell her my longest recognised kill 'was 845 metres', which seems to impress her.

She claims she isn't a 'gun nut' as we discuss her personal armoury, which consists of her service Glock 19 and a 'little' sub-compact Glock 26. She also has a Sig Sauer P229 as her personal weapon.

When she asks Pig, I confirm our preference is the H&K USP handgun.

'I've never fired those,' she replies.

I am curious why she joined the Secret Service, so I ask, 'So why the Secret Service as a career, Hannah?'

I notice the other conversations all stop so obviously it's a topic everyone is interested in.

She takes a moment and then says, 'When I was fifteen, I went to the local seven-eleven for some drinks and whilst in there, a crazed gunman comes in to hold the place up, screaming, "On the floor or I will shoot you." I, like everyone else, dropped to the floor, people screaming everywhere. It was pandemonium.

'He then shot the cashier in cold blood. The poor man was standing there, his hands in the air, no threat at all and BANG, he just shoots him. Dead before he hit the floor. He then reached around the screen to grab what cash and cigarettes he could and took off, screaming all the time. It was very scary. I vowed then and there to have a right to be armed in public, always.'

Mary, Stacey and Suzie have all gone over and given her hugs as the telling appeared to have brought back the bad memory.

Not me, she hasn't satisfied my curiosity, so I ask, 'Okay, I understand, but why the Secret Service and not the police, or follow your mum into the Marines or defence forces?'

I'm getting a dirty look from Suzie now; maybe I've crossed another line.

Hannah again takes her time before saying, 'I never wanted Mum's life in the Marines or army life generally. I had enough of that growing up. The police force was never an option. They do not have a good reputation here in Washington – it is a crime-infested city. So, it came down to the Secret Service, besides there is a bit of prestige attached as well,' she adds with a smile.

Mary then adds, 'It's not at all easy to get in either but she stuck at it and now she is in line to join the Vice President's protection team. A very prestigious appointment.' This is spoken with overwhelming pride as she smiles at her daughter.

'Wow that's awesome – congrats!' says Suzie and we all join in.

Hannah replies, 'Thanks. Hoping to hear something definite in the next couple of weeks. Then off for more detailed training. Will then be living out of a suitcase as we travel wherever she goes. I'm pretty excited about the opportunity. Might even get to visit Brisbane for the G7 summit, as it might be the VP' – she pronounced it VeeP like the TV series – 'who attends. I have sat in on a couple of pre-planning meetings as it is already on our planning radar.'

I look at Suzie and say, 'When is that on?' I have heard talk about it coming up. Quite a feather in little old Brisbane's cap, holding a G7 summit!

Hannah replies, 'Early next year. February, I think.'

We are back inside now, enjoying the air conditioning, and Albert says, 'That must have been very frightening, Hannah. What about you, Mary? What is the most frightening thing you have experienced?'

Mary says, 'That would be coming under enemy fire for the first time. My first foot patrol in Afghanistan. We didn't sustain any casualties but I quickly realised war is for real and I was certainly glad

I had taken all our training seriously. You quickly understand why the drill sergeants keep drumming it into you.'

Uncle Albert reaches over putting a comforting hand on Mary's shoulder – under the watchful eyes of Hannah!

He then looks at Pig and I, saying, 'No doubt you two have experienced some pretty scary stuff but I want you all to listen to this. It's a recording I made whilst walking the National Trail. This is a five-thousand-kilometre hiking, biking or horse-riding trail from Cooktown in far north Queensland all the way down to Healesville in the Yarra Ranges on the outskirts of Melbourne.

'After my wife Steph died, I decided to do something totally different. The girls thought I was mad but it is very hard, sad and draining caring for someone you love dearly as they are ravaged by an aggressive cancer. Not as bad obviously for the sufferer but bad enough.

'So I set off with "Spark", one of Steph's favourite horses, and Bluey, of course, our Australian purebred cattle dog, bought a pack horse then organised supply drops all along the route and headed up to Cooktown. I had to promise the girls so I took a sat phone so they could check on me – mind you, they made me agree to call them both separately once a week. They also insisted I take an EPIRB – an Emergency Position Indicating Radio Beacon. I was surprised they even knew what they were!

'It's five thousand kilometres so I expected it to take me some four or five months. Just me, Bluey the horses and nature. After what I had been through, it was bliss – no hospitals, no phone, no radio, no TV. So peaceful and calming.

'Anyway, I'm well on my way. It was 'round day forty and as dusk approached, I was in fairly thick scrub so I stopped and set up camp. This entailed my swag on the ground, a good healthy fire to cook on and not much else. I hobbled the horses as per normal so they could wander and feed, fed Bluey and me, and as darkness set in, I settled down in my swag.

'Seemed like a normal night. But not long after dark, I heard both horses snorting and even poring the ground, which they only do if something is scaring them or disturbing them. They aren't usually frightened of animals, even wild dogs and as I hadn't heard any dogs barking, this wasn't the likely cause.

'Bluey isn't a "people dog". Never left Steph's side, mind you, he normally roamed far and wide but always kept me in view. He knew where his next feed was coming from but at night, he would find his own spot normally a few meters away from me. Tonight, he kept squirming closer and closer. That's all right; the evening chill had arrived so he was now so close to me, I could feel his body warmth. Then I heard it. Or, more precisely them.'

Here, Uncle Albert pauses and turns to Hannah, 'Would you mind turning all lights off? You need to hear this in total darkness.'

Weird, I think but get up and help Hannah close all the blinds and cover power lights on the TV and other appliances.

Once he is happy with the darkness, he continues, 'Now, listen to this,' and presses play on his phone.

What follows is a series of snorts and guttural noises, almost human-like but at the same time, very animal-like. Sort of subhuman noises as if they are carrying on a conversation. 'They', I assumed, were Yowies, Australia's version of the American 'Bigfoot'.

They got louder as the two (I presumed) Yowies got closer and closer. As the noises seem almost on top of him, he stops the recording and says, 'By now, I have my back to the nearest big tree, my pistol in my hand. I had added wood to my fire so it is blazing. Bluey is cowering beside me and these two animals are still closing in on me.'

'How did you know it was two?' asks Pig.

'The noises were coming from slightly different directions, both heading north but maybe about ten metres apart. They actually went either side of us, didn't seem to slow down, just went about their business. They obviously knew we were there. Clearly, they didn't consider us a threat to them; otherwise, I'm sure I wouldn't be here to tell this tale.'

With this, he turns the recording on again and, I have to say I have been in some scary shit, some tight spots, but these grunts and noises are making the hair on the back of my neck stand up. Suzie is clutching my hand tightly too.

The noises quieten as the animals move further away until Uncle Albert once again stops the recording.

With the lights back on, I look around the room. Everyone is wide-eyed and clearly disconcerted by what we heard.

'What did you find the next morning?' I ask.

'At first light, I was up – well, that wasn't unusual. On a journey like this you only walk, and ride in daylight hours but I had to go looking for the horses. They were much further away than normal but with the coming of daylight, they seemed to have calmed down. As had Bluey. I did find a couple of imprints in a bit of a damp spot.' He again fiddles with his phone and pulls up a photo showing a huge footprint. He had placed an enamel mug (you know, an old-fashioned picnic mug) to give the footprint size some perspective.

I take a size thirteen boot and this was far bigger than my feet.

We all take turns looking at the photos and Uncle Albert adds, 'I also found some spoor and took a sample of it. I handed it over to a member of the police stock squad I ran into on the track a few days later. But he didn't seem too interested. I found out later that Kilkivan, the nearest town to where I was at the time, is a known Yowie hotspot.'

After a bit more chatter, Hannah asks me, 'What about you, Mort? What's the scariest thing you have experienced?'

Well, there has been a few, I think before saying, 'I reckon the time an Afghan or maybe Russian sniper and I locked eyes, both about to shoot.'

Silence, Suzie once again grabbing my hand.

'What happened?' Mary asks.

'He blinked,' I reply.

'What do you mean?' Hannah asks as I think Mary gets what I mean.

'He blinked, meaning he hesitated and missed. I didn't and likely shot him before he even fired. We were only five hundred metres apart.'

A bit blunt maybe but no sense carrying on with 'what ifs'!

Hannah again. 'What about you, Julien?'

Pig answers immediately. 'That would be coming to and discovering my leg was trapped under our bushie. Then the pain hit. Wasn't a pleasant experience.'

Again, the tone of his reply doesn't invite follow-up questions.

Uncle Albert, perhaps sensing the need to move on quickly, says to Stacey, 'What about you, dear?'

Stacey is silent for a couple of moments before replying in a quiet, soft voice, gripping Pig's hand tightly, 'Lying in my bed as a ten-year-old, waiting to see if my stepfather was going to "visit" me. I spent two years living with being scared out of my wits, waiting for the nights when he would visit. He always threatened "to beat the shit out of me and my mum" if I told anyone, so I didn't. I ran away from home when I was twelve and lived on the streets. Haven't seen or spoken to my mum since.'

Shit.

We all take turns to go over and hug Stacey, who continues to hold Pig close.

Suzie, Hannah and Mary linger, trying to give Stacey strength.

Me, I just want to find the bastard and beat the shit out of him. I glance at Pig, our eyes lock, a slight nod. Agreed, we will find this arsehole.

Mary, needing to move the subject on, asks, 'Suzie, you're the only one who hasn't told us your scariest moment.' It sort of seems heartless moving on from Stacey's sad tale but equally, we can't dwell on it.

The girls are all still in a huddle, holding each other anyway.

Suzie looks over at me and says, 'That would be when I got kidnapped by a bent copper, a policeman, and then Mort comes smashing through the door and kills him whilst he has a gun to my head.'

This gets even more gasps with Hannah and Mary casting appraising eyes my way, whereas Uncle Albert is simply aghast.

Suzie continues, 'Afterward, Mort took me down to your place, Albert, to keep me safe, whilst he went back. He and Julien then took down the Jackal bikies stockade, killing the ringleader of the bent police ring. It even brought down our State Government who were complicit with the bikies and bent police.'

Uncle Albert. 'Shit, I remember all that being on the news. That was you two?' he asks, looking at Pig and I.

We nod before I add, 'All this is covered by our "Official Secrets Act" so please don't go sharing this story.'

Suzie has been fiddling with her phone and now brings up the video showing me in full combat gear, rocket launcher on my shoulder at the fire position and starts sharing it around.

I have to admit I do look an intimidating figure. The video had been shot by a news helicopter but quickly had a suppression order against it.

I didn't even know Suzie had it on her phone. I remember when she was shown it and thinking about it now, I realise it makes sense she would have asked for a copy.

'Wow, they should make a movie or TV series about your story,' Uncle Albert says.

'Yes,' I quickly reply. 'We' – I indicate to Pig and I – 'can be executive directors and be on the big bucks, like you!'

Quick as a flash, Stacey says, 'Well, we can be your executive assistants then!' meaning her and Suzie. I'm quite relieved Stacey seems to have recovered from the raw memories we had unwittingly evoked from her.

Hannah then adds, 'You could get the Hemsworth brothers to play the leads and Margot Robbie can be Suzie! They are all Queensland locals, aren't they?'

'Be buggered,' is Suzie's quick response, 'if it means cuddling up to Chris Hemsworth, I'll be playing myself!'

'Mmm,' adds Hannah in a dreamy voice. 'Liam Hemsworth, now he can leave his shoes under my bed anytime!'

We all have a laugh at where the conversation has ended up. We have disclosed more than we should have here but I'm comfortable no harm will come of it.

It's time to get going now. We have a flight to catch in the morning, so we say our goodbyes and head back to the hotel in our Uber. Suzie once again thanks Uncle Albert for the use of the Shelby tomorrow.

22

I am cruising down Highway 1, alone in the Chevy Suburban rental. Suzie, Pig and Stacey are somewhere up ahead in the Shelby Mustang Uncle Albert had organised for us – well, for Suzie, really, she being the one who got so excited at the thought of driving one.

When we picked it up, as arranged, Carlos had met us at San Francisco Airport, handing it over almost reverently. Suzie was so excited; it was fun to watch. She rang her father (not minding the seventeen-hour time difference!) and said, 'Hey, Dad, listen to this,' then started it up and gave it a few revs before asking her dad, 'What do you reckon this is?'

He responded with a few options, getting 'nope' each time until she put him out of his misery after a few more pumps of the accelerator, telling him, 'It's a 2021 Shelby Mustang GT!'

There was silence for a few moments (we had made her put the call on speaker so we could all share the moment), then he came back, 'You have got to be kidding. A real Shelby?'

'Yep, and a lovely dark blue with black striping too!' his daughter answered. 'And I get to drive it from San Francisco to LA – well, I have to share the driving with the others but how cool is that, Dad!'

'You lucky so and so,' he answered. 'How did you manage that?'

'Well, Mort's uncle Albert has a car rental business over here, offering Mustangs, Corvettes, Harleys and Honda Golden Wing bikes for hire for people wanting to drive the Route 66 Highway across America. So, he offered us his personal Shelby when he heard how keen I was! Cool, ah!'

'Shit, honey, that's awesome. Make sure you have fun and BE CAREFUL.'

'Yes, Dad,' she said before giving it a few more revs and hanging up!

Her smile split her face from ear to ear and no one else was game to suggest they would take the first drive. Suzie was up! 'I might ring him back once we are out on the highway and I open it up, just for fun,' she said more to herself than any of us.

We head south on old Highway 1, the scenic route, the 'driving route'. We are sightseeing, so we are not in a rush. We have a few days before our flight home to Australia from LAX, and the girls say they 'only' need two days for shopping!

We all have a bit of a drive of the Shelby. It is powerful and certainly sounds good, and we stop at Santa Cruz for the first night.

Next morning, the girls head out in the Mustang and then Pig joins them after our afternoon coffee break when they change drivers, with Suzie taking the wheel. I'm thinking, I'm sure I put on deodorant this morning but no one wants to share my ride. It is a Suburban, so nothing hot, fast and fancy like the Shelby Mustang.

Naturally, I'm watching my mirrors, always on the lookout for the law, knowing they are mucking about up front in the Mustang and suddenly I see a couple of matching white Chevy Tahoes seemingly keeping pace with me, a little ways back, so not too close, but suspicious enough for me to slow down and see if they move up and pass but no, they remain at a similar distance behind me.

Bugger.

I dial up Campbell, asking, 'Are you keeping tabs on us?'

'No. What are you talking about?' is his reply. I explain what's going on, giving him our location and he assures me nothing he is aware of, so not official.

I call Pig, telling him, 'I've got company. Check your mirrors,' which he does without saying anything but Suzie sees what he is doing and says, 'Nothing back there. I'm watching closely for cops. What's going on?'

Pig answers, 'Mort has company. Two Tahoes matching his speed.'

There is an almighty screech through the phone and a squeal from Stacey in the back, so I ask Pig, 'What the hell was that?'

'That's Suzie doing a handbrake turn.'

By now I can also hear the Shelby at full noise as she ramps it up through the gears. There's no doubt she is pushing it hard and not for fun now.

We agree they will head back past me and the two Tahoes before swinging around and following them at a discrete distance, whilst we wait and see what may be eventuating.

A few minutes later, I tell her to back off as I can hear them coming. We don't want the Tahoes to notice.

Pig and I discuss possibilities. The fact the Mustang hasn't attracted any attention suggests whoever is behind the Tahoes has picked our trail up through the Hertz rental system, as I had used the FBI-issued ID to rent it, whereas there is nothing officially recorded for the Mustang.

I say to Pig, 'That means Campbell has a leak as he and his team are the only ones who are aware of those identities.'

Shit. FBI with high-level leaks.

We continue on heading south at the speed limit, wandering down Highway 1 with dusk approaching and I comment to Pig, who, as demanded by Suzie, has put his phone on speaker in the centre console so they can all hear the conversation. 'I'm guessing they are waiting for dark to make a play for us. No doubt try and box us in on a suitable piece of road.'

No one says anything for a few minutes, then Suzie speaks up, sounding quite composed and, frankly, forthright. 'Once it gets dark, I can come up behind the back car, no lights, and give him a bump and with the right timing, I should be able to put him off the road.'

I'm a bit surprised at the casualness of her approach and ask her, 'How can you do that? The Mustang is a lightweight compared to a Tahoe.'

She replies, 'It's not about weight; it's about timing. You would need to be pushing the speed and also a windy bit of road will help but remember, I spent years driving stock cars and we used to do this for fun. Some of the boys used to try and gang up on me so I got pretty good at dodging them and putting them into the fence. Dad and his mates used to run a book on how many I could 'fence' in each race!'

Pig and I are silent and Suzie goes on, 'Pig, you have a pocketknife on you?'

He grunts in the affirmative, so she continues, 'Good because the first tap is going to set off the airbags so I'm going to need you to burst them instantly – mine first then yours – so I can then concentrate on putting them out of the running. Then Mort,' she goes on, 'the first car still won't be able to see me and when I'm in position, I want you to slam your brakes on hard, hand brake and all, and with any luck, I will be pushing them into the back of you. If it goes to plan, you and Julien can then disarm them and we can get away.'

'Okay, Suzie,' I say. 'I like your plan. Plenty of gaps but we don't have any other options. Stacey, how do you feel about this? Sorry, we can't drop you off beforehand now either.'

Stacey replies, 'No way in hell I'm going to miss this. Might be scary as shit but we are the good guys we will win. Besides, I'm going where Jules is going.'

My phone rings, telling me I have another incoming call, so I put their call on hold and hear Campbell seeking an update, so I tell him none yet, we are working on a plan. I have not told him we are split in two cars; the fewer people that know that the better, especially right now. Before I hang up, I tell him, 'Campbell, you need to understand you have a leak.'

Silence, then, 'How the hell do you reckon that?' with a defensive, belligerent tone.

'You and your team are the only ones who know what names we were travelling under and the only way they can have connected us to the rental is through the Hertz rental system. Someone on your team has sold us out to the Columbians.'

There is a long pause, then he sighs and swears.

I reply, 'You need to get it sorted. I'm going dark now as I don't know who is reading your mail. I need to sort this immediate issue out then you will be hearing from me again. Clear?'

'Noted,' is the reply before I hang up.

Whilst I have been on the phone, it has become noticeably darker so I pick Pig's call up again and they too have noticed how much darker it has got.

I then receive a text from Campbell saying backup has been dispatched from San Luis Obispo – ETA to our position twenty to twenty-five minutes.

Suzie, who has certainly taken the initiative now, tells me she has Julien running the road ahead through the GPS, seeing how soon we might have a few curves. Nice sweeping 'S' curves would be great, she says, seemingly oblivious to the scenario we are discussing could well be life or death. There's no doubt she's up for it!

She and Pig identify a few good bends a few kilometres ahead so she tells me to start building speed. Almost at the same moment, we both notice the Tahoes increasing their speed. Almost as if they too had picked the road ahead as a good ambush spot.

I have the Suburban growling now as the speedo heads into the nineties but the two Tahoes keep gaining on me. As that's the point, I don't try to outrun them.

Pig lets me know I'm about two kilometres away from the start of Suzie's S's and as it's now fully dark, I keep pushing.

Two kilometres pass in a flash and then Suzie, as calm as you like, starts counting down, ten, nine, warning me they will initiate a hit on the back Tahoe on one.

I'm now running at close to one hundred miles an hour so have to really focus as Suburbans might have the grunt to travel at that speed but are not designed to go around curves easily at these speeds either. But that's exactly what Suzie is banking on.

Through the phone, I hear her say 'three, two, one' and then a BANG, followed by a squeal of brakes and some muffled swearing from Pig as the airbags go off. He apparently quickly deflates Suzie's then his.

All the while, Suzie is focused solely on the car in front. Now she has clear vision again and as the Tahoe is careening around a right-hand bend, she pushes the Mustang into the right rear panel, having dropped into second gear before impact, she now plants her foot, forcing the rear of the Tahoe right around until it connects with the steel wire barrier. She immediately hits the brakes hard, giving the Tahoe room.

The driver manages to regain control but before he has a chance to do anything, Suzie is back into him, this time on the left rear panel as they careen into a left-hand bend. This bump is intentionally harder, forcing the car into a full three-sixty spin. Suzie expects this and again applies her brakes hard, thereby staying clear of the spinning vehicle. Then as it slides sideways across the road, in the middle of another three-sixty, she quickly flashes in, hitting it amid ships before again braking hard. But this hit is the last one. The Tahoe seems to take a life of its own, spinning around, and then connecting hard with the wire rope barrier and this time the barrier can't hold it and the Tahoe flips over the rope, crushing a stanchion and disappearing down the side of the canyon.

There is a loud explosion from down below so we don't need to be worried about them re-joining the battle anytime soon.

I ask over the phone, 'You all okay?'

'Yes,' comes a chorus of replies.

'How's the car, Suzie?' I ask.

She answers pretty well straight away. 'All good mechanically as far as I can see. Now let's sort out car two.'

They are still tight on my tail, clearly being paid for results as they haven't backed off to see what has happened to their colleagues.

Still running without lights, Suzie quickly comes up behind car two and without hesitation rams into the back of it, sending it careening off to the side of the road but the driver brings it back under control and they immediately come under fire from both rear windows.

Pig calmly reassures the girls, saying, 'Don't worry, it is very difficult to shoot a car behind through the side windows. You can't get your arm around far enough.'

Stacey replies, 'Alright for you to say!'

I immediately say, 'Let's do this now.'

Suzie answers, as cool as a cucumber, 'On the count of three, hit your brakes hard with everything you have, Mort. One, two, three.'

I hit the brakes with everything, the Suburban fishtailing a little but

I hold it straight, applying the handbrake as well once the worst of the speed has dropped.

I hear more squealing of brakes behind me, then the roar of the Mustang as Suzie again hits the Tahoe from behind, this time aggressively pushing it into the rear of my Suburban.

There is a loud smash as we collide and as soon as I have come to a halt, I'm out, gun in hand, running back to the driver's side of the Tahoe. As quick as I am, Pig is quicker. He already has the passenger rear door open and I hear the retort as he fires, slamming the door and reaching for the front passenger door and bang, he fires again.

At the same time, I do the same. The driver's head is still buried in the air bag so I shoot him in the left knee. I open the rear door and do the same. This bloke is a little worse for wear, having not been wearing his seatbelt. Serves him right for taking potshots at my fiancée. Without saying a word, Pig and I kneecap all four. Still, they are alive, which is likely better than their colleagues down in the canyon. I then grab the driver's phone from the phone holder attached to the windscreen and pull out his wallet from his rear pocket. Pig has done the same with the front seat passenger, who had been holding his phone in his hand.

Pig and I nod over the hood of the car. Whilst we have been busy, Suzie has disengaged the Mustang from the rear of the Tahoe and moved up in front of my Suburban.

Fortunately, we have all come to a stop on the side of the road so the Tahoe isn't blocking the road; hopefully that means no one will stop too soon.

Pig jumps into the Mustang and me back into the Suburban.

Now we find the Mustang no longer has any headlights, nor I any taillights, so we agree we need to travel in tight convoy, the Mustang tight in behind me.

We head off at speed and I dial up Campbell to tell him he has a mess to clean up and the location and I will be back in touch once we are clear. Then I tell him, 'You will have to cleanse any record of the guns you gave Pig and me,' to which he replies, 'No worries there, they are throwaways!'

Fifteen minutes later, two black Suburbans roar past heading north so we guess these were the 'back up'. With any luck, they will get to the scene before any State Trooper or Sheriff's deputy. They can then control and cleanse the scene.

After driving for thirty minutes, I pull up at an overlook, Suzie pulling in beside me. We get out. Suzie and I have a long hug and squeeze and I tell her, 'You were awesome back there, so proud of you.' She hugs me tighter letting a little sob escape. I squeeze her even tighter, then add, 'You have to understand it was them or us. You have no reason to feel guilty about injuring or possibly doing worse to those thugs. They are vicious thugs – members of a drug cartel. No reason to feel any sorrow or anguish. They would not have hesitated to kill us. That was what they were there for after all.' She doesn't answer, just hugs me tighter, reaction no doubt setting in. Pig and Stacey seem to be doing the same.

We quickly converse and Pig and I break down the guns, throwing each component off in different directions, making it likely impossible to find, even if they know where we had thrown them from.

Pig then tells me Julio, the front passenger, had his email and their intranet site open on his phone, so Pig had already uploaded all the emails, phone numbers and as much data off the intranet as he could get and saved it all to our cloud-based server.

'Shit,' I say, 'good job,' and we fist bump. He adds that he got a link from Midge, so they were 'sucking up' all the data available off the intranet site direct to Midge. Right now, we don't feel safe dealing with the FBI.

Scary shit.

We agree we have to run hard and hopefully get to LA and disappear before they throw a cordon around the area. Both the Columbians and the police. Pig asks Suzie if she wants a break driving and she replies, 'No, I've got this.'

I ask Pig to drive the Suburban and I will travel with Suzie as I have a few phone calls to make. I have to crawl over the back seat of the Suburban to grab my prepaid phone out of my duffel as the tailgate won't open because of the damage.

We head off, having decided to cut across to I5 before we hit San Luis Obispo, taking Highway 46 and 58.

We are good for fuel, which is a relief as we would certainly stand out if we had to refuel. Travelling tight is very demanding but Suzie has it under control, so I hit the phone.

23

First call is to Uncle Albert. If he is still in Washington, it's nearly time to wake up anyway! Of course, as I am now using a throwaway phone, he doesn't recognise the number but answers anyway, unlike many these days.

I tell him it's me and then explain, 'We have had a bit of a problem. We came under attack and, well, Suzie used the Shelby as a stock car, doing a fair bit of damage to the front end.'

This is met by silence for a moment before he replies: 'Are you all okay?'

'Yes,' I reply. 'Which is more than we can say for the others.'

'Well, that's the main thing then. Cars can be repaired – that's what insurance is for.'

I'm reassured by his measured and understanding tone and then move on to the main point of my call: 'Carlos, your LA agent, he's clean, isn't he? I don't want to step from the frying pan into the fire?'

'Shit, yes, not opposed to a bit of backyard work but never with the gangs or anything.'

I pause before continuing, 'We are heading south on the I5 and I'm hoping Carlos can help get these cars off the road as once it's daylight, we will stand out like dogs' balls and I'm sure people will be on the lookout now.'

Suzie, of course, is taking this all in as she drives, looking at me with mounting concern.

Uncle Albert comes back, 'Let me call Carlos and see what he can get sorted. He has cousins all over the place, so I'm sure he can help.'

'Great, thanks, Unc,' I reply and he answers, 'Hold on, Mary wants a word.'

Then Mary comes on the phone, asking, 'So you were attacked?'

'Yes, but I'm not saying any more for now.'

'Does Campbell know?'

'Yes, and his team have to be the source. That's why I'm staying dark for now, so do not pass on anything you learnt from Albert please.'

'Okay, but I need to understand the full story when you can.'

'Okay, when time permits,' I reply, not really understanding why she needs to know so much. But then we have learnt she is pretty high up in the right circles of power there in Washington and clearly, there is a cross-over with the FBI and NDA (and whoever else!).

I hang up and Suzie reaches her hand over, putting it on top of mine. I flip my hand over and give her hand a squeeze and we stay holding hands silently for a little bit.

A little while later, my phone rings and it is Uncle Albert so I answer, saying, 'Hi.'

He replies, saying, 'Carlos will meet you at his cousin's panel repair shop in San Fernando,' and gives me the address.

I say, 'Hold on,' and use Google Maps on my phone to input the address and get an ETA of forty-five minutes.

I relay this to Uncle Albert, who continues, 'He will have a "loaner" car for you to borrow as well, so you can disappear further into the city.'

'Awesome. Thanks for this and keep a tab on the repair cost as Uncle Sam will be paying!' I hang up. I explain to Suzie what is going on and then ring Pig to let him know we will be exiting the I5 on the San Fernando Mission Boulevard exit, telling him Carlos will meet us with a loan car.

I ask Pig to put his phone on speaker so we are all able to listen and I say to them all, 'When we get to this address, please don't touch anything, anywhere. We don't want to leave our fingerprints or DNA anywhere we can avoid. Unless it's critical, don't go to the bathroom. Too much risk of DNA being left behind. Not much we can do with the two vehicles but, if possible, I want to get them crushed and quickly, so this should eliminate that risk. Then when we get into the loan car, again, please do not touch anything. If you have a pair of gloves, please put them on.'

Pig interrupts me here, saying, 'I have a box of disposable gloves in my backpack so we can all put a pair of those on.'

'Good,' I continue. 'We all need to understand what we have done will create a reaction from the Colombians. They will not want to let this go unpunished. We won't be using those IDs again, but they will likely leave no stone unturned in trying to identify and pursue us. We have caused them to lose face. They won't tolerate that. Sorry, but we need to be looking over our shoulders until we head home.

'My plan is, we will only use the loan car to get to a large shopping mall where we will park it in the car park, split up and take separate taxis to the Fashion Island Shopping Mall at Newport Beach, as the hotel runs a shuttle from there to the hotel.' (We are booked into the Pendry Newport Beach Hotel.)

'I will hold off letting Carlos know where the loan car is for a couple of days to ensure our trail has gone cold if anyone has traced us that far. We good?' I conclude.

Suzie gives me a silent nod with a concerned look on her face and I hear Stacey asking Pig his thoughts and he adds, 'We might make it two separate taxi or Uber rides, just so they can't fluke finding just the one taxi driver.'

I reply, 'Good idea. We just need to ensure these aren't taking us in a direct route to Fashion Island, so maybe you take a taxi to Long Beach and we will go to Anaheim, then a second journey to Newport Beach. Also, let's avoid Uber, their records are pretty comprehensive. We can pay cash in a taxi, so harder to trace.

'Also, when we are in the loan car, let's keep conversation to a minimum. Unlikely it will be bugged but let's not take any chances. I know I might sound paranoid but why take unnecessary risks? Suzie, once we get there, do you mind finding a large shopping mall, further in toward LA but not too far please?'

Pig replies, 'Deal.'

Then Stacey pipes up, 'As Suzie is driving, I'll find a shopping mall if you like.'

My turn. 'Deal!'

***

Twenty minutes later, we exit the I5 on San Fernando Mission Boulevard before taking a left and a right, getting into the depths of the suburb.

We pull up at the address, which already has the roller door up, so we quickly drive both cars in and out of sight.

I hear the roller door start coming down as I exit the Shelby.

Good.

As I get out of the Shelby, Carlos is already coming over, a look of consternation on his face.

'My goodness, how did you do all this damage? Both cars, how did you do this?'

I reply, 'Carlos, the less you know the better,' broadening my look to include a newcomer whom Carlos introduces as his cousin Edwardo, both of a similar small stature with swished back, black wavy hair, ensuring he too understands ignorance is best.

There is no one else in the building.

Good.

Pig and I join Carlos and Edwardo as they slowly walk around both cars, muttering at the damage. There is no doubt Carlos is quite upset at the state of the Shelby. Uncle Albert had told us how fond of the car he is.

Once they have finished, I ask, 'Can they both be repaired adequately?'

It's Edwardo who replies, 'Yes but it will take a long time and the repairs will be obvious.'

Mmm. Plan B then.

'Can you arrange to have both cars crushed, on the QT – quietly?'

They start talking in Spanish, so I quickly and firmly say, 'In English, please.'

They stop and start again in English, discussing where and who they could get to crush the cars quickly.

Edwardo pulls his phone out, looking for a number, so I put my hand up in the stop sign and ask, 'Sorry, this has to be done TOTALLY without record and in secret. Can you do this and what will it cost?'

Carlos says, 'But the Suburban is a Hertz rental. You can't crush it. It has to be returned to them or they will keep charging you.'

I smile and say, 'It will be returned to them in their system and I'm sure they will eventually realise it is missing but it and we will be long gone by then.'

I can't admit to them that Pig – or if need be, Midge – will access (we don't hack, remember!) the Hertz system and 'return' the vehicle in their system at LAX where it was supposed to be off-hired.)

They are naturally puzzled by this but Edwardo confirms, 'Yes, I know a wrecker's yard who we can pay to do it tonight. It will likely cost five thousand dollars for each car. They can stay here in this workshop today; I don't have anyone coming in here today. Carlos and I will deliver them to the wreckers tonight, so no one else will see them.'

I nod. 'Good, let's do that. Give me your bank account and I will deposit the ten thousand dollars plus a decent bonus for you both now.'

Carlos pipes up. 'Albert told me not to worry about any costs. He said he will cover it.'

'No. This is on me.'

As I say this, I open Google on my phone and access one of my Cayman Island bank accounts. When I'm ready, I glance at Carlos who has pulled his phone up and when he sees me looking at him, he reels off his bank account details. I nod and pay him thirty thousand dollars, a tidy bonus for the two of them; hopefully enough to keep their mouths shut!

Once I have completed the transaction, I say to Carlos, 'I have paid you a total of thirty thousand K, so ten K for each of you plus the cost of having both cars crushed. Trust you will respect our privacy and not reveal anything about us or these two vehicles to anyone. I will also pay Albert for the Shelby, so he is not out of pocket. We good?' I ask them both.

They both nod and we four shake hands, Pig and I giving them both an intimidating stare as we do this.

I'm not sure how much Uncle Albert has said to Carlos about what has happened but clearly enough for him to not ask too many questions.

He adds, 'You can borrow the F150 over there,' pointing to an older

Ford F150 dual cab with a canopy so I say, 'Great, thanks. I will let you know where you can collect it from.' We share phone numbers, me giving him my prepaid number so it can't be traced.

Pig and I head back over to the girls who have started unloading the Suburban as we hadn't bothered putting any luggage in the Shelby. You would be lucky to get any of our suitcases in it anyway!

However, as the back door won't lift, I'm struggling to pull the luggage over the back seat when suddenly there is a pop noise and Edwardo has managed to pop the back door open with a small wrecking bar. Handy things, these!

This makes it much easier to unload the luggage and Pig goes over and brings the F150 closer so we can get this loaded. We have all donned the disposable gloves before arriving and if either Carlos or Edwardo notice, they aren't saying anything.

Once we are all loaded up, Pig and I give both the Shelby and Suburban a final once over to ensure we haven't forgotten anything but no, good to go.

Pig and I shake hands with Carlos and Edwardo again, thanking them for their help and stressing the need for secrecy.

Before we all get in the F150, Stacey hands me her phone with Google Maps showing directions to Westfield Fashion Square in Sherman Oaks, about twenty minutes' drive away. I nod my thanks.

This time, I jump in the driver's seat. Suzie and Pig deserve a break from the night time drive. We roll out the roller door and I'm reassured to hear this being closed behind us.

We are off.

24

I follow the directions on Google Maps whilst also keeping a close eye on my mirrors. Nothing.

I'm obeying the speed limit as we don't want to attract any attention, so it's a full twenty minutes later when we approach the Westfield Mall along Riverside Drive. I pull into the first drop-off zone and Pig and Stacey quickly get out, grabbing their luggage before Pig comes up to my window and we fist pump. They head inside. We move off down Riverside Drive before entering the car park at the end of the complex. I head toward the back and park amongst a number of other cars and small trucks.

Suzie and I look at each other and with a sliver of a smile she aims her fist at me so we too fist bump and exit the F150, grab our luggage – which of course now comprises three large cases (two of them a bright matching pink, I might add!), plus my backpack and Suzie's smaller cabin bag. Yes, I'm wheeling two of the large bags, including one of the pink ones! So, Suzie only has her cabin bag and one larger case. I am a gentleman after all!

We enter the mall through the Macy's entrance and enter the mall proper where I spy a Starbucks up ahead. Gotta like that!

Yes, we join the queue but still quickly have our coffees. Whilst waiting, I Google where the nearest taxi rank is and we head there.

Only two couples and a family group are in front of us so we are quickly seated in a Ford Escape, a small SUV, and easily get all our luggage in. The next taxi in line is a Prius; as some of you might remember, I'm not fond of Priuses after being knocked down by one not so long ago.

Besides, I very much doubt we plus our luggage will fit.

I tell the driver Disneyland Hotel Anaheim, having seen it is one of the largest, so should be easy to get lost in the crowd.

Whilst chatting in the taxi, we realise how hungry we are, having not eaten since lunch yesterday so after Googling the nearest Denny's, I change our destination to the Denny's restaurant closest to the hotel.

Forty-odd minutes later, I'm paying the taxi driver and yes, I remember to tip him an extra twenty dollars so he doesn't remember me as being a tight arse!

We grab our bags and head inside Denny's. Over the years I have heard much about the Denny's restaurant chain from my various American colleagues but this is a first for me.

I have always understood what great value their breakfasts are and, more importantly, at the moment, their service is always quick and efficient. AND their coffee is claimed to be the best!

Time to find out.

It's not long and we have ordered our (late) breakfast and are quickly on our second coffee.

Yes, it gets the nod and the waitress, certainly no spring chicken but quick and efficient and fast with the coffee refill, does too!

In no time at all we are fed, caffeinated and out of there.

The taxi queue is a bit longer here, so patience is needed. This time it's an aging Ford Crown Victoria (seen plenty of these in cop shows over the ages!) that pulls up in front of us. No matter to me, we will certainly get our luggage in this old girl!

This time it's a shorter ride and we are quickly exiting the taxi at the Fashion Island shopping mall outside the Whole Foods market.

A short walk around the corner and there is the hotel shuttle, golf buggy 'thingy' waiting for us.

Good timing!

We jump in, much easier than lugging our luggage the six hundred metres to the hotel. (Yes, I know it would be good 'incidental exercise' for me to push the luggage up the rise to the hotel but discretion is the better policy at present – or so I tell myself!)

When we get to check in, there is a note from Pig and Stacey saying they are in suite 201.

We get ourselves checked in, the bellhops having grabbed all the luggage from the bus/buggy and in no time at all we are opening the door to 401, a large, airy corner suite. One I'm guessing is two floors up from Pig and Stacey.

Once the luggage arrives and yes, I remember to tip him too. I turn toward Suzie who is looking a little distraught and I suddenly realise the last few hours of effective silence have weighed heavily on her, after the traumatic events of last night.

I silently take her into my arms and let her have a cry. As you know by now, I'm not the sympathetic type and to be honest, the way Suzie had handled herself last night with such assurance and aplomb I had assumed she was coping well. Yes, I know, I made an ass of myself by making such an assumption.

Now we are in the privacy of our hotel room and one that I am one hundred per cent confident no one, the cops, the FBI or the Colombians can track us to. Yet.

Suzie has her cry as I hold her tight (but gently), stroking her hair (yes, I know it's a futile gesture but all I can muster). We have been through a few of these teary sessions now, so I think Suzie would be shocked if I did anything else. Well, that's my rationale anyway!

Once she has settled down a little, I suggest she grab the shower first while I start unpacking. We now have four days here, a day longer than originally planned. So, I plan on unpacking a bit so we don't feel like we are living out of a suitcase the whole time. Then again, I'm not unpacking fully, as you never know, we might have to leave in a hurry. Plan for the worst, hope for the best.

Surprisingly (or is that deliberately?), I finish my unpacking before Suzie is out of the shower. So, yes, you guessed it, I join her, getting a delightful squeal for my trouble – but not much else!

Once we are both showered and refreshed, I text Pig and suggest we meet up in the lobby and wander over to the Cheesecake Factory for a feed. Pig and I haven't experienced it yet and as the girls tell it, awesome food selection. And as it's too early for the dinner crowd and too late for the lunch crowd we might avoid too long a wait.

'Deal,' comes back the reply.

'When?'

'Fifteen,' I reply.

In fifteen minutes, we wander out of the lift to find Pig and Stacey waiting for us, sitting together holding hands. I instinctively wonder if they had had a similar scene to Suzie and me?

But before we head off, Pig puts his hand on my arm and pulls me away from the girls; whilst they notice, they stay where they are.

Pig starts, 'Midge has rung a couple of times. They are ecstatic with what we have given them. When he last rang, the cartel still didn't realise we were inside their server, so Midge was trawling everything and anything. Biggest cache of data they have mined, ever, he claims. They have access to all their internal and external emails, other encrypted services, the lot. They can even see how much money they have in the various bank accounts – hundreds of millions, he says.

'He says we will be in credit with DEA, FBI and every other department for the rest of our lives! He's assured me he is monitoring all communications so if our names, false or real, come up, we will know instantly.'

I smile at Pig, we fist bump. Awesome result, I think.

He continues, 'He also said he has organised four special phone handsets, one for each of us. Looks and works the same as a normal iPhone but fully encrypted and also can never be tracked or traced but we can use our own SIM cards. Matteo who lives here in LA has them, so we just have to contact him to arrange a meeting.'

'That sounds like a deal,' I reply. 'Will be good to meet Mateo too after the way he helped us crack that hacking ring last year.'

'Okay, I will text him and see when suits to meet, maybe for a coffee,' replies Pig.

We re-join the girls and agree to walk to the restaurant, avoiding the little shuttle and as we wander off down the drive, I reach for Suzie's hand and hold it. We move our arms in a rhythmic swing, just to lighten the mood a little.

It's a ten- or so-minute walk to the Cheesecake Factory and yes, our lucky day, as there is only a short queue and they all seem to be larger groups.

We are asked to wait, but not given a beeper thing and sure enough after only a couple of minutes we are called to our table.

With our menus open, the girls suddenly seem to relax, recounting what they had had last time before discussing what they might have this time.

Me? As soon as I see it, I know what I am having. Meatloaf and mash!

Suzie ends up having the buttered chicken; Pig, the shepherd's pie; and Stacey, the Baja chicken tacos!

As it turns out, we are all happy with our selections. We decide not to make complete 'pigs' of ourselves (he he!) and determine to take a slice of cheesecake with us back to the hotel instead.

A slice each, that is.

All right, all right, I'll tell you what we all chose!

Stacey decides on the original.

Pig, the caramel apple.

Suzie, the fresh strawberry.

Me, the key lime.

Suzie wants to share, which I reluctantly agree to – the key lime is special!

Again, all bloody delicious!

Pig gets a reply from Matteo during dinner who suggests a quick meeting at Starbucks here at Fashion Island at eight-thirty tomorrow morning.

Pig explains to the girls we are all getting replacement phones in the morning, with some resistance from both Stacey and Suzie, both claiming they like the colours of their existing phone covers.

Yes, you guessed it, pink for Suzie and purple for Stacey. (She claims it's mauve but it's really purple!)

Pig assures them their covers will still fit. Looking at him, I'm thinking, he's hoping anyway!

On the walk back and to avoid either of the girls asking, I say, 'We all need a good night's sleep and put the last thirty-six to forty-eight hours behind us, but tomorrow morning Pig and I will be putting our heads together to discuss our options.'

Not surprisingly, Suzie stands firm, saying, 'That's fine but potentially it's our lives as well as yours at risk, so we won't be excluded from any discussions.'

I'm not surprised by her reaction, as we had discussed it briefly before heading out to eat. And, I have no intention of excluding her or Stacey from our plans, but Pig and I do need to discuss options, if any. Also, I am keen to have a further chat with Midge.

Once I explain my rationale, both girls seem mollified. We head to our rooms but not before Pig gets in a parting shot, saying, 'Remember we are only two floors down, so we don't want to be woken by your snoring!'

But I'm ready for him, turning, smiling, and saying, 'Nor us by your bedhead banging on the wall!'

Gottem!

Well, maybe a tie.

Suzie also comes quickly to my defence, saying, 'It was only that one night, so it must have been the booze.'

Thank you, Suzie!

Once they exit the lift, I whisper to Suzie, 'Maybe we should rattle the headboard, ah!'

Subtle, aren't I?

She lets me kiss her, then pushes me away as the lift door opens. She keeps hold of my hand as we walk to our room, so there is hope!

25

Next morning and with the girls deciding on a lie-in this morning before they head to the gym, Pig and I meet for breakfast in the ground floor café but not until I had taken myself off for a nice long leisurely run early this morning. Good to get out and clear the head.

After our quick breakfast, we head over to Starbucks to meet Matteo. Having never met him before, we aren't sure who or what to expect.

We need not have worried as when we walk in, a young Latino couple – both covered in tatts, nose piercings and pink and green 'punk' style haircuts – raise their cups to us, so we walk over and he confirms he is Matteo and then he introduces us to his partner Matilda. Pig went up and ordered our coffee – no waiting when you take straight black! Naturally, I ask how they recognise us and Matilda pipes up and says, 'Well, just the size of you is a dead giveaway, knowing some of your background!'

Back at the table, we naturally start chatting about the recent hacking where Matteo had assisted us in capturing two Chinese 'students' red-handed with the proceeds of the crime in their bank accounts. A masterpiece of international crime detection and timing! Matteo even identifies the two students as members of AP40 – a world-renowned Chinese hacking organisation. They are still sitting in prison awaiting trial, with extradition applications also pending to face further serious hacking charges to be laid by the US Attorney General's office.

It turns out Matilda is Matteo's partner in business as well as life, and they both come across as well-versed in the arts of tracing and tracking hack attacks.

Pig asks the question we are both keen to know, 'So, how do you know Midge?'

Matteo smiles and says, 'I'm, well, we are lucky, as in my early days I was a "hacker for hire", willing to do anything, particularly if it was challenging. Then one day I got a message in my inbox, an inbox I didn't share with anyone. The message simply said, "Keep going, Matteo, and you will be arrested, keys thrown away." At the time I was working three different hacks on government departments and big business. I had no idea which one had triggered the warning. Scared me shitless, I can tell you. Suddenly, I realised I wasn't the best out there. Someone had cracked my "impenetrable" shield, even knew my name. Shook me to my core. I didn't know which job to not proceed with, so I sat back and did nothing on any of them for three days. Then another message comes in. "That's better." This time I reply, "What do you want me to do?"

'He keeps me waiting another two days, so I'm getting really edgy when the next message comes in. "Why not turn your skills into a business? I can help you."

'This was all happening at the same time that Matilda and I were getting together. At the time, she was working for a government department in their IT department, tasked with tracing any breaches. So, when I told her about this and because she wasn't too happy with me being a hacker anyway, she managed to get me a contract with her department, trying to access their data. The pay was quite lucrative, so

I dropped the three hacks I had been working on and turned to the commercial field. That first contract was fun actually, as I was trying to access the department's data, and Matilda was trying to stop me. Made our evenings fun, trying to guess what the other's next moves were! I eventually managed to gain access, which pissed Matilda off!' Here they share a smile. 'Then she resigned and came and joined me.' He stops and turns to Matilda and smiles, taking her hand, and says, 'We make a good team!' getting another smile in reply.

'Then one day we were at our local Starbucks, having our morning coffee, and this tall skinny white dude sat down, smiled and said, "I'm pleased you heeded my advice. You're now doing good work and I have a couple of new jobs for you. Turn back to your old ways and the future will be very dull, black even." He nodded at us both and then left.

'Was all a bit scary actually. Knowing someone was able to monitor our moves. I had always thought I was one of the best, but Midge is way out of my class. A couple of days later, another message appeared with two contacts needing our assistance. This one was signed "Midge" – that was the first time we had a name. Of course, I checked the name out on all the websites, dark and real, but no mention of Midge anywhere, which just made it scarier.

'We bid for those two contracts, won them, cleaned up their problems, got paid good money and we haven't looked back. We both really get a buzz out of fighting cybercrime now, so no turning back.'

Well, the telling of the tale is a longer explanation than I am expecting. Pig and I have both finished our coffees, so I ask if anyone else would like a refill but no, just us two. My turn to shout!

When I return to the table, Matteo has four phones out on the table and Pig has his out, removing his sim card. I then do likewise. Matteo explains these are very new technology, not yet widely available but guaranteed to be untraceable and untrackable. Works for me!

Pig asks, 'So a normal phone cover will fit these?' getting a nod from Matilda. I smile at him, knowing he is relieved at the answer!

Just then, Pig's new phone starts ringing. Midge's name appears on the screen but no Australian artist tune this time!

Pig gets up from the table to take the call after showing Matteo and Matilda who is calling.

With Pig on the phone, the two of them take their leave, exiting Starbucks and I watch them get onto two Vespa scooters parked outside.

Mmm, I muse, another example of not being able to judge a book by its cover – their personal style and appearance totally at odds with their work in life!

With them gone, Pig re-joins me, still on the phone to Midge, and I hear him say, 'Okay, give us twenty to thirty minutes and we will call you back when we have access to iPads.'

He hangs up, looks at me with a serious expression and says, 'Midge was ringing to tell us they have intercepted a message from Chico Garcia, the West Coat Head of the Garcia cartel and brother of Diego' – (who we had helped get arrested back in New York) – 'ordering his four lieutenants to a meeting at his ranch on Friday at midday to discuss.'

Here, he presses play on his phone and I hear, 'The gringos who escaped from Julio the other night have disappeared. We need to find them and teach them a lesson. We cannot allow people who attack us to go unpunished. We also need to put urgent plans in place to help Diego and ensure no one else tries to take over our East Coast operations.'

Pig presses stop and we look at each other. Without saying anything, we both get up and throw our now-empty coffee cups into the bin as we exit Starbucks for the short walk back to the hotel.

Once away from the café and heading back to the hotel, we start discussing what we have learnt.

Pig: 'Midge says his ranch is a heavily fortified old winery near the town of Ramona just west of Escondido and the I5 heading south to San Diego.'

I reply, 'Yes, might be an opportunity to do some more serious damage to the cartel on this side of the country now as well. Friday. We fly home Friday but not until eleven p.m.'

I look at Pig, he nods and we fist pump. Nothing else to be said. But plenty of preparation is to be done, starting with detailed planning. Good timing that the girls are planning on shopping the next two days!

As we walk into the hotel, we see Suzie and Stacey still sitting in the restaurant finishing their breakfast. We dutifully kiss our partners and order another coffee to drink whilst the girls finish theirs. (Yes, I know – we are addicted to the stuff!)

Pig pulls out the two phones, handing one to both girls, then starts to help Stacey with hers, getting his hand slapped out of the way! I know better than to try and help Suzie so I leave her to it. Pig gently reminds Stacey to turn her photos to auto-upload, getting a frustrated nod in reply.

I ask where they are planning on shopping today, having not taken too much notice when they were talking about it at dinner last night.

I get a quizzical look from Suzie, implying the question, 'Don't you listen?'

But she answers anyway, 'We are heading to Citadel Outlets first then on the way back we are stopping at South Coast Plaza, which is another huge shopping centre.' Suzie, looking at me, says, 'Macy's have a whole store there of home furnishings, so I might buy a new sofa or something.'

I don't bite, knowing she is simply winding me up. Well, I sure hope she is only winding me up!

'At Citadel they have outlets for Armani, Guess, Hugo Boss, Polo Ralph Lauren, Michael Kors, Kate Spade, Coach, so should be able to fill the car up there alone, ah, Stacey!'

Stacey smiles and nods, looking like she too is very much looking forward to this shopping expedition, armed with Pig's Visa!

I reply, 'What, no Lululemon?' (Suzie's current favourite activewear brand.)

'Actually, yes, they are there too,' she replies, again with that smirky smile!

We had booked a rental for the next three days whilst at the hotel, with Midway Rentals, a local company, booked in Suzie's name as she will be the primary driver. And her name had not been used or mentioned on any documentation whilst in the eastern states, so I'm confident it won't trigger any alerts. Suzie also takes the opportunity to stir me for as she looks through their range of cars for hire, she says to Stacey, 'Look, we can even hire a Bentley convertible. Now that would be shopping in style!'

Whilst Stacey smiles at her, I do not give her the satisfaction of answering, knowing she is just winding me up.

Certainly hope so!

Now as it nears nine-thirty and the shops open at ten, it's time for them to get moving. They have to take a taxi (no more Ubers this trip!) to Midway to pick their car up on the way.

As we leave the table, it's Stacey who asks, 'So what are you two going to be doing today?'

I let Pig answer. 'Not much, chilling out I guess,' is his reply. Suzie is giving me a look as if she doesn't believe him but I have my innocent face on!

26

With the girls gone on their shopping expedition, Pig and I adjourn to his room (yes, with fresh coffees!) and give Midge a call. Now we are in private, Pig puts the call on speaker and Midge runs through again what he had shared with Pig earlier. After he has finished, I say, 'We see this as an opportunity, Midge, to strike hard and fast, assuming they are still unaware you are in their system. (Midge grunts confirmation.) As in football (of any code), attack is always the best form of defence so to nullify their hunt for us by attacking and destroying the hierarchy of the Garcia cartel is a very attractive proposition. Don't know how we might be able to do it yet but if we do come up with a plan, we can't do it without you providing support, weapons, resources, et cetera. What are the chances of getting something like this approved in the timeline we have?'

Phew, a big speech for me!

Midge is silent for a few moments but that's fine, we are patient guys – learnt that the hard way.

Eventually, he replies, 'Guys, if anyone can pull something like this off, it is you two. I reckon I can get you any resources and weaponry you need but would expect any approval would be more tacit approval – you know, provide the tooling, et cetera, knowing what it is going to be used for without making any official commitment or approval. Might even be better if we don't share your plans with anyone.'

Pig and I ponder this, thinking of the ramifications if anything goes wrong.

We have been around the block enough times to know, despite the best-laid plans, something can always go wrong. Plan for the worst, hope for the best.

Pig and I look at each other. As usual, no need for words, we are on the same wavelength. We nod.

'Okay, Midge, but we want you in our corner. What we discuss with you, remains with us three, so no one else is aware of how or when we might strike. Are you happy with this?'

'No issues with me, my friends,' he replies.

'Okay, walk us through this ranch of Chico's?' I ask.

Midge starts, 'Well, it's just outside the little town of Ramona in San Diego County. Population about twenty thousand. I'm sending through what images and details we have now, so you can review them while we talk. It is on a little side road just off "Mussey Grade Road". I have it marked on the maps.'

(As he says this, our iPads light up with incoming messages – not email or messenger but a new highly restricted data sharing app Midge had shared with us previously.)

Pig and I open the app and start reviewing the maps and data he has shared.

'As you can see, the perimeter is heavily fortified, eight-foot electric fence, V-shaped razor wire on top, then inside he has a two-hundred-yard cleared area and he has armed guards riding around on ATVs constantly. There are also loose guard dogs roaming freely in this border area. These are supposedly vicious half-starved dogs. I've seen a video of one of them attacking one of the guards who was off his

ATV having a leak. This area is then sectioned off with another lower five-foot electric fence, so keeps the dogs away from his family, staff and visitors. The fences are also hidden from the house and road by thick trees and shrubbery.

'The driveway entrance is manned by armed guards, not visible from the road, so they don't scare the locals but from the video I've seen, they are in the face of any unexpected visitors. Chico, like his brother, is a mean and vicious son of a bitch. Wouldn't surprise me if the grounds are full of bodies.

'He also has pretty sophisticated anti-drone radar running 24/7. I know the DEA have lost a few drones when they thought they had some new undetectable technology, but these simply disappeared like all the others. Frankly, the DEA techs are still scratching their heads, not being aware of any radar system that should have been able to identify their drones. They even sent up a second one, believing the first one must have failed, they were so confident in their new technology. It disappeared just like the first one.

'Chico and his wife are involved in the local scene, members of the local country club, wife involved in a couple of charities, kids went to the local primary school when they were young. The two youngest are away at college now; the eldest Gabriel is now one of his lieutenants, hasn't earnt that right but given it by Daddy. He is the flash playboy type, pretty useless at everything, I understand. Drives the Ferrari, you know the type. He's been called to this meeting.

'The house is, as you would expect, a fortress in its own right. We believe the house has secure blast-proof fire doors more the size and style of water-tight doors on ships in case of an accident. So, he can quickly move into a separate area of the house and lock these doors, ensuring he is secure from any outside attack. The house also has a large cellar, used as a wine cellar but also fully stocked against any outbreak of war or whatever. You know "doomsday preppers" style. None of this has ever been confirmed as all his staff are very loyal to him – they know what happens to loose lips.

'He has been married to his wife for nearly thirty years but again, we believe he has a mistress living there with him. There have been a few of these over the years; some simply disappear, never to be seen again. We expect there are multiple bodies in the grounds from people he has murdered or has had murdered.

'The property used to be a winery, or at least a vineyard, and Chico still has a small section where he cares and cultivates the grapes and turns them into wine. You, of course, won't see any of this in the shops but he is apparently quite proud of his wine and shares it with his friends and lieutenants.

'We have seen from other internal staff memos he has issued overnight that the meeting will be held in the cabana, adjacent to the swimming pool. The cabana, just so you don't get the wrong idea, is a thatched-roof-type structure, about the size of a three-car garage, no sides but with a full kitchen servery, barbeque area and separate toilets and changing rooms.'

Midge goes silent, letting us look through what he has sent us.

I look at Pig as I start to reply, 'Well, doesn't look like a full-frontal assault will work. We would need a platoon or two and no doubt would incur significant casualties. Can you send through any images you have of the outdoor areas, the pool and cabana if that's where the activity's going to be?'

Then before he can respond, Pig pipes up, 'And a topography map of the area too, please.'

I nod my agreement; he is on the same wavelength as me!

No surprise there.

'On their way,' is the prompt reply from Midge.

Like before, our iPads beep, indicating incoming files.

I open the images, clearly taken from a satellite at some point and whilst continuing to look at these, I ask, 'How old are these images?'

Midge pauses. 'Ah, let's see. Two to two and a half years old.'

'Any chance you can get updated ones please?'

'Sure can. I will organise for new ones this afternoon. We have so many satellites up there now – only takes a couple of hours to get one situated where we want it. At least in this part of the world.'

Then Pig passes his iPad over to me, saying, 'See this little state park? It has a high point of 1650' about 465 metres, might give us sufficient elevation over the ranch.'

I look at where he is pointing and see a little state park – Dos Picos County Park – with an elevation of 1650'. From the map, I calculate the distance from the ranch at around 1250 metres and comment, 'That will be some shooting!'

He looks at me and smiles. We nod. We are up for it!

'Okay, Midge,' I start. 'Can you get us a really detailed topography map of this area? We need to get out there and have a look for ourselves.'

Then, addressing Pig, I say, 'I'm thinking the Sako TKIV2000 with suppressor? What do you think?'

This is one of the newer and most accurate sniper rifles now available. Neither of us has ever fired one before, having used 'Betsy', a SR98, in my time in the Australian Army but with the claimed accuracy of up to 1500 metres with this model Sako, I reckon it's the way to go.

Pig nods in agreement, adding, 'We would need to be able to test fire them to zero them in.'

I nod, then to Midge: 'Any chance you can source two Sako TKIV2000 sniper rifles with suppressors? And we would need to sight these in over a similar distance.'

'Two?' he asks.

'Yes,' I reply, 'if we are going to take down five at once we will both need to be firing.'

'Okay, on it,' he replies. 'Will let you know how I go. Shouldn't be too long. Anything else suit if the Sako's aren't available? I have no idea what sniper rifles we use in the armed forces. Anything else?'

I say, 'If no Sako's available, let us know what you can supply, please. Also, two H&K USP handguns or if easier, any of the Glocks.'

'Okay, will see what I can do.'

We hang up from Midge and fist bump.

Wow, we have set ourselves a hell of a challenge!

27

We are buzzing!

We decide to head down to the café for refreshments and coffee. Yes, yes, I know but it stimulates the brain!

We grab a muffin and coffee each and wander out to an outside table. Pig has brought his iPad so we will know if Midge sends anything through.

We need to make a plan. And make a list of everything we are going to need.

Shit, it is going to be difficult telling the girls what we are planning, I suddenly think.

We chat generally about a plan and what options, then decide we really need to get out there and check it out for ourselves.

We can't simply jump in a cab and wander around the locale, though. Nor would it be prudent to use a rental which too can be traced.

No, we quickly decide we need a work ute (pickup truck in American!), something that will fit in down around that area. An older F'y (F150), Dodge Ram or Chevy Silverado.

We continue making a list, then Pig decides he will use the notes app on his iPad, two columns: one for him, one for me.

The list looks like this:

	Mort	Pig
Truck	X	
Work clothes	X	X
Suitable work tools (rake, shovels etc)	X	
Range finder/Binoculars		X
Drone		X
Disguises	X	
Yoga mats		X
Backpack to carry rifles		X

We decide we, like our ute, need to fit in, hence our need to visit another op shop to get some well-worn work gear. Unlike New York, the commonly worn gear for gardeners, et cetera, that we have seen here in California seems to be jeans and old t-shirts. Should be easy to find. Again, like New York, we agree we will do this separately so as to not arouse suspicion.

Likewise, I will need to find a salvage yard or somewhere selling old tools, rakes, shovels, picks, et cetera, so we can pretend to be working whilst in the county park.

The 'binis' and range finders are obvious; we won't scrimp on these either, sticking with trusted brands we know are reliable. The yoga mats are to lay on the ground in case our firing positions happen to be on rocky ground. Yes, I know, getting soft in our old age!

The drone; we want to launch this over the county park once we are close so we can see who or what might be going on before we blunder in. Might also help identify a suitable shooting spot.

Pig says he has always wanted to visit one of the big sporting goods stores here in the States. He looks up Mr Google and finds there is a Bass Pro shop an hour away. 'Cool.'

We stop for a breath, so to speak. I look at Pig and say, 'You know, we have to be doubly careful with this. Whilst through Midge, someone will be helping us, knowing what the outcome should be. But that doesn't mean someone else, with their own agenda, doesn't want a different outcome for their own purposes and we could become "collateral damage".'

We have seen firsthand the risks when two separate agendas go down at the same time.

We agree to be doubly careful.

After some thought, Pig says, 'You know the biggest risk is the guns. The Sako's are unique so the bullets will be easily matched back to these weapons. So, if anyone wants to tie us to the assignations, they will have to prove the weapons were in our hands at the time of the shooting.'

I nod; he is right.

We contemplate this in silence until…

'Barrel borer!' Pig exclaims.

A barrel borer is a little metal cylinder attached to a small wire. You set the diameter of the borer to suit the diameter of the rifle (in this case, .338), pull the borer through and it puts very small grooves into the barrel, thereby changing the signature of the gun so bullets fired from it prior to being 'bored' won't match it. Highly illegal, of course, but it is exactly what we need.

I add, 'Boom! We run it through before and after the shooting, then the bullets won't match what they have on file or afterwards.'

We sit there contemplating again before I say, 'Sergeant Chris!'

Pig smiles and nods, saying, 'I was just trying to remember his name. I wonder if they have locked him up yet!'

I'm busy going through my phone. Sergeant Chris is a former sergeant in the US Quartermaster's office. We had met a few times in Afghanistan. Bent as a two-bob watch. But want anything – girls, porn, cigarettes or illegal weapons – he could source it. No doubt making a mint as he went.

He got out of the military just before they arrested him. He has since set up business in Dubai.

Yes, I still have his number! I send him a text, not being sure what the time difference is between California and Dubai. I ask, 'Sergeant Chris, how they hanging? Need a .338-barrel borer within 24 hrs nr Newport Beach CA. P&A? (Price and availability if you're not sure!) You choose pick up point. NO ID. Thks, Mort n Pig 😊 '

Pig has watched over my shoulder and we smile, thinking of a few nights of heavy drinking we had shared with Chris, a big burly country boy from Idaho or somewhere, back in the day!

I then start looking up used pickup trucks – or utes, as we call them.

Heaps and heaps of them available. I identify a number of likely dealers along Harbor Boulevard in Costa Mesa who seem to have plenty of suitable stock so I'm off.

Whilst we wait for our separate cabs to take us shopping, we agree once I have my truck, I will call him with a plan of picking him up so we can go get our work clothes. He is tasked with finding two different op shops close together so we can do this at the same time.

***

My cab arrives and I tell him to drop me off at the Famers Market on Harbor Boulevard Costa Mesa. That way he can't confirm where I have gone.

Whilst in the cab, I text Pig to suggest, 'Maybe pick up a camo shelter as well.'

He replies, 'Good idea.'

Once there, I grab a coffee (naturally!) and head on down the road.

I also grab a box of plastic gloves from a 7-11. You know why we need these!

It is in the third yard I visit that I find just what I'm looking for – an older Toyota Tacoma. Smaller than the usual breed of pickups, but this also has a long lockable toolbox in the rear tray plus ladder racks. After taking it for a test drive and haggling over the price, we agree on a deal and I sign the paperwork. The dealer isn't too fussy and for one thousand dollars off the price being cash (I had withdrawn two thousand dollars off my prepaid Visas while at the farmers market), he left the purchaser section of the transfer form blank. I have no intention of lodging the transfer papers anyway. Fingers crossed we will be finished with the ute within forty-eight hours.

Before driving out of the dealers' yard, I don a pair of surgical gloves, wiping down the steering wheel, instruments and gear lever, and door handles et cetera from my test drive.

Good to go.

I find a Salvation Army thrift shop just up the road still on Harbor Boulevard, so I pull in to buy my work clothes, work boots, well-worn work gloves and an Anaheim Ducks cap, then decide I might as well get Pig his as well. We are basically the same size after all. Except Pig 'only' takes a size eleven boot!

My lucky day as they also have a decent range of hand tools, so I grab:
- A ladder
- Two picks
- Two shovels
- Hedge clippers
- Telescopic pruners
- Tie-down straps
- Two tarps

- A broom
- A rake

Done and dusted!

A text to Pig telling him I'm on my way ETA fifty minutes. He replies: 'Bring coffee.'

Of course.

It's not hard to find a Starbucks as I near the Pro Bass store and I wander in. Pig has told me to look for him in the hunting section and sure enough, that's where he is. He has ordered the Vortex top-of-the-range binoculars that also double as a ranger finder.

When he sees me, he says, 'I just had a text from Stacey. They are heading back to the hotel.'

I nod, saying, 'Yes, I received the same message from Suzie.'

He continues, 'Their range of drones is disappointing. They only carry their own brand and you need a separate remote control so I can't use my iPad. It does come with a high-definition camera, which is all we really need.'

I shrug, saying, 'Beggars can't be choosers.'

'I also heard from Midge and it looks like we are good to go. Will give you the details once we are outside.'

He has a trolley, which already has everything else we had talked about, so he wheels it to the check out, pays and we wander out to our new wheels.

He pauses when he sees it, then shrugs, saying, 'Well, not flash so will fit in well, I guess.'

We load our new purchases in the back seat of the ute and head back to the hotel, having both texted 'our girls' that we will be back in an hour or so.

As soon as we are underway, Pig brings me up to date by saying, 'Midge rang whilst I was in the taxi so I gave him a call back when we arrived and before I went into the store. He confirmed they can get us two Sako TKIV2000 sniper rifles with suppressors. They are flying them in overnight. He has also arranged for us to visit Pendleton Marine base just off the I5 South interstate heading toward San Diego. We have to do this tomorrow evening at seven p.m. so we can gain access without proper identification. We can collect the guns and as much ammo as we need then. We are to meet a Major Houlihan at seven p.m. tomorrow who will provide "dark" access onto the base and specifically to their range for test firing the weapons.'

On the way back, we debate how and what we tell the girls. So much has changed since they left this morning.

We decide eating in tonight would be a good thing. Maybe pizza?

So Pig texts Stacey, asking, 'Hi, you okay if M&S join us for pizza in our room tonight?'

She replies, 'Sure, why not? Happy to stay off my feet. You sort the pizza!'

Pig can't resist texting back, 'Okay, will do. I prefer you on your back anyway.' He sends it with a heart! (He doesn't realise I can read what he is typing!) Then when he looks at me with my own smirky smile, he suddenly realises I have seen his message and he even blushes!

The reply is a face with tongue poking out.

I then pull my phone out and have Siri (I'm driving, remember) send a text to Suzie saying, 'Hi P&S have invited us for pizza in their room tonight. Suit you? We will bring some beer and wine back.'

'Sounds good. Where are you?'

I choose not to answer the second question but nod to Pig, saying, 'You better sort the pizzas!'

Then a few miles before we get back to the hotel, we see a Safeway supermarket on the next corner so I wheel in and we go in and buy a six-pack of Budweiser and a couple of bottles of New Zealand Sauv Blanc.

As I'm driving toward Newport Centre, Pig says after a few minutes silence, 'We will need a storage shed. Somewhere to park the ute once we have the weapons tomorrow night. Can't afford to leave them on the side of the road. Besides, we will need somewhere private to pull the guns down and clean them and bore the barrels.'

I nod, saying, 'Yes, you're right. We will have to find somewhere local that's suitable.'

Pig buries his head in his phone for a few minutes and then says, 'There are a couple around both, about ten to fifteen minutes away from the hotel.'

'Do either of them offer after-hours access? You know, so we don't have to front up and get a key?'

A pause as he is checking before coming back, 'Yes, this one does. Offers access 24/7 and uses codes not keys. Looks like you book and pay online, and a code is sent by text. You punch this number in at the entrance and again at the door to your shed and that's it.'

'Okay so we will need to wear our disguises but won't need to talk to anyone or front a camera. Good. Book it.'

'Done. Booked from seven p.m. tomorrow for forty-eight hours.'

After another pause, Pig and I discuss how we can explain what we are planning to the girls.

Really only one way to do this. Tell it to them straight.

Besides, might be good to hear the plan out loud anyway.

I then add, 'We also need to be careful of talking when we are on the base as they will be able to identify us from our voices. We will have to try and not say a word whilst there and zeroing the guns in.'

Pig nods his agreement.

28

We park the ute on a side road on the other side of the shopping centre from the hotel, not wanting anyone to connect us with it.

We leave most of our purchases in it, only taking the drone and binoculars with us – the only things of value.

Plus, the Bud and wine!

Pig has ordered the pizza via Uber Eats and as it is due a couple of minutes, after we walk in, I leave him at reception waiting for the pizza and head up to our room.

Of course, after getting a nice warm welcome (making me suspicious of how much Suzie has spent!) and hearing about their day of shopping, she then asks what we have been up to.

'All in good time,' I reply, hoping to avoid saying too much until we are altogether.

'No, you don't,' is the reply I get. 'What have you two been doing? You're up to something.'

I try to side track the discussion. 'So what have you bought today?'

I know it's not working from her shaking head.

Oh well.

I take her hands and we sit down on the couch. Suzie already has a look of concern on her face.

'Midge rang this morning to tell us Chico Garcia has called all his lieutenants to a meeting at his ranch on Friday.'

'That's the day we leave,' Suzie butts in. I nod, acknowledging that's correct – better than saying, 'Yeah I know that!'

I continue. 'He has called them together to start hunting us – "the gringos that have disappeared". So, Pig and I have been making plans, based on attack is the best form of defence.'

Suzie now has a worried look on her face and I gently touch her face. My fingers caress her cheek and I say reassuringly (I hope, anyway!) 'Don't worry, we excel at making plans and being thorough. This is why we are still alive today. We always analyse all risks to counter them. You know that.'

Not surprisingly, she doesn't look convinced but I continue anyway: 'That's why we suggested pizza, so we can sit down and explain our plan to you both, so you will see how thorough our plan is and you can help de-risk it by thinking of any holes in it.'

I had thrown this last bit in, in the interest of involving them in the plan, thereby providing them with ownership. Well, that's my hope.

I lean in and give her a hug, which turns into a bit of a long kiss, with me thinking, it's a bugger Pig and Stacey are waiting for us!

29

After taking a couple of minutes to refresh, we head down to Pig and Stacey's room and knock. Stacey lets us in.

Pig already has a can of Bud open; on seeing me, he pulls the ring tab on another for me, then pours a glass of Sauv Blanc for Suzie.

We are all standing so we clink glasses and I say, 'To the future.'

The pizzas are sitting in their boxes and Stacey has put plates and napkins out. She picks up the knife and starts serving slices onto the plates.

Pig beats me to the first one (he is a Pig, after all!) but not by much.

We eat in silence for a few minutes before I say, 'Okay, we need to have a serious discussion. As you know, we escaped from the ambush up on Highway 1 – thanks in large part to Suzie's daring driving skills. Our attackers were members of the Garcia Cartel. As a consequence of escaping them and in fact injuring and maiming some of them, we now have a target on our back. We knew this would be a consequence of our actions. So far, we have two things going for us.

'One – they do not know who we are. Whilst they obviously found out our false names from an FBI stooge, we have to trust no one inside the FBI knows our real identities, except Campbell, Hunter and maybe their boss. I trust them implicitly. So, we can be reasonably confident they will not be able to identify us. BUT I do not want to spend the rest of my life looking over my shoulder and worrying about you all. You are all family to me, so threaten you, there will be consequences. Serious consequences.

'Two – unbeknown to the cartel and through Pig's quick thinking, we know everything they are doing and saying. This is a huge advantage. One that won't last forever as I am sure someone will twig that Julio has been logged in since before the attack. The damage is done long-term. The FBI and DEA have all they need to shut them down already. But that doesn't necessarily solve our problem. Again, I do not want to be looking over my shoulder for the rest of my life.

'This morning, Midge shared a message they intercepted where Chico Garcia, the head of their West Coast operations, has called all his lieutenants to a meeting at his ranch here in southern California at midday on Friday to discuss how to track us down and teach us a lesson – make an example of us. Pig, Midge and I plan on using this information to strike whilst Chico and all his lieutenants are together and take them out.'

Before I can continue, it's Suzie who cuts in, saying, 'And how do you plan on doing that?'

'I'm just getting to that.'

Pig has his iPad open and leans onto the table we are all sitting around and continues, 'This is a map showing Chico's ranch, just outside the town of Ramona inland from the I5 toward San Diego. Midge advises he has armed guards and attack dogs patrolling the perimeter, so a full-frontal attack is not an option. Besides, we would need a platoon or two and no doubt there would be significant casualties. So that's a no-go.'

Whilst Pig continues his briefing, I grab another slice (well, two, actually) of pizza and open fresh cans of Bud for Pig and me. Yes, I top up the girls' glasses too, getting a nod from both, who are both watching and listening intently.

Pig goes on. 'On the other hand, we see this little state park Dos Picos County Park has an elevation of 1650 feet or 450 metres. We are hoping it will have a clear view back over the ranch.'

'How far is that from the ranch then?' This time it's Stacey getting in first.

Pig answers, 'Approximately 1250 metres, so over a kilometre.'

I add helpfully, 'That's fifteen to sixteen footy fields, twelve soccer fields, eleven American football fields, end on end.'

The girls' mouths drop and Stacey says, 'What? How can you hope to shoot someone from that far away?'

Suzie looks at me in consternation but then seems to remember the conversation back in Washington where Mary had confirmed our status as 'world-class snipers'.

I answer, 'That's what we are trained to do. Both of us.' As I say this, I indicate Pig and I together.

'Besides, we have requested new, state-of-the-art sniper rifles. These are reputed to be accurate up to 1500 metres, so in our hands I am confident we can do this. Depending on wind and weather conditions, of course. And finding a suitable firing position.'

I take up where Pig had left off, giving him a chance to grab the last slice of pizza.

'We won't know until we can go down there in the morning and check out what the view is like and whether it will be suitable. We need an anonymous vehicle to do that, so today we bought a ute, like a tradie's ute, one that will fit in and not look out of place when we do our recon tomorrow and, hopefully, if our plans come together, when we do the hit. The ute is parked on the street on the other side of the shopping centre so it isn't likely to be connected to the hotel and as best we can tell, there is no CCTV coverage on the street where we parked. That's why it's on the street and not parked in the shopping centre car park. CCTV coverage would have shown us getting out of it. We have already fixed the number plate so it cannot be recognised from the cameras.'

'How come?' This again from Stacey as Suzie knows how we do this.

And it is Suzie who explains, 'They have some chemical mix they spray onto the number plates, so it is clear to the naked eye but blurry when seen on film. That's why they never get any speeding fines at home.' As she says this, she gives me a smile, letting me know she has worked this out and no doubt why she so confidently speeds when in the Camry. Little does she know I have done the same to her mini!

Pig takes up the plan. 'In the morning, Mort and I are heading down to Ramona to do a recon. As well as the ute, we also bought hand tools – you know, shovels, picks, a ladder and gear so we can make it look like we are workmen maintaining the park. We also bought a drone and top-of-the-range view finder. We are lucky in one respect; the meeting is taking place out in the open, in the cabana next to the large swimming pool.

'Then tomorrow night at seven p.m. we have to meet a Major Houlihan at the Pendleton Marine base just off the I5 South to get our sniper rifles and handguns. We will also use their range to zero the guns in. So, sorry you will need to have dinner on your own tomorrow.'

Suzie looks at Stacey and says, 'Well, I reckon they can shout us to Flemings, that fancy steakhouse over the road from the shopping centre, don't you?'

She gets a smile and nod from Stacey and I add, 'Yeah, I fancied having a feed there too.'

'Tough luck, sounds like you will be too busy,' is the reply I get from Suzie but she says it with a nice smile!

I continue. 'On the assumption that we can find a suitable firing position in the park or surrounds – that is why we bought the drone. This will be a lot quicker than doing it by foot. We will then also work out an escape route or two and finalise our plans so that on Friday it should be a simple in and out. Being so far from the ranch will only improve our chances of escape as I am sure this is way beyond any defensive planning the cartel will be doing.

Then again, as always, our motto is 'plan for the worst, hope for the best'.

There is silence for a few minutes as we all contemplate the plan.

Then Suzie – her legal training kicking in, maybe – asks, 'Okay, what are the biggest risks and how can they be eliminated?'

I nod to her, acknowledging her good question.

I then look at Pig before saying, 'Being honest, if our plan comes together, we see little risk of being caught before or after the assault, as, being so far away and, again all going to plan, there will be a major distraction to keep the cartel and the authorities busy. I see our biggest risk coming from within the FBI or DEA, for whilst by providing the weapons for this assault they are giving us tacit approval, we know from past experience there is always someone within the ranks with a different view of things or an ulterior motive.

'We will be minimising any possible connection between us and the guns. For instance, we will be checking the weapons for any tracking devices. We will naturally use gloves so we don't leave any fingerprints. We have already ordered a "barrel borer" – a little device, totally illegal of course, which we will pull through the sniper rifle barrels both before and after firing so the bullets will not match the gun signature they have on file or be a match for it when they get the weapons back.

'We have already demanded and been granted "dark access" to Pendleton Base so we will not be recorded as visitors. We will be hiding our identity enough to be unrecognisable in any CCTV footage they take as well. I have even bought wigs for us both and we have tinted contact lenses and of course, baseball caps. We haven't told them yet but we will demand this Major Houlihan pick us up from a Starbucks ten minutes up the highway, so we don't present at the base ourselves.'

Suzie again: 'How will you get there?'

'We will drive the ute down and park it somewhere nearby, then have him drop us back to the ute with the weapons,' I reply. I then add, 'These sniper rifles are 1200 millimetres long and no doubt will come in metal cases, not easily hidden, that's why I bought a ute with a long toolbox in the tray.'

'Okay but if the ute is going to be sitting at the Starbucks with CCTV coverage, aren't you and the ute exposed whilst you are away?'

Mmmm. 'Well, yes, but we theorise it is a small risk and one we can't see a way around it,' I reply.

Suzie is looking at me intently and says, 'If Stacey and I drop you off in your disguises and with your number plates unrecognisable, this will avoid the ute being parked there and exposed to any form of identification or tracking. You can text us and we can then come back and pick you up, maybe from a different location, so they won't know where they are dropping you and they won't be able to set up any surveillance.'

Pig and I look at each other and he gives me a small nod, so I reply, 'Good idea but that means you will miss out on your meal at Flemings.'

She smiles and says, 'Not an issue if it means helping you both be safe!'

Nice.

I reach out and take her hand and give it a squeeze.

In the silence that follows, Stacey asks, 'Major Houlihan, wasn't that "Hot Lips"' name in the M*A*S*H* TV series – you know, the character Major Margaret Houlihan?'

I smile, saying, 'Yes, it is, that's why we think this is a false name, so keeping the officer anonymous.'

With no more questions, I then address both Suzie and Stacey, saying, 'Okay, now you know what we will be planning, we need to be basically packed and ready to go before any of us leave the hotel on Friday, and then we need you to stay close to the hotel on Friday. We have a late check out at five p.m., so that isn't an issue. Tomorrow, you can do more shopping away from here and on Friday, you can stay local at the Fashion Island shops or maybe Newport Beach. Then if the shit hits the fan, we will come back here grab you and jump in one or two taxis and head to the airport early.'

I'm non-plussed by Suzie's reply. 'Well, actually, we are sort of over shopping, to be honest, so Friday we had talked about just hanging around the hotel.'

'Shit, YOU are over shopping? Can I have that in writing, please!'

She gives me the sweetest smile and reaches out for my hand, giving my fingers a squeeze as my heart melts. (Ah, I know, I know.)

30

Seven a.m. the next morning, Pig and I are on the road. First stop, a Starbucks. Of course.

Here, we use their toilets to change into our work gear. We don't worry about the disguises as yet but do don the caps that suit our work attire.

Whilst we enjoy our coffee, we also review the updated satellite images Midge sent through overnight of the ranch and surrounds. These include Dos Picos Park so we already have a good idea of what we will find. The detail in these satellite images is extraordinary, seemingly a lot better than we were used to when in the field. Newer and newer technology, I guess.

One thing we are keen to explore is there appears to be a track leading from the park direct onto Highway 67 some six kilometres (three point seven miles) further south from Ramona. If this is passable, this can be our escape route, no need to go back toward Ramona through, what we hope at least, will be growing pandemonium. Bonus.

With Pig driving, I take a closer look at the images of Chico's ranch.

These images are very detailed. You can see the guards driving their ATVs randomly around the perimeter. I count four of them all circling in different directions and different distances. I can also count six dogs but there could be more; if they were sitting or standing still, they would not be clear.

The buildings, of course, haven't changed much from the previous images Midge had shared with us. But I zoom in on the cabana and pool area. I don't see anything of concern here. The area is flat, lawned and paved; certainly no protection when bullets start flying.

It is an hour-forty, give or take, to Ramona. Not, I hasten to add, that we will be going into the town, rather avoiding it on the assumption there will be plenty of eyes in town looking or at least noticing anything or anyone different.

This means we take Highland Valley Road off the I5 rather than the direct route on Highway 78. We meander around the edges of small subdivisions before ending up on Highway 67 south of Ramona. Just where we need to be.

A right turn and then a left and we are on Mussey Grade Road. We have agreed we won't even drive past Chico's ranch, being absolutely confident we would be recorded. There is no need anyway, with the satellite images Midge has provided and the overview we hope to get from Dos Picos Park.

A short time later and we are turning right into the County Park. Right at the entrance are picnic tables, all empty, so we grab our coffee and muffins we had bought before exiting the I5 (we bought two coffees each, being unsure when we would have another chance!) Preplanning, you see.

Pig pulls the drone out and quickly has it airborne, as usual, doing ever-increasing circles checking to see who is around. We know there is a camping ground and see half a dozen RVs and tents in here, some people feeding the ducks and fishing in the nearby lake but that's okay; we are headed for the more isolated area of the park. The higher elevation.

Well, looks like we have the rest of the park to ourselves except for a couple walking their dog at the other side of the park, where there is some sort of 'Mountain Retreat', which we will steer clear of.

Next step is to check out for any possible vantage points; we need to be able to confirm we will be able to see the ranch and the cabana – sort of important, ah!

From the satellite images, we have already identified a couple of likely spots so the drone is simply checking access and to ensure there is no one around.

All clear, so back in the ute and heading toward the summit. We can only go so far in the ute, then we have to hoof it on foot. No matter, done that about a zillion times.

As we are only doing a recon, we take the binoculars and range finder. We head on up the track following the route we planned earlier when reviewing the satellite images.

We check out two of the identified spots and whilst they do have vision over the ranch, the angle isn't ideal.

Upward and onward with Pig commenting it will be a longer haul back to the ute afterwards. Still, we have to find our shooting spot.

We next exit the track by a craggy rocky outcrop, large boulders all tumbled and jumbled. This looks promising.

Without standing on top of any of the boulders and thus providing a silhouette, we find two adjacent firing spots. We lay down in our preferred positions, Pig on the left because he prefers to lay on a slight angle so this enables us to be close together.

Through the binoculars, we can clearly see ranch staff going about their business, even easily see staff setting up tables and chairs under the cabana, getting ready for tomorrow, I guess. The pool is off to the right of the cabana.

I use the range finder to see the tables being set up in the cabana are

1240 metres away. Doable. I share this with Pig. He agrees. The pool is slightly further at 1285 metres.

We look at each other and nod, then wriggle around a bit more to make ourselves more comfortable.

Yes, this will do.

We fist bump and I say, 'You have the three on the left. I will take the right.' I then point to something we had identified on the satellite images sitting adjacent to the cabana and say, 'Perfect, there is our distraction right there!'

Pig is smiling with me.

We then look around for ways to affix the camo shelter, not so much to give us protection but to avoid us being seen from any aerial surveillance – i.e. Chico's drone, or even the satellites way above. But most important it will prevent sunshine reflecting off the barrel of the rifle. It is matte black rather than shiny metal but still! We find a couple of straggly trees off to each side that we can tie the shelter to. Should work fine.

We don't talk too much as we take one last look around, then head back to the ute, even though our drone recon showed no one was in this area of the park – no sense taking any risks.

Once back at the ute, we again check the satellite images to see if there is another way to get the ute closer to our 'sniper hide'.

After scrolling around a fair bit, we see a narrow track that heads off from the main track way back just inside the park; this meanders around and passes directly below our hide.

Back down the track, we go until we find this side track, missing it the first time as it is quite overgrown. Still, we engage 4x4 and ease our way along.

Whilst overgrown, it is only with grasses and weeds, no small trees or scrub we need to worry about. It takes us twenty minutes but we eventually come out near the hide and luckily there is even room to pull off the track. It is even under cover of trees so not visible from very far. Bonus!

Twenty minutes is better than a thirty-minute walk each way with our gun packs on. A bit awkward if we happen to pass any other hikers. We do plan to have rakes sticking out the top of our gun packs, making it look like we are carrying tools. Well, hopefully.

This track will mean we won't have to worry about that.

Not much else to do here so we head back to the ute and instead of turning right back toward Ramona, we turn left and follow the road until it peters out into a trail. We again engage 4x4 and follow this monitoring our progress on Pig's GPS, making sure we are headed toward Highway 67.

Sure enough we emerge onto the highway before turning right and following Google Maps back to the I5.

A successful morning. Pig texts the girls to say we are headed back to the hotel. But not before we find another Starbucks. Here, we sit outside enjoying the sunshine and recap on what we had found.

Concerns? We have a couple:

1. The sound of the gunfire will carry. Even with the suppressors it is likely to be recognised as gunfire. With the six of so campers in the campground we only need one of them to recognise gunfire and call the cops.

2. Exit. If someone does call the cops, having to exit the park past the campground is an issue. Clearly if anyone is suspicious, they will be checking and likely report us leaving.

Suddenly, Pig grabs his iPad again and I lean over to see what he's looking at. I see he is following the side track where we plan on parking below the hide. This time he continues to follow the trail further away from the entrance. It meanders around a little but eventually comes out on our exit road, just before that turns into a track. Bingo! We fist pump and Pig says, 'I saw that track as we came out and wondered if it was the same track.'

Great, scratch concern number two!

After grabbing another coffee to go, we get back in the ute and Pig dials up Midge so we can bring him up to date.

He answers on the first ring we look at each other, eyebrows raised as this is most unusual. Normally there is no answer and he calls us back. Rightly or wrongly, we assume maybe this mission is critically important to someone else other than just us!

After the pleasantries are out of the way, Pig brings him up to date, thanking him first for the new images received overnight before confirming we have identified a shooting spot but not getting into any details. We trust Midge. Implicitly. But he does not need to know the operational details.

Midge in turn confirms the weapons will be ready for our seven p.m. meeting with Major Houlihan tonight and texts us a phone number so we can liaise directly with them. We don't know whether it is a he or she, maybe a female with a sense of humour! Or hot lips!!

Before we hang up, I say to Midge, 'Boy, those images have come a long way in the last few years, compared to what we had to work with in Afghanistan.'

'Yes,' he replies, 'they certainly have. Ever changing, that area of technology.'

I then ask, 'We don't want satellites above us tomorrow. Can you arrange that?'

A pause then he replies, 'I guess, but why?'

I reply, 'We don't want any proof we were there. We don't want such proof falling into the wrong hands.'

Another pause. 'Okay. Don't really understand what the risk is but sure, I can organise that.'

Good.

We sign off as we head back to the hotel, having changed back into our regular gear whilst at the Starbucks.

We are only a few minutes from the hotel, walking from where we had left the ute when I receive a message from Sergeant Chris. 'Good to hear from you, Mort, thought you had retired 😊 Yes, can help $500 and you can collect from the 7-11.' He gives us an address on Balboa Boulevard, Newport Beach. 'ETA 5pm today. Have shipped it already to ensure you get it in time, so please pay by PayPal ASAP.' He gives me the PayPal account details.

Pig had been reading it with me, so we share a smile and fist bump as we walk.

31

We end up having a leisurely afternoon around the pool at the hotel, the girls getting plenty of attention in their recently purchased bikinis. Pig and I are watching closely, mind you!

We decide to eat at the local PK Chang's – a chain of family styled Asian food, renowned for their quick and efficient service and of course, excellent food – so it's an early dinner to enable us to be down near Pendleton Marine base by six-thirty.

We will grab the barrel borer on our way back.

Suzie handed her rental back today, so Pig and I walk over to the ute, then collect the girls outside Whole Foods.

As we head south, Suzie having taken over the driving, I text Major Houlihan, requesting they pick us up at Starbucks, giving them the address.

I get a reply pretty quickly, saying, 'That wasn't the plan?'

I reply, 'Please 😊 😊'

Who can resist!

Not Major Houlihan, it seems as they reply, 'Okay. ETA 6.45pm.'

Now Suzie has a timeline, so she speeds up a bit as we want to be there well before 6.45 so we can suss it out, making sure we don't have a 'welcome committee' and ensuring the girls are long gone before the major or anyone else gets there.

It most probably seems we are totally paranoid but hey, I want to have a life when this is over.

Whilst travelling, Pig and I don our wigs and insert our coloured contact lends, Stacey fussing over us to ensure the wigs are sitting just right. Well, she fusses over Pig more than me but hey, so she should!

We cruise past the Starbucks, looking for any unusual or suspicious vehicles but don't see any, so Suzie drops us off around the corner from Starbucks and therefore out of range of any CCTV they have.

We go in and order three coffees, long blacks, because if Major Houlihan is army, long black will be their drink. Anything else will raise our suspicions!

Right on time a tall, athletic-looking soldier walks in, looking around. We both know immediately he is Major Houlihan. A soldier always knows. Especially an officer!

The three of us nod, I hand him his coffee, he takes a sip and nods his thanks.

We exit and outside there is an official US Army Suburban. Black of course.

Pig and I both get in the back seat, easier to stay away from any cameras that way.

He doesn't say a word and that suits us. He starts up and we are on our way to the base approximately fifteen minutes away.

A silent fifteen minutes.

We arrive at the base entrance. Time to see if this has been cleared as promised.

Sure enough, again not a word was spoken, the guard sees our Major at the wheel, checks his clipboard, raises the boom gate and we are in.

Clearly the major knows where he is going as he travels through the base until he comes to a stop outside a building labelled 'Armory/Range'.

Turning the car off, he turns to us and nods, then exits the car himself.

Like good soldiers, we follow through the entrance and follow signs to the range, grabbing the requisite earmuffs as we go.

Arriving at the range, we are met by an armoury sergeant, an older man. He looks at us closely as if he might recognise us. Don't want that. He too doesn't say anything but leads us over to where he has the two Sako's set up on the bench, along with two Glock 17s and boxes of ammunition for all.

He then asks, 'Have you used the Sako before?' Pig and I shake our heads in the negative.

'Okay, I have been assured you are experienced snipers so I'm not going to cover the basics but I will show you how to dismantle and reassemble these before we take you to the range.'

The major is standing back observing and I reckon not missing much.

The armoury sergeant is quickly into his spiel about dismantling and reassembling the Sako's and it becomes clear to him (and the major) that we do know what we are doing here.

After about ten minutes of this, he is satisfied we know how to do this and he suggests we head to the range.

Pig and I grab our Sako's, whilst the major picks up both Glocks, checking they are both empty first. Good man. If I had any lingering doubts that he was a Marine they are gone now.

Turning the lights on in the range itself, he comments, somewhat sceptically, 'I'm told you want the targets at 1370 yards.' I do the math in my head – yes, that's about 1250 metres – and nod.

Pig has set up his gun on the left, so we both slide down, wriggle around a bit to get comfortable. The range is earthen so as to simulate what it would be like outside.

Not in any rush, we both take our time, getting a feel for these new guns. I work the bolt and pull the trigger gently a few times and with my earmuffs on, I can only assume Pig is doing the same.

The armoury sergeant has his field binoculars set up behind us on a raised platform.

I'm ready.

I raise myself up and load a round into the rifle, checking to see it is a .338 magnum, which the rifle is designed to fire.

It is. The whole box is. As you would expect.

Time to shoot this thing.

I snuggle back down, sensing rather than seeing Pig sitting up anticipating I'm ready to shoot.

Time stands still. I am back in the zone. It's been a while since I have had to shoot over this distance. Truth be told, whilst I have practised over this range, my longest confirmed kill is 'only' 845 metres, so somewhat shorter than this bugger.

Still, time to find out.

I have slowed my breathing. The trigger has a fine touch to it, bullseye engaged. I hold my breath, slowly release it and ease the trigger.

BOOM!

Shit, loud in here even with earmuffs.

Before I can check the target myself, I can hear murmurings of approval from behind and Pig next to me.

Yes, I have jagged the left edge of the inner circle. I'll take that as a first shot!

I adjust the sights slightly, reload and once again assume my position, breathe out slowly and pull. BOOM!

Again, murmurings and I see I have missed the bullseye to the right this time. Still a kill shot in real life, but I quickly make another sight adjustment and settle down again and reload.

Breathe in, hold, slow release and pull the trigger. BOOM.

No need to listen to the whispers behind; I know as soon as I shoot, that's a bullseye. It's often the way with any good craftsman or sportsman. You know a good golfer or cricketer knows when they have a good shot. A marksman is the same.

I repeat the process four more times, drilling the bullseye each time.

Satisfied, I withdraw from the mound with Pig giving me a smile and we fist bump.

Both the major and armoury sergeant give me congratulatory handshakes, with the sergeant saying, 'You certainly have done this before.' I smile.

Pig's turn.

He goes through the same process as I did and when he is ready:

BOOM.

His first shot is off in the outer circles to the right. He makes an adjustment before going through his routine again.

BOOM.

This time he is a little closer but still off to the right.

Two further adjustments before he too centres one through the bullseye.

Like me, he then repeats four times, ensuring he is comfortable.

Once he is happy, he too gets the congratulatory handshake and the same comment from the sergeant.

I resume my position on the mound. I want to simulate shooting four rapid shots as we will need to do tomorrow.

The sergeant pulls the targets in. I hold up four and with eyebrows raised, he adds three more targets, side by side, gets my nod of approval and sends them back to the 1370-yard mark.

I resume my position.

Same process, acquire target, breathe in, release slowly, finesse the trigger.

Boom.

Reload.

Acquire target, breathe in, release slowly, pull the trigger.

Boom.

Reload.

Acquire target, breathe in, release slowly, pull the trigger.

Boom.

Reload.

Acquire target, breathe in, release slowly, pull the trigger.

Boom.

Four through the bullseye but a couple on the edge so not perfect, but certainly four dead targets.

Now Pig's turn.

He repeats exactly what I have done but not quite as well.

He has two in the inner circle and two in the bullseye, so again four kill shots.

One and a half seconds. That is all it takes for these bullets to travel 1250 metres, so one and BANG.

I do the count for each of Pig's shots and he is somewhere around one and a half to two seconds per shot.

The average human reaction time is somewhere around one and a half to three seconds. We have been hoping to have two down inside the three seconds, thus making the last shot the riskiest; they will have had time to react.

His timing is pretty good.

We fist bump once he rises up.

Now for the simple bit, zeroing in the Glocks.

The sergeant puts fresh targets side by side at fifty metres (fifty-five feet). Pig and I stand side by side, both assume our preferred shooting stance and on the count of three from the sergeant, who seems to know what we are going to do, we fire.

Once, twice, three times, four. Rapid fire.

Nowhere near as noisy as the Sako's, of course.

The sergeant pulls the targets in and again no doubt we have both scored four kills shots but I get a slightly better score than Pig. As expected. I would have been bummed if I hadn't!

Comfortable we have the weapons and skills to achieve our goals tomorrow, we nod our thanks and shake hands with the sergeant, having met our desire to not speak and thus allow anyone, if they have the desire, to be able to prove we have been here from our recorded voices.

They both help Pig and I dismantle the Sako's and load them into their travel cases. Long metal cases with wheels on the base, so you pull them along just like luggage. Once loaded, Pig pulls his phone, engages his 'tracker identifier app' (not one you will get on the App Store!) and checks the cases, inside and out.

Good, all clean.

Both the major and armoury sergeant watch on in silence.

With the major leading the way, we head back to the front door and load our weaponry into the Suburban.

The major jumps in the driver's seat and once again, Pig and I get into the back.

As we exit the base through the armed entrance, I lean over and show the major the address we want to be delivered back to.

This time a little further south at a service centre off the I5.

No disagreement or reaction this time, he simply nods and heads to the I5 south on ramp.

Again, no chance for him to set up any surveillance when we are only about ten minutes away.

This, of course, was all prearranged with Suzie and Stacey who should be already at our rendezvous.

Pig had already sent Stacey a text saying our ETA was ten minutes, getting a smiley face as a reply.

The major drops us off to the side of the service station, the side where we had asked Midge to disable the CCTV footage for an hour, so once again no one will be able to prove we were there or had loaded two gun cases into the toolbox of our ute.

After a routine trip back, we stop off at the 7-11 and I collect the barrel borer. It is only tiny about one hundred millimetres long and diameter of .338' or 8.5 millimetres, so just a little box. But it might just save our lives!

We decide the girls and Pig will jump in a cab from here and I head off to the storage centre, enter the given code at the main entrance and again at our lot number, twenty-two. Up goes the door and I drive the ute in and lock it.

After closing the door after exiting, I pull a hair off my head, lick it and place it across the bottom of the door and onto the concrete floor.

If this is gone in the morning, I will know someone has been in there. Simple but effective!

It's a bit far to walk back to the hotel so I walk down the road to a service station and call a cab.

One must have been loitering around the corner as he turns up in seconds. I get him to drop me off at Whole Foods and walk to the hotel.

32

D-Day.

No need for an early start but I'm still up at the crack of dawn.

Anticipation, I guess!

I take myself off for a nice easy run, using up some of the restless energy. I have always found I think better when focused and running does that for me. Focuses and relaxes.

The terrain around Newport Beach is pretty flat and level so no 'puff points' as in hills, a nice and easy jog.

I even remember to do my cool-down stretches on arrival back at the hotel, with one of the valets offering a towel and cold bottle of water.

Appreciated!

Pig and I had agreed we would leave at eighty-thirty a.m. to collect the ute and give us plenty of time in case of delays or accidents on the freeway.

Suzie is awake when I return to the hotel and I realise, not surprisingly, a little apprehensive.

I try and give her reassurance that all will be well but the simple fact is, all we can do at this point is control what we can and hope for the best.

Very reassuring, I'm sure.

We have breakfast in our room, a long lingering goodbye and I'm down in the lobby waiting for Pig, right on time.

As is he, getting out of the lift behind me.

The doorman whistles up a taxi and we are off to the 7-11 adjacent to the storage facility.

Coffee to go of course. Make that two, so we don't have to stop again!

I go and collect the ute, whilst Pig uses the toilet to get changed whilst he waits for the coffee.

Before opening the roller door, I check the hair I placed at the base to see if the door has moved.

No, it hasn't.

Yes, paranoid. But alive!

I then change into my workwear.

I collect Pig from the 7-11, and we head south on Highway 73, which merges onto I5 South. Not long after, we come to a standstill.

Bugger.

No signs and nothing on the radio, so we just have to chug along. This we do for twenty minutes, using up all our spare time. But then again that's why we factored in an extra thirty minutes.

In the middle of this, Midge calls to wish us good luck and assures us there have been no messages showing anything out of the ordinary at the ranch.

'Good luck, dudes,' he finishes. 'Waiting with bated breath on the outcome of your exploits. AND I'm not alone, you have a VERY high-level audience today.' And he's gone.

No pressure! We bump fists.

Suddenly, the traffic clears and off we go.

Don't you find it weird how jammed-up traffic just suddenly clears and there is no apparent reason for the holdup?

I do.

We manage to pick up about five minutes so are only fifteen minutes behind schedule when we enter Dos Picos County Park. Hopefully for the last time.

Same routine as yesterday, we stop at the first picnic table and Pig launches the drone. This isn't a favourite obviously as he has not given it a name. He ignores me when I ask why.

Now we know where we are headed. We take a quick check over the camping ground to see if there are any more encamped there but no, looks like only the same RVs and tents as yesterday.

Pig quickly swings the drone over toward our 'hide', following the track to see if anyone else is on it.

Bugger, yes, there are a couple of mountain bikers peddling along, close to our hide.

He leaves the drone hovering behind them so they can't see or hear it and we wait.

We sit tight for ten minutes by which time they are comfortably past the hide and still heading away toward our exit.

Pig leaves the drone airborne as we get back into the ute, continuing to monitor them whilst we make our way along the track.

Once we arrive at our parking spot, the bike riders are still peddling away from us so he brings the drone back toward us and then past us, back along the track, to ensure we are as alone as we need to be.

Yes, we are, but Pig is going to be monitoring the track and our surroundings until it's time to leave.

Control what you can.

11.25 – still plenty of time to get ourselves set before the meeting starts at twelve.

Parked ready for a quick getaway, if needed, I pull out the shelter and head up to set this up first.

With really only enough room for one without being exposed, Pig waits at the ute. The guns are still packed in the toolbox. (Yes, I checked to make sure they were there before leaving the storage unit!)

It doesn't take long to set the shelter up. I crawl around on my knees, showing I'm getting old or soft, as those loose stones and rocks hurt!

All done. I clamber back down to the ute, grab the two yoga mats and the rangefinders next and retreat back to the hide. These are quickly positioned and it's now time to bring up the artillery. We both don our holstered Glocks, remove the weapons from their carry bags and climb up and into our little hide. The toolbox is closed but not locked, all in the interest of a speedy exit once the deed is done. Pig's prosthetic makes clambering up the relatively steep, rocky slope rather awkward, but never once does he complain.

I let Pig get into position first, as it would be difficult for us to try and do this at the same time. Once he is settled, he again checks the drone, but no, no suspicious-looking people to be seen.

I too don't take long to settle into my comfortable shooting position, bring the rangefinder to my eyes and review what is going on 1250 metres away.

It's as clear as day, no sign of Chico or any of his high-level guests yet, but that's not surprising. Pig notes the wind is barely ruffling the leaves, so should not impact the bullet trajectory.

I use one of the table settings to tune in my sights, imagining it is Chico's head.

This may seem vicious and violent but I remind myself, How many lives have he and his cartel destroyed today, this week, this month, this year?

Suddenly, I know I am doing the right thing; the only thing that is right for me.

In position and ready. Ten minutes to spare.

It is not even ten minutes and then sauntering out from the main house wearing speedos (brief swimmers), a sleeveless top and a towel over his shoulder is Gabriel, Chico's eldest son and a ranking lieutenant.

He drops his towel on a nearby sun-lounger along with his top, dives into the pool and starts swimming leisurely laps. It is a large pool, about thirty metres at a guess, and he swims effortlessly.

The pool is side on to where the meeting chairs have been set up.

Then two more men are heading toward the cabana. The older one is Chico and the other, from images we have been shown, must be Angel Sanchez.

I look behind them and see a group of four men who have followed Chico out of the house but have stopped about midway between the house and cabana under a marquee. His security detail, I surmise. There is a table set up there with coffee pots and snacks along with chairs. So clearly this is their station. Good, not too close.

Chico and Angel take a coffee each off the buffet table and sit down, side by side. Chico, as expected, has taken the middle chair. He has a small collapsible table set up in front of him, which has a laptop and TV screen set up on it. Angel sits to his right. My side!

Next to appear are Jose Lopez and Santiago Smith; yes, Smith is an odd name but that is what his passport says, according to Midge when we queried it. They too grab a coffee; Jose even brings the coffee pot over to top up Chico and Angel's cups.

'Brown nosing,' mutters Pig, I smile, helping to ease the tension. They take the two seats closest to Chico on his left. Pig's targets.

It's now a little after twelve. Chico checks his watch. Gabriel has stopped swimming and is leaning on the end of the pool, maybe letting the others know he is different, doesn't have to do as Daddy would expect!

It's not until ten past twelve that the final attendee, Diego Gonzalez, comes rushing out of the house, not running but hustling across to the cabana. When he gets there, he bends down into a sort of bow to Chico, obviously apologising profusely for being late. He takes a seat on the left. Pig's.

I suspect Chico is not someone used to being kept waiting.

Chico leans forward and starts the laptop, having ignored the fact Gabriel is still in the pool. No doubt he can see the images on the screen from the pool anyway.

I look at Pig. We nod.

It's time.

I confirm, 'I've got Chico, Gabriel and Angel. You the three on his left plus the bonus.'

Bonus? You just have to wait and see!

We both take our time, preparing, and just as I'm about to bring Chico's head into the sights, Pig places a warning hand on my shoulder. I glance over and he points to the small drone screen he has set up to the left of his position.

The two mountain bikers are almost directly below us, slowly riding back past our ute, looking around, wondering where we might be.

Shit.

Talk about bad timing.

Once past the ute, they start to speed up. We can see them both talking but the only consolation is we can see they have their iPhone buds in. Hopefully listening to heavy rock! Randomly, local Queensland heavy metal bands 'Parkway Drive' and 'Pantera' come to mind. They wouldn't hear any shots if they happen to be listening to them!

As they ride further away, I continue to monitor the meeting happening over a kilometre away.

A waitress has refilled all the coffee cups (they are drinking from cups, not mugs – go figure!), also offering a plate of muffins.

As we are behind the TV screen, we have no idea of what is on it but hopefully they haven't got hold of photos of us.

We leave it ten minutes. The bikers have got further away and with the track twisting and turning through gullies and over ridges, hopefully there is enough distance to diffuse and distort the sound of our shots.

We again look at each other and nod.

Time to refocus.

I pan my sights over my targets. Gabriel is still in the pool, leaning on the edge. This will be a difficult shot as he is side-on to me. He will be last. Chico will be first. Of course.

We had agreed that we need body shots – such as biggest body mass – as over this distance we need to maximise our chances of success.

But it's Chico's head I'm zoning in on.

I know Pig is waiting on my first shot before he will fire.

Time.

A deep breath.

I slow my breathing. The trigger has a whisper touch to it, the sight firmly set right on Chico's nose, centre of the head. Another deep breath, a slow release and I caress the trigger.

BOOM.

LOUD. Glad I'm wearing earplugs.

It's only a second and I hear Pig firing his first shot as well.

One and a half seconds, that is how long these bullets take to hit their target over this distance. The best possible reaction time is theoretically one point five to three seconds. No time to waste.

Reload, acquire target – this time Angel, immediately to Chico's right – breathe in, feather the trigger.

Boom.

Just after I pull the trigger and move the sight looking for Gabriel, I see in the periphery of my vision in my sights Chico's head exploding. Gotcha!

Reload.

One and a half seconds.

Acquire next target. Gabriel, he still hasn't moved. Body shot this time, maximum mass.

Breathe in, release slowly, pull the trigger.

Boom.

Reload. Just in case.

I hold my sights on Gabriel, waiting, and suddenly I see him tense, reacting to what is happening right in front of his eyes.

I instinctively hold my breath; will he move sufficiently for my shot to miss?

No. Suddenly the pool is turning red around him. Looks like I have hit him a little lower than planned – gut shot maybe. That will hurt, but not for long with a .338 magnum splitting his gizzards out.

I run the sights back over Angel. Yes, looks like a clean head shot. Chico, I know, is cactus. I keep panning to the left and see Jose, Diego and Santiago all slumped and collapsing to the ground.

Pig has one last shot to make.

BOOM, there it goes.

I have his target in my sights, in case needed, so one and a half seconds later I see I won't need to pull the trigger as his armour-piercing shell hits the propane gas tank sitting away to the left of the cabana.

We wait.

BOOM. Well, 'boom' doesn't really cut it. This isn't a rifle firing – this is a propane gas tank exploding.

Shit.

BIG and loud, flames reaching skyward.

We look at each and smile and fist bump.

Massive. Simply massive.

Awesome.

One hundred per cent success.

Except…

There is now a loud rumbling noise. We both put our eyes to our range finders just in time to see the whole house explode.

F…k!

Double F…K!

Can't claim we had anticipated that. The flaming gas from the propane tank must have passed through the pipeline to the house and is now exploding throughout, likely coming out of the gas appliances throughout the house.

There are flames coming from all over the house, windows exploding, explosion after explosion.

Wow, we wanted a distraction. We sure do have one!

33

Three hours later.

We exit our taxi back at Whole Foods back on Fashion Island, dressed once again in our polos and shorts. No welcoming party – we had told the girls to wait in our room so that's where we head.

We enter to a nice warm welcome each, long lingering hugs and kisses. Nice.

'This is the welcome I should get every time I get home from work,' I say. Suzie just hugs me tighter.

We eventually disentangle and I turn to see Pig is pouring us a fresh coffee the girls had ordered up, two pots actually, plus a plate of muffins and sandwiches.

Thoughtful, aren't they?

No time to waste for although our flight isn't departing until eleven tonight, we want to leave the hotel as quickly as possible in case someone has managed to track us. Not sure how it could be done considering all the precautions we have taken but we are alive because we minimise risks.

But no, Suzie, supported by Stacey, insists on a full replay. We don't have a choice, so Pig and I sit down and walk them through the setup and execution of our plan.

Then we explain the house explosion.

Pig continues, 'We couldn't hear but I'm sure there was much screaming and yelling from the staff as they ran as fast as they could away from the house and the cabana area.'

I continued, 'I panned back over where Chico's security detail had been standing, about halfway to the house, but whilst it looked like some had started toward the cabana, I suspect when the explosion happened, they were discouraged, then with the house exploding behind them, they had spread wide and far. No concerted effort to identify where the shots had come from. Good.'

I continued. 'It was time to skedaddle. Pig had checked the drone monitor, all clear. We don't need to say anything. We put our rifles aside, roll up our yoga mats, Pig gets ready with his first load, his Sako, range finder and mat and makes his way down to the ute. I do likewise, getting there before him. His prosthetic certainly slowed him down in that terrain. Never a word of complaint though. Our Pig is tough,' I add with a smile his way.

I continue, 'I head back up, breaking off a branch as I go. I pick up all seven cartridges, pull down the camo shelter, take a close look to see if I can see any thread or other tell-tale signs we had been there, then using the branch as a broom, I clean away any evidence showing we had been there, even brushing the sides of the adjacent boulders for any marks in the dust. I stood back, checking closely. No sign that I can see, and I'm looking for them, and know what to look for. I walked backward toward the brush through which we climbed from the ute, brushing my footprints as I go. We have done this before, remember.

'Pig had finished packing the ute by the time I got back and had moved it onto the track ready to go. I loaded the shelter under the covering tarp on the tray. I go back to where the ute had been parked and again using my branch, I brush away the tyre marks and our boot prints, again walking backward to the passenger door and climbing in, a little awkwardly for sure, but confident we had left no signs. Pig engaged gear and we were off. We shared a look, a smile and a fist bump, of course. We know better than to congratulate ourselves as we still need to make our exit and escape.

'I look at my watch, just after one p.m. We didn't encounter anyone else on our exit from the park and once again used the trail to head back onto Highway 67, and then followed Google Maps to the I5 north. As we left the park, there was certainly a chorus of sirens in the background, so I'm pleased we found the back way out, thereby not being seen by any eagle-eyed emergency services or police.

'Back on the I5, no stopping for coffee. We need to get out of the area and back to Newport Beach, back to you as quickly and safely as we can. Once on the I5, we did relax a bit and Pig said to me, "I thought we agreed on body shots – you know, maximum mass."

'I smile back at him, saying, "That was a statement shot. Like 'take that arsehole'!"

'We shared another smile. No traffic snarls this time and we were back at the storage facility in just over an hour and a half. Of course, we had rung you to say we were on our way back and yes, it was a complete success – so far.'

Pig takes up the storytelling:

'Midge was on the phone within the hour. I put his call on speaker so we could both hear and his first words were, "Man oh man, you dudes just keep delivering! What an outcome. We don't have a body count yet." Pig butts in, "One hundred per cent as targeted." Midge takes a moment to digest before saying, "So, the explosions were just a distraction, cover for your exit?" "Yep," I reply succinctly.

'"Man oh man, I'm just passing that on. As you wouldn't allow us to have a satellite coverage, we don't yet have eyes on the ground to confirm that. We will have someone there in about thirty minutes but FBI is there now, so they will be able to confirm."

'"Tell them to check by the cabana. That's where they are, not in the house," I add. "Righto, hold on, I will quickly pass that on," he says.'

I continue: 'We continued to chat; Midge was obviously in awe of what we had done. Nice but not necessary. At the end, he closed off the conversation by saying, "Guys, I have got to tell you, you had a very high-powered audience today so don't think your efforts went unnoticed." To which I replied, "Well, as long as they don't have any ulterior motives, that's fine." And we signed off.'

Pig and I then share another grin.

We aren't emotional types (if you haven't noticed!) so a grin and a fist bump are about as good as it gets for us.

Pig's turn to continue: 'When we arrived back at the storage shed, I punched in the code, then drove in. It was all pretty routine. Mort grabbed the carry cases the Sako's came in, opened them and removed his rifle from its carry case. He used the barrel borer to give the barrel a different "signature", and gave the gun a quick clean and wipe down. We weren't concerned about fingerprints as we have never touched them without gloves on. My name's Willy not Silly!'

I take over: 'I then did the same with Pig's Sako as he gave the cab of the ute, both front and back seats, a good clean and wipe down. Again, an over-the-top precaution no doubt, but worth the effort to be sure. Once we finished all the cleaning, we stripped down and changed back into our holiday clothes, bundling our work wear into a couple of black plastic bags. Ready for disposal.

'With the rifles back in their cases, I leant these against the front wall of the storage unit. Placed our Glocks, still in their holsters, against the rifle case along with all the remaining ammunition. Once done, I pulled the door back up and Pig backed the ute out.

'I pulled the roller door back down and locked it, jumped in the ute and we headed off to the suburb of Irvine, nearby. We found a couple of industrial bins in a small industrial complex, threw our work clothes in, one bag in each, keeping the "evidence" separate.

'Once we had done this, we parked in a Costco supermarket car park, leaving the tools in the back and the keys in the ignition. That way someone will hopefully steal it and further obliterate any signs we have used it. We picked up a coffee and taxied back to the Fashion Island Shopping Centre, again using Whole Foods as our drop-off point. It was then a pleasant five-minute walk to the hotel. To see you!'

As our recounting of the events comes to an end, Suzie starts flicking through the news channels and sure enough, there are images of the house on fire in the distance, taken from a helicopter, which isn't allowed any closer due to risks of further explosions, it would seem.

The breathless reporter is saying, 'In a breaking story, a house has exploded down in San Diego County. Emergency services are on site along with the FBI. There is no word yet on if there are any casualties, but we can see a number of ambulances lined up on the edge of the property. The house is rumoured to be the home of cartel boss Chico Garcia. Police and FBI are not commenting at this stage.'

'Right, we need to keep moving. Pig, you right if we meet in the lobby in thirty minutes?' I ask.

He nods, filling his mug again and with Stacey holding his hand, they head back to their room.

I reach over to Suzie and give her a kiss and hug and suggest she come and scrub my back but I only get a smile and a push toward the bathroom. Ah well.

Whilst waiting for Suzie to finish packing her carry-on, I text the location and access code to the lock-up to Major Houlihan, saying, 'You will find your goodies here.'

Thirty minutes later I have settled the accounts and everyone else is settled in the minivan Suzie had booked for the transfer to LAX. We need the minivan to get all the extra luggage the girls had bought. Stacey has also ended up having to buy an extra suitcase.

Nothing is said on the journey other than typical small talk and chat as we approach LAX. I ask the driver to drop us at the Daily Grill at the Westin Hotel, saying to the others, 'So we can have one last decent feed before we leave.'

No objections but the driver does ask, 'What about your luggage, sir? You won't be able to take it all into the restaurant.'

Mmm, good point.

He continues, 'Sir, I am happy to wait for you and then take you to LAX after your meal if that suits you.'

Before I can respond, Suzie jumps in. 'That would be great, thank you. What will that cost us?'

The driver turns his head to address Suzie. 'I would charge an extra fifty dollars, Madam.'

I nod and say, 'Deal!' and give him a smile.

I was planning on using this stop as one last block out in our journey, so if anyone is on our tail, they would be hunting for us in LAX, not at a nearby hotel.

But even to me this is extremely unlikely, so I accept the convenience of the offer.

He duly drops us off at the Westin and gives me his card so I can give him a call when we are ready again.

34

Six hours later.

We are sitting and lounging around in the Qantas First Lounge in the Tom Bradley Terminal at LAX – one of the benefits of being Section V: we are honourable Platinum Qantas members!

It's after ten at night and our flight home is due to board in twenty minutes. We have been sitting around for a few hours now and we're keen to get on board and head home.

Suddenly, Pig says, 'Twelve o'clock,' and disappears. Twelve o'clock is straight ahead, so I glance up from the magazine I'm browsing. I see Campbell with an older, smartly dressed woman and a tall, bald, black American. Campbell and my eyes meet and he smiles. Good start, I think. Suzie, who is sitting next to me, has looked up as well and is watching.

They are in discussion with the Qantas hostess and I see ID badges being shown. As I watch, the hostess leads them to one of the meeting rooms on the left side of the lounge, lets them in and closes the door. Then she comes directly over to me. 'Mr Ireland, Ms Amanda Reynolds of the FBI has asked if you can join her, please.'

I nod and stand up; Suzie immediately stands as well, saying, 'I'm coming too.'

I follow the hostess over to the meeting room; she knocks and opens the door. I enter, followed by Suzie and the hostess closes the door.

Campbell gives me another smile but it is the woman I am focused on, clearly the boss with a real air of authority about her. The tall bloke, well, he's looking daggers at me.

The lady smiles, reaches out her hand and says, 'Mort, I am Amanda Reynolds, Deputy Director of the FBI. I am very pleased to meet you.' We shake hands and she then says, 'You know Campbell here.' We smile and shake hands, she then says, 'And this is Raymond Atwell, Special Agent in Charge of our LA office.'

He seemingly reluctantly shakes hands and has quite a scowl on his face. I wonder what his problem is.

I then introduce Suzie as my fiancée and she shakes hands with the three of them.

Amanda then says politely, 'We were hoping to have a word with Mort in private?'

I smile and say, 'I'm happy for Suzie to stay. She has been with us this whole trip. Besides, she is my lawyer as well.'

A little frown crosses Amanda's face, but she doesn't push it. We all sit down, Amanda on one side flanked by Raymond on her right and Campbell on her left.

I take the seat directly opposite Amanda and look her in the eyes.

Campbell asks, 'Where's Pig?'

I reply, 'Likely taking a leak.'

He smiles at me and says sincerely, 'We don't have any backup, Mort.'

This makes Amanda quickly turn and look at Campbell, puzzled, and I reply, 'He will likely join us shortly then.'

Amanda now has to ask, still looking at Campbell, 'Why would we need backup?'

Campbell slips another smile my way and explains, 'As we have seen, they don't take chances. Ever. They don't know why we have suddenly turned up here unannounced, so Pig will be checking for any backup, and if so, would stay out there to neutralise them if need be. Mort would take care of us.'

Raymond snorts at this, squares his shoulders and says, 'There are three of us.'

Campbell again. 'Sitting like this, side by side, we are easy meat for Mort. I've seen him take six out one night in the mess.'

Amanda is now giving me another appraising look, whilst Raymond seems to have lost some of his cockiness.

Silence. I'm quite content to wait patiently because Amanda and Campbell, I suspect, have flown direct from either New York or Washington for this little meeting. A six-hour flight. Gee, they didn't waste any time jumping a plane then, I'm thinking. Bet they haven't flown commercial!

As if on cue, Pig opens the door and walks in, nodding to the three of them before sitting down opposite Raymond.

As you know we are both big, intimidating units, sitting shoulder to shoulder across a narrow table full of suspicion, the threat emanates from us.

We are dangerous.

Of course, Pig has been listening through my phone because, as soon as he raised the warning, I opened our private messenger app.

Another pause as I think Amanda reappraises the situation.

She eventually continues. 'Mort, Julien, Suzie, we are not here to threaten you in any way. You have carried out an extraordinary mission today – in fact, over the last two to three weeks. You have provided us with two, three even, separate excellent outcomes. We came tonight simply to discuss how you achieved this and, well basically, to debrief and thank you before you head home.'

Raymond snorts (Pig might be getting jealous!) again and seemingly can't resist: 'Bloody amateurs, come in guns blazing and destroy all the hard work we have been doing for years, wiping out our surveillance and resources. We have people on the inside of the cartel. We don't need rank amateurs coming in guns blazing.'

I'm not taking any of his shit.

I lean across the table, taking up his personal space and start: 'Four days. Four days it took us to place a wire on Diego over in New York. You, the FBI, have been trying for months – shit, years, for all I know. The very same day we succeeded; you were able to arrest him. For attempted murder. So even you could lock him up for life. Then you, the FBI, leaked our identities. We came under attack.

'Not only did we repel these attackers, we, through Pig's quick thinking and know-how, provided you full, unfettered access to the Garcia cartel's finances, connections, administration, their bank records. Shit, it will take an army of forensic accountants years to unravel it all.

'Then, learning Chico and all five of his lieutenants were all going to be at a meeting this afternoon, we took the obvious course of action. We eliminated them. Sliced the head of this bloody big viper. The bloody big viper that you, through your efforts or lack thereof, have allowed to prosper and grow.'

I lean even closer and he leans as far back in his chair as he can, so I finish, 'How's your progress coming along?'

Phew. I don't normally have that much to say but this bloke has pissed me off.

He is looking with what may be fear in his eyes before responding, 'If I find you have broken any laws, I will bring you before a court and we will see…'

I cut him off mid-sentence, saying, 'Exactly what I would expect a small-minded bureaucrat to say. You will never win this battle when you are hamstrung by having to play by your rules when your opponents don't play by any.'

'ENOUGH.'

Amanda has not raised her voice but the authority is clear to us all. She lets the silence settle.

She is looking at Raymond as she says, 'There will be NO witch hunt. Understood?'

He nods and I ease back into my chair, my point well and truly made. I hope.

Amanda now takes a deep breath and I glance at Campbell, who looks like he has been enjoying the encounter.

'Mort, Julian, Suzie. Firstly, I need to apologise on behalf of the FBI. You were right, we did have a leak and yes, the cartel did manage to gain your mission names. We can only apologise and be thankful you all came through unscathed. For the record, they squeezed one of my team whose teenage sister was being held by them. Sad situation really. He has now lost his job, so has little prospect of helping his sister out of the hole she has dug for herself.'

Again, she pauses.

'Now before we get to today's events, can I ask what happened to the car – or is that cars? – that you were travelling in on the Highway 1?'

I reply, 'Never to be seen again.'

I can tell she wants to ask more but the abruptness of my answer seems to dissuade her.

Suzie is looking at her watch and I realise we are approaching our boarding time. Amanda, seeing Suzie looking at the time, says reassuringly, 'Don't worry, your flight will not be leaving without you. We have advised both Qantas and air traffic control we will be delaying the flight for a short time only.'

Suzie and I nod. Pig hasn't said boo, or even made any gesture, simply sitting there watching Raymond, who is clearly becoming uncomfortable being the sole focus of such close attention.

'Today. Do you mind giving us a brief run-through of your planning and execution of your plan today please?'

I nod. Knowing something they don't, I see no harm in spelling this out.

I start, 'Once we had confirmation you could supply the Sako rifles, it was a matter of finding a suitable firing spot. We found one – we inspected it yesterday and laid out our plan. We continued to monitor the intel still coming through in case we needed to change anything. But once we found the ideal shooting spot, it wasn't likely to change.

'We set up twenty minutes before the scheduled meeting started and, whilst we had to wait for a couple of mountain bikers to get further away, when ready, we pulled the trigger.

'Once finished, we tidied the spot up, making it fairly difficult to recognise, left by a predetermined back exit, and made our way back to LA, off-loaded the weapons and back to our hotel. Then here to LAX for our flight home tonight.'

No notes had been taken but Amanda does have some questions:

'Thank you. Again, I am in awe of your ability to plan and execute such a mission on such short notice. But I am curious why neither of you spoke whilst on the gun range last night?'

'We had identified this was one area where we could not control. We did not want to provide any evidence we had been there. So, we did not speak, we wore disguises and sat way back in our seats, making it difficult for any decent CCTV photos.'

She butts in here, saying, 'But here you are talking freely, surely even more dangerous here than at the range?'

'If any of you are recording this conversation, you are going to be disappointed. Pig is jamming the signal so all you are getting is static.'

I'm watching Raymond when I say this and sure enough, the look of shock and disappointment shows briefly.

Amanda nods and continues, 'And the searching for the bugs on the weapon cases. Surely if we are providing the weapons, that's proof enough we are on your side.'

'We have been around a few missions over the years – not here in your country but working for you in other parts of the world. The one thing we have learnt, there is often someone with a different perspective than that of the mission's main goal. We prefer to be paranoid and stay alive.'

Again, I am looking directly at Raymond as I say this. My point and my look are not lost on Amanda either.

'We have retrieved the weapons, thank you. And, for the record, we have not found the spot from which you shot. We will avoid a long and thorough investigation into the shooting as with the house explosion. We are saying all died in the fire. Simpler that way.'

Pig and I smile at each other. It is Campbell who speaks up. 'What? Is that why you planned the explosion?'

'No,' I reply, 'the house explosion was a bonus. We had only hoped or expected the gas tank to explode and that would be sufficient distraction to help us get away. The house explosion was not anticipated.'

Raymond pipes up, 'Just as well there were no casualties then, isn't it?'

I again look him in the eye and say, 'Yes, it is. But let's be clear, there are no innocents living or working in that house. It is always worth reminding ourselves: how many lives has the cartel destroyed, today, this week, this month, this year? Suddenly, a couple of cartel members lives being collateral damage dims when viewed in this light.'

Raymond even nods his head slightly in acknowledgement of this point. Wow!

Amanda looks at her watch now as the Qantas lounge hostess can be seen hovering outside the meeting room door, joined by Stacey who must also be wondering what is going on.

'Okay. Again, thank you for your time tonight. We, the FBI, and our country are indebted to you for your efforts. You have provided us with excellent outcomes and we certainly appreciate the courage and bravery you have shown in executing these missions.

'I repeat, there will be NO witch hunt. The shootings will never be mentioned, as the official line on all six deaths will be fire-related. Your names are not mentioned anywhere, nor will they be, as I agreed upfront. That we can manage.'

As she finishes, she stands up and extends her hand to me, Suzie and then Pig whilst Campbell follows suit.

But before Raymond can get up, I lean over aggressively in his face again, saying, 'If our identities ever become known, you better run because you won't be able to hide.'

We don't bother shaking hands. Suzie is heading to the exit followed by Campbell and Pig when Amanda looks at me, saying, 'Mort, a moment please.'

I wait whilst the others all leave the room. Amanda again looks me in the eye and says, 'I know I am repeating myself but truly, the people of our country are indebted to you for what you have achieved. You never said a truer word earlier when you said, "We can't win this war playing by the rules." But if we choose to not play by the rules, sadly, that way leads to anarchy.

'Please send me an invoice for your services I will ensure it is paid. Here, this is my personal card. My cell phone number is answered 24/7 so if I can assist you at any time, ever, please call me. I don't share these details very often. Please do not share them. Oh, and Midge asked me to give you this.' She hands over a pen drive. 'He also asked me to say, "Awesome job"!'

I nod my thanks at what she had said and say, 'A pen drive – that's a bit retro for Midge, isn't it? Please thank him for me.'

She laughs and says, 'That's exactly what I said to him! He said to tell you it's to do with some case you're working on where the voice has been synthesised. He has managed to "un-synthesise it" and matched it to a voice for you. Mary offered her congratulations as well.'

'Cool, say hi back to Mary for us. An interesting lady,' is all I say as we exit the room. I even turn the lights out.

Pig, Suzie and Stacey are already at the lounge door with the hostess who is ushering them all out and into one of those airport people carriers.

Looks like express delivery to our plane!

THE END!

Shawline Publishing Group Pty Ltd
www.shawlinepublishing.com.au

SLP
SHAWLINE
PUBLISHING
GROUP

Milton Keynes UK
Ingram Content Group UK Ltd.
UKHW050049190624
444315UK00016B/1205